I0566682

Sweet Thang

Deatri King-Bey

Sweet Thang Copyright © 2016 Deatri King-Bey

ISBN-10: 0-9829673-4-9
ISBN-13: 978-0-9829673-4-8
Library of Congress Control Number: 2016902123

Editor: Lynel Washington
Proofreader: Paulette Nunlee
Photographer: Amanda Aponte
Cover Models: Daetriel Ortega & Chris Bukky

This is a work of fiction. All of the characters, events, incidents, names, organizations and places portrayed in this novel are either products of the author's imagination or are used fictitiously. Any resemblance to actual persons, living or dead, business establishments, events or locales is entirely coincidental.

All rights reserved. Except for the use in any review, the production or utilization of this work in whole or in part in any form by any electronic, mechanical, or other means, now known or hereafter invented, including xerograph, photocopying and recording, or in any information storage or retrieval system, is forbidden without the written permission of the author, Deatri King-Bey.

Visit Deatri Online: http://DeatriKingBey.com

ACKNOWLEDGMENTS

I thank God, my family, friends, readers and editors for sticking by me. Love you all.

Chapter One

Los Angeles…

First Sean's contact for his upcoming feature article didn't show, then he found some jerk had parked in his assigned space in front of his condo, forcing him to park two blocks away in a metered spot.

Sean smacked the elevator button for the seventh floor. "What next?" he grumbled under his breath.

A hot shower and hotter sex were his choices for "next," but with the way his day had gone, he didn't see that happening. He nudged his shirtsleeve off his watch. Barely past three, his fiancée wouldn't be home yet; there were too many shopping hours left in the day. Thinking what Nakia lacked in other areas, she made up for in the bed put a grin on his face. A small script tattoo above her bikini line that read *Sex on Demand*, told the entire story.

By the time the elevator reached the seventh floor, he'd reached a hardened state. A hot shower, X-rated movie and self-gratification would have to do until Nakia arrived home.

The sound of a man grunting and flesh pounding flesh greeted Sean as he opened the door to his condominium unit. An easy-going smile curled his lips. He quietly closed the door. Nakia loved X-rated movies as much as he did. He quickly undressed to the sweet music of a porn movie he didn't recognize. Briefs dropped, he headed for the bedroom.

"Oh sheeee…" Nakia moaned.

"Come on! Come for me." The video man panted.

Hand wrapped around his engorged dick, Sean stroked from base to tip. The quality of his new surround sound was so good it sounded as if a sex scene were actually occurring in his room—bed creaking and all!

Instead of seeing Nakia sprawled out on the bed with her dildo slipping in and out of her luscious, pink pussy, Sean saw some bastard fucking his fiancée. Rage engulfed Sean. He worked his ass off to provide for Nakia, and this was how she thanked him. Two choices loomed before Sean: choke the shit out of Nakia or walk away. Decision made, he turned and walked into the living room for his clothes.

1

I can't believe this shit. He jerked his briefs and pants up.

"That's the spot, big daddy. Oh God please don't stop!"

Unsure if he could maintain control, Sean grabbed his shirt and snatched his keys off the end table.

"You like this shit, don't you, baby?"

Feet barely in his loafers, Sean stalked out and slammed the door. The elevator would take too long, so he darted down the stairwell—not to runaway, but to save Nakia's life. Cooling time was a must before confronting her.

He stopped just short of the burgundy Mercedes parked in his space. *I'll bet this shit belongs to "big daddy."* Fighting the urge to smash the windshield, he stepped away from the car. When he went off to college to become a reporter, he left any destructive ways back in juvenile hall.

"Sean!" Nakia exited the building. "Wait."

"Stay the hell away from me." Without glancing back to see her approach, he headed for his car. "I'll deal with your ass when I'm ready. Just get your shit out of my condo."

"Please, Sean, don't do this."

Though he heard her running up behind him, he continued onward. "Woman—and I use the term loosely—stay the hell away from me."

She grabbed onto his shirt, and it felt like someone had stabbed him in the back. He spun around to fight, but stopped himself. He'd never struck a woman before and wouldn't start now.

"Please, Sean, please…" she tearfully pleaded as she held the silk, Kimono robe he'd given her for her birthday closed. "Give me a chance to explain."

Unaffected by the quiver in her voice or the tears streaming down her face, he barked, "What the hell is there to explain?"

"I love you, please give me a chance. Please, baby, don't throw all we have away. We can work through this."

"I'm not throwing shit away. The second you opened your legs for someone else, there was nothing for us to work through. I don't share." He spied her screw partner easing out the building, and sure enough, he went to the Mercedes.

"We can talk this through."

He drew in several non-calming breaths. "I won't stand here arguing with you in the middle of the street. You'd better

2

tell *big daddy* not to leave, because you and your shit need a ride back to your car." He stepped around her to return to his condo.

The first thing Sean did when he re-entered his unit was yank Nakia's coats out the entry closet and toss them to the floor behind him. Might as well start at the front of the unit and work his way to the back to clean out all signs of contamination—Nakia.

She rushed in. "Sean..." She grabbed her coats off the floor. "What the hell are you doing?"

"Dumb-ass question." He pulled several hatboxes from the built-in closet shelving and dropped them on the stack of coats. "You have two hours to get your shit."

* * *

Atlanta, two months later...

"I'm a lost cause, Granny."

The overstuffed armchair cushioned Bertha's frail body as she turned from watching two teens tossing a football in the neighbor's yard across the street to face her favorite grandchild. Playing favorites was a definite no-no, but Bertha couldn't help herself where Joy was concerned.

Slouched on the sofa, Joy ran her fingers over her face and drew out a long sigh.

"Being a tad bit melodramatic today, aren't we?" Bertha said slowly, keeping the chuckle in her voice at bay.

"I'm a thirty-three-year-old, sexually-frustrated virgin whose only confidant is her ninety-six-year-old granny. Can you get anymore lost?"

"Melodramatic and sarcastic." Bertha giggled. "What a combination. Your future husband best watch out."

"Where did it all go wrong?" Joy drawled, then pushed off the couch and crossed over to Bertha. "I'm serious. Originally, I was waiting until I fell madly in love, and now... now I'm an oddball—a scared, horny oddball at that."

"Fear is needed to make you more cautious. Just don't let the fear paralyze you. And there's nothing wrong with being a virgin."

"I'm not saying there is something wrong with being a virgin, but at my age it makes me, yet again, an oddball."

"You've never been an oddball."

Joy sucked air through her teeth. "And you said it with such a straight face. Come on, Granny. Unlike my sisters and brothers who were planned pregnancies, I was an *oops*—menopause child."

Bertha pursed her lips. "You weren't an *oops*. Your mother was the head of the maternity department; she knows how the birds and the bees work before, during and after menopause."

"Then why are my siblings twenty some odd years older than me? My parents didn't even want to raise me."

Bertha knew the reason. Emily had missed much of her other children's lives and had suddenly wanted a chance to be a "real mother" before she couldn't have children. Within a year of having Joy, Emily couldn't "just be mommy" and returned to work part- time. By the time Joy was three, Emily was back to her old workaholic self. "Your parents wanted you. They love you." This wasn't the first time Joy had said something along these lines of late, which troubled Bertha.

"You know how kids are," Joy rambled and toyed with the floral-print curtain. "They tease each other over the silliest things, and I had 'Gramps and Gram' for parents, which set me apart and I was raised by my grandparents."

Though Bertha would never admit it aloud, Joy was always the oddball, which Bertha liked. "We're so much alike." When Bertha was Joy's age, she had long, dark, curly hair, a slender yet curvy body and big brown expressive eyes, but their similarities went well beyond looks.

"Yeah, Mom thinks we're both crazy." She faced Bertha. "By the way, Mom and Dad are back from their cruise. We've been summoned to dinner, tonight. Mom's been calling you all day."

"Whoever invented caller ID needs a raise."

"She knew you weren't taking her calls, so I've been charged with bringing you, but since I'm not going, I thought I should at least tell you about it. You want me to order a car for you?"

"Your mother will pitch a fit when you don't show."

"Won't be the first or last time." She winked a mischievous brown eye. "You going?"

"Of course not. How many times have I told her to stop expecting me to show up when she asks the day of the event? Anyway, I have a date."

"Awww man…" Joy slowly lowered and shook her head. "My granny dates more than I do. Shoot me. Shoot me now."

"Not that type of date." Bertha playfully tapped her arthritic hand on Joy's side. "My date is with that computer." She motioned at the end table beside the chair. "Those folks who invented the Internet also deserve a raise. Do you like Orbitz, Travelocity or Expedia best?"

"Oh no." Hands on her hips, Joy faced her grandmother. "You're about to get me into trouble again, aren't you?"

"Of course not. I want to leave in two…" She took in Joy's jeans and oversized, denim, button-up shirt. Why her sweet little thing of a granddaughter chose to hide behind such unflattering, baggy clothing was beyond her. And she could use a haircut, too. Bertha noticed women nowadays wore shorter, snazzy styles. With the natural curl of her hair, she'd look good with one of those geometric cuts like Halle Berry often wore. "Make that three days. We need to go shopping."

"And just where do you think *we're* going and for how long?"

Bertha paid a lot for her pearly white dentures and showcased just about every tooth in the set with the smile she flashed Joy. "Where have I always wanted to go?"

"California. But I still have six weeks of school left, and did your doctor clear this trip? You've never flown before, and you haven't been feeling well."

Bertha harrumphed and sunk into the corner of the oversized chair with her arms crossed over her chest. "He's conspiring with your parents to keep me prisoner. The only cure for growing old is death, and I plan to see the sunset on the Pacific before I die."

Brow raised, Joy asked, "Now who's being melodramatic? And they aren't trying to keep you prisoner." She settled in the chair next to her granny.

"Then why did they take my car?"

Shoulders hunched, Joy said, "I don't know, maybe it has something to do with your driving seven miles an hour. You have a chauffeur at your disposal twenty-four/seven. Let's make a compromise." She sat forward, dug into her back pocket and pulled out a letter. "Check this out. I was accepted into that writer's summer retreat I told you about."

Eyes wide, Bertha drew her hands to her mouth. "Oh Lordy be! I'm so proud of you. I can't believe you're actually going to do it."

"Yes, ma'am, I certainly am, and since it's in Los Angeles, I thought I'd take my favorite person in the whole world with me—that is if her doctor clears it."

Excitement welled up in Bertha. For years she'd prayed Joy would chase her dream of becoming an author. "They have doctors in Los Angeles. I'm going, but if this program is half as intensive as you've told me about, we won't get to spend much time together. So now we're taking two trips to California. Mine will be for fun."

"Granny, I'm a fourth grade teacher. I can't afford to take us twice."

"I'm paying for the fun trip."

"Thanks, but I can't allow you to spend so much money on me."

"You have always been entirely too difficult," Bertha grumbled.

"From what I hear, you're four times as bad as me." She cuddled up next to her granny. "Save your money for my trip to you. I've found this great senior center that does all kinds of neat trips and things. You can hang out there while I attend the workshops. And if you don't want to go out, you can watch T.V., read, surf the Internet, nap. The center has it all. I can only give you a hundred bucks a week for pocket change, but that's enough for at least two field trips a week."

Bertha blinked rapidly to keep from tearing up. Of all her adult children to great-great grandchildren, Joy was the least secure financially, but always went out of her way to make her granny's dreams come true—no matter what the cost emotionally or financially.

"I can afford this, Joy. Indulge an old woman. Come with me. I know you don't want to hear this, but the children will be fine with a substitute teacher. You'll only be gone a week, maybe two."

"Why the rush?" Joy asked, concern clear in her voice.

"I've been waiting my whole life. Why should I have to wait any longer? Tonight I'm booking our flight to California. I'm going with or without you."

Mouth and eyes opened wide, Joy gasped. "That's not fair. You know I'd never let you go alone."

"I certainly do. And you know I'll leave without you. Now how long before we can leave."

"You are so wrong for this," Joy mumbled. "This is blackmail, extortion or something."

"It most certainly is. And I'm paying for everything. Now how long?"

Joy stared at Bertha a long while, but Bertha didn't crack. This was too important. Time was too short.

"I guess three days will be enough time. But I can only be gone a week."

"Excellent! And don't tell your parents we're escaping Alcatraz. They'll try to stop us."

"You're preaching to the choir." She gently placed her hand on her grandmother's hand. "You think you're dying, don't you?" she asked softly, slowly. "That's why you're in such a hurry to get to California."

Joy's eyes had darkened to sorrowful black pools. The poor child couldn't hide her emotions if she wanted to. Her eyes would tell on her every time. Bertha sandwiched Joy's hand between her own. "This is our last summer together, baby. I've had a good life, but I'm tired. This old body I'm stuck in is giving out on me and won't last much longer."

Tears trickled down Joy's cheeks. "I don't want to lose you. I don't want to be alone."

Bertha wiped the moisture from her own face. "I'll always be with you. If not in body, in spirit. You remember that." After a long while, she forced a smile to her face. "Now let's stop all of the doom and gloom. Grab that laptop for me." She motioned to the end table on Joy's side of the armchair. "I've been busy all week."

* * *

Joy forced thoughts of her granny dying out of her mind and did her bidding. "Why are a bunch of naked men on your desktop?" She appreciatively brushed her fingers over the eight fine specimens of men. Oh how she longed to do this—and so much more—to a real man. Thinking her granny was the original "hot mess," all she could do was shake her head. "I'm taking your Internet privileges from you if you continue this behavior, young lady," she teased.

"They aren't naked."

"Granny, a piece of cloth on a dick does not count as clothing." Both women giggled. "What am I going to do with you?"

7

"Pick three—no, make that four."

"What are you up to?"

Bertha remained silent too long for Joy. The two never had trouble communicating. When Joy was twelve, she'd decided to shock her granny by asking her what a blowjob was. Without missing a beat, Bertha had answered, "That's when a woman sucks a man's penis. But don't do that, you'll go blind." The memory still tickled Joy. A few years later, Bertha explained oral sex didn't lead to blindness, but she had told Joy the lie to discourage her from trying at such a young age. Here it was twenty-one years later, and Joy still hadn't tried.

"I think you should pick this one." Bertha touched the image of an olive-complexioned man with short, wavy hair and an athletic build.

"I already have a very nice calendar of naked men. By the way, thanks for the calendar. You're worrying me. What aren't you saying?"

Bertha fiddled with Joy's hair a bit. Maybe she'd have it cut. It had grown too long and uncontrollable. Her mother wanted her to have it relaxed, but Joy refused—out of rebellion mostly.

"Out with it, Granny."

"When we're in California, you're losing your virginity to one of these men."

"Granny!"

Wide eyed, Bertha blinked several times. "What?"

"Don't give me that innocent look. You know exactly what." Joy couldn't believe what a crazy turn her life had taken. Yes, Bertha had always been a tad bit eccentric and ahead of her time, but this was *way* off the "Bertha Hot Mess" meter.

"If you don't like these men, I have more for you to choose from."

"First off, there is no way I'm having my *granny* pick the man I lose my virginity to. Secondly, there is no way in hell I'm doing anything with anyone off the Internet."

"Get with the times, Joy. The dating scene has changed. The Internet is the way to go. Match.com, e-Harmony… The list goes on and on."

Eyes closed, Joy allowed her head to lull back onto the overstuffed chair. "All I asked was for someone to shoot me." *This is only a dream. In a few seconds, the alarm will sound and scare me half to death. Or better yet, please scare me to death.* Time passed, but no alarm sounded. "Dang." She opened her eyes and faced Bertha. "Please tell me you haven't contacted these men for their services."

Silence.

"Granny?"

"Of course I didn't. I knew you'd act like a prude. But I did sign you up for a group or two." She wedged a pencil between her fingers and pressed the left mouse pad button with the eraser to open a browser window. "Your user ID is Sweet Thang."

"No, no, no, no, no you have not been pretending to be me. What are you thinking?"

"I'm thinking I've run out of time. You're right. It's a damn shame your only confidant is an old woman. I'll always be with you, but I won't always be here. You've got to come out of your shell, baby. This is a safe way for you to test the waters."

"Granny, the Internet *is not* safe." *Inhale... exhale... inhale... exhale.* "I know you're trying to help, but chatting with a bunch of hard-up, put-their-stuff-in-any-hole men is not the answer. And I was using hyperbole. Yes, you're the only person I tell everything, but I'm not some anti-social virgin who's afraid to meet people. I choose to spend my time with you because I love you and enjoy your company. Though I never want you to die, I realize our time is limited. I'm only thirty-three. I have plenty of time to run the street, and if for some reason I die tomorrow, I haven't missed out on what life has to offer because I've had you in my life for my entire life."

"I love you so much, baby." Bertha choked back tears. "I know I'm the reason you won't give yourself to a relationship. You'd need to put that man first until your children come along."

"I'm not blaming you. I live the life I want, and I'm happy." She chuckled nervously. "Horny as hell, but happy."

"I just worry about you."

"And I love you for it." She hugged Bertha. "Now what have you gotten me into? You didn't use my real name, did you?" She clicked on her username and her profile appeared. She liked the picture of her hand Bertha had used instead of a headshot.

Lips pursed, Bertha waved her off. "Of course I didn't use your real name. I signed you up for the community group. You can meet people with common interests as you. It's actually very interesting. You should give it a try. I like community chat room thirteen the best. You may even get a few ideas for your future novels from it."

"An idea is coming to me now. This guy meets a woman in the chat room. They get to know each other online, and he falls for her. But then he finds out she isn't the thirty-three-year-old woman she'd claimed to be, but a ninety-six-year-old granny pretending to be her granddaughter."

"That's the spirit!" The women laughed and toured the groups Bertha had signed Joy up for. Though Joy had heard stories about the Internet groups, what she saw was truly fascinating.

"I think I'll write a novel based off some of the things that occur in chat rooms. There's so much material here to work from."

Bertha yawned. "You should. It's time for me to hit the sack. Can you book the flight and hotel for me?"

"Can't I change your mind? At least until you've seen Dr. Slater again. First thing in the morning, I'll make an appointment for you."

"I'm not changing my mind. Make our arrangements." She kissed Joy on the cheek. "Time for bed, *Sweet Thang*," she teased.

"Troublemaker. And Sweet *Thang*? Really, Granny. *Thang*?"

"You are my sweet little thing. I had to jazz it up for the younger crowd. I know what I'm doing."

"You scare me."

After Joy set the laptop on the end table, she helped her grandmother into her wheel chair. While Joy was at work, a nurse's aide helped Bertha. "When Mom finds out, she'll probably have me arrested for kidnapping."

"Probably?" Laughing, Bertha wrapped her arms around Joy's neck for her to lift.

"You'd just best not do anything to get us caught."

Chapter Two

Sweet Thang: Why are you angry?

Angry White Man: I'll bet you think you're the first person to ask that.

Smile spread across her face, Joy readied to type her reply. They'd been debating about the war on terror for hours. She hated to admit it, but Bertha was onto something; the community chat room was great. A few men had propositioned her for cybersex, but they accepted "no thanks" and moved on. And the freedom was amazing. Since she would never meet these people, she could say whatever without worry of consequences or what anyone thought.

She actually agreed with almost everything Angry White Man said, but defended the opposing position to make things interesting. He was highly intelligent, which she admired, but his moniker fit him perfectly.

Sweet Thang: Then you'd lose. So are you angry with anyone in particular, or the world in general?

Angry White Man: Since you must know, women. You are a bunch of lying, conniving, manipulative, cheating, useless sacks of flesh.

Sweet Thang: LOL! Why don't you tell me how you really feel? Who says I'm a woman?

Angry White Man: Okay, *Sweet Thang*, I know you aren't going to LIE and say you're a man.

Sweet Thang: How do you know I'm not a gay man or a straight man who isn't afraid to express himself? You've assumed I'm a female because of a moniker that is completely made up. For all you know, I could be a space alien.

Awaiting his reply, Joy crossed her arms over her chest and watched the screen. She hadn't had this much fun with someone of the opposite sex in… a really long time. Bertha suffered her first stroke shortly after her husband passed when Joy was twenty. The sicker Bertha became, the closer to home Joy stayed. When both of Bertha's legs were amputated below the knees six years ago, Joy moved in with her grandmother. Since Joy couldn't devote the time needed for a relationship, she just didn't see the point in dating.

Angry White Man: You are correct. I've assumed things I

shouldn't have. I still think you're a woman, but I don't know. You're deeper than most women, so maybe you're a gay dude.

Sweet Thang: Oh no you didn't just say women are shallow.

Angry White Man: LOL! Hell yeah, your ass is female!

Lips pursed, Joy typed,

Sweet Thang: Okay, okay, so my ass was born connected to female parts. So who is she?

Angry White Man: Here we go… I'm not talking about her. I'm still too angry, Miss Nosey Thang. My turn. What makes you so sweet?

Sweet Thang: My granny picked out this name. She's always called me a sweet little thing. I'll be in your part of the country in a few days. Where are the hotspots?

A large amount of time passed. They'd entered the private room because the others in the community accused them of boring them to death and taking too much screen space, but the private rooms weren't as reliable. She'd already been kicked out of the private room twice.

Angry White Man: You're the same as the rest. I'm not some hard-up bastard, trolling the Internet in search of a woman. You need to move on to the freaks group for companionship.

Joy abused the keyboard when she typed.

Sweet Thang: You're reading comprehension skills aren't the best, are they? I didn't say I wanted to go out with you. I don't even know you. You have a serious projecting issue. Let me assure you, you have nothing to worry about from me. I'm a thirty-three-year-old virgin, taking my granny on the vacation of her dreams before it's too late. I don't want you in any way, shape or form. Well, that's not quite true. I'd like to pick your brain, but I don't have to meet you personally for that, so you are safe.

Unable to believe she'd revealed her virginal status, she let go of the embarrassment and readied to defend herself. She'd read a few posts in the freaks group where the members literally set up sex parties and partner swaps. She didn't have anything against the members of the group, but she wanted no parts of it.

Angry White Man: You're either lying about being a virgin or lying about your age.

Sweet Thang: Of all the things I just said, you focus on the virgin part. That tells me *exactly* where your mind is. I have no need to lie about either. Newsflash, Mr. Angry White Man, just as not all men are angry, not all women are out to get you or want you.

The sound of a car pulling into her driveway caught her attention. She glanced out the window and saw her parents' white stretch Lincoln limo. *Oh great.*

Angry White Man: You really are a virgin, aren't you?

Sweet Thang: It doesn't matter. Forget I said anything. I hate to rush off, but my parents are here to tell me what a failure I am. How about we meet up tomorrow? I want to hear your views about climate change.

Angry White Man: Damn, you *are* a heavy-hitter. Okay, I have a little research to do. Tomorrow, same time, same room.

* * *

Sean shut down his laptop and set it on the coffee table, then leaned back on the couch. After Nakia moved out, it took some serious internal scanning to pinpoint what had gone wrong. What scared him most about this breakup was he was pissed Nakia would actually cheat on him, but not hurt. They were compatible in the bedroom, but... *Damn.* It hurt like hell to admit he'd become the type of person to just want a faithful sex partner. At least that's what he'd thought he'd settled for. He'd met Nakia when he was on the rebound from a woman who'd sliced and diced his heart and served it on a platter. He had sworn never to give anyone the chance to serve him up again, but he never intended to become a heartless bastard. He'd just wanted to guard his heart.

He'd accomplished his goal and protected his heart, but Nakia hadn't fulfilled other needs he was quickly realizing he couldn't do without. He'd met Nakia at one of the hotspots in town he'd heard about in the freak chat room. He chuckled. Sweet Thang was correct; he *had* been projecting. The way she'd called him on his behavior impressed him.

Sweet Thang. Since Nakia's departure, he would go into community chat room thirteen daily to conduct his women-ain't-shit blast, but Sweet Thang had come out of lurk-mode and began talking politics. He'd noticed her a few times over the past month, but she never said anything until today. He'd replied to her comments with the advantage of being well read and an investigative reporter. He'd known this would shut her up so he could continue on his women-bashing quest, but she'd countered with reasonable arguments. The next thing he knew, hours had passed, and he'd found himself laughing and enjoying himself with a woman, and it had nothing to do with sex— something he'd never shared with Nakia.

A real live thirty-three-year-old virgin. I wonder how that happened. The way she'd gone toe-to-toe with him in their debate had shocked and turned him on. Obviously, she was a bookworm and an Internet news junkie. How else could she have been able to compete with him? And she'd mentioned a grandmother. Oh yeah, he could see it now... the little bookworm afraid to go three steps away from her granny. She had even allowed her grandmother to choose her screen name.

He'd never been with a virgin before and wondered just how sweet and tight Sweet Thang would be. His cock jumped to life. He hadn't had sex since the morning he'd kicked Nakia out. Not that he hadn't had the urge or opportunity. He just wasn't ready to be bothered with the drama associated with women.

He unzipped his pants and freed his now-throbbing member. "I miss the soft touch of a woman, too." Eyes closed, he wrapped his hand about the base of his dick and stroked, but imagined the inquisitive hands of a sweet, little virgin exploring him. Soon, she'd tire of just touching and want to taste.

Oh yeah, he could feel her hot mouth suckling his exposed dick. Initially, she'd be timid, but would soon lose all shyness. His hand stroked faster, gripped tighter. Her moans would mix with his as his fingers tangled in her hair, and soon, soon, she'd get her first real taste. Cum shot out of his dick. He drew in a sharp intake of air. It took him a few moments to regroup. This wasn't as good as the real thing, but would do, for now.

Wondering what Sweet Thang was up to, he glanced at his laptop.

* * *

Joy closed the door behind her mother. "Welcome back." She sank into her mother's loving embrace. "I missed you," she said honestly. She didn't agree with her mother on much, but she never doubted her love for her.

Emily pulled back slightly and gently pinched Joy's chin. "I missed my baby, too."

Though Emily was closer to eighty than seventy, she was still the most beautiful woman in the world to Joy. Flawless milk-chocolate skin, wavy, silver hair trimmed in a short, sleek style and big brown eyes that sparkled with youthful mischief, Emily stayed in top shape and dressed to kill.

"I have the most beautiful mother ever!"

"You've always been my joy." Emily took Joy's hand and led her to the sofa.

Joy smiled. Her brothers were dubbed Emily's heart, the twins were her pride and Joy was her joy. "I'm serious. I hope I look half as good as you when I hit fifty, let alone seventy-six. Where's Daddy?"

Emily delicately rested her hands in her lap. "I asked him to give us a few minutes alone." She finger-combed Joy's unruly hair behind her ears. "I'm worried about you. Why didn't you come to dinner?"

"There's no reason to worry. I'm doing great, really."

"No, you're not. And Mother's right, I'm part to blame."

Brows knitted together, Joy drawled, "Oh no. When did you speak with Granny?"

"Before our trip she paid a visit and laid into all of us 'old folks' for 'stunting your creative growth,' " Emily said with lots of pizzazz.

"Yep, that sounds like Granny."

"She had a mouth full for all of us from the twins to your dad. She said we need to give you freedom 'to be.' " Emily lowered her head. "But that's the problem. We've given you more freedom than the others, and look at the results: You have a dead-end job, use your granny to keep from meeting people and don't take care of yourself. Look at you. You're a beautiful young woman, but no one would know with the way you dress and carry yourself. I love Mother, but she's always been... A little different."

"She raised you and you came out fine. How many other women your age have come close to the accomplishments you have? Granny is ahead of her time, your time and mine. She's a true free spirit."

"I'm grateful to Mother for all she's done for me. She encouraged us all to reach for the impossible. I can hear her now." Back straight, she flopped one hand on her hip and pointed at Joy with her free hand, as Bertha often did in her younger days. " 'No daughter of mine will be a maid, secretary, teacher or housewife. Don't allow anyone to force you into a tiny box. You define who you are. Go build your own box and stand on top of it!' " Both women laughed lightly.

"You do Granny entirely too well."

"I love that woman. I couldn't ask for a better mother. She instilled such confidence in us I knew I could be anything. But with you… You needed something more structured, more traditional, more focused."

Joy held her tongue in order to keep the peace. Bertha had been Joy's main caregiver shortly after Emily had returned to work fulltime, and she didn't like anyone putting her in a negative light. By the time Joy came along, times had changed so drastically that being an elementary school teacher was no longer one of the few boxes women were allowed to explore but was one of many options. Bertha saw no reason to dissuade Joy from reaching for that teaching star and explained this to her many times.

"I know you like teaching, but at least consider moving to the university level. Heather has agreed to pull a few strings—"

"Sorry to interrupt, Mom, but I'm not leaving my job. I love the kids."

The way Joy saw it, all of Benjamin and Emily Warren's children—besides herself—were huge successes in their parents' eyes. First, there were the twins who were only fifty-four, yet Heather was the vice president of a university, and Helen was senior partner at a law firm. The oldest of her siblings, Marshall, was the CEO of a software company; and Joy's favorite sibling, Jonathan, owned an investment firm. Her brothers and sisters each followed the career path their parents had set out for them, and were seemingly happy with their choices, but Joy couldn't follow suit.

"Just consider it, darling. If you don't want to teach at the university level, Jonathan has also agreed to start training you—"

"Again, thanks but no thanks." Tired of the same old song, Joy barely followed the conversation, and in the back of her mind began preparing her arguments for her debate with Angry White Man tomorrow. She could hardly wait. Arguing with him was invigorating.

Emily took Joy's hands into her own. "I only want what's best for you, darling."

"I know, but it's not like I'm out there selling drugs or my body. I'm teaching the future leaders of our world. I don't make a lot of money, and being a fourth grade teacher isn't prestigious, but I'm proud of and love what I do."

"Your father and I aren't getting any younger. We're worried about you. Who will take care of you when we're gone?"

"You mean besides Marshall, Jonathan and the twins?" Joy teased. "And I know you've set up a trust fund for me through Jonathan."

Emily smiled. "We all love you. You're my smartest, brightest, sweetest child."

"That's a lot of 'est.' "

"You also have the hardest head. I know you'll want to fight me on this, but please, please just hear me out. Your father and I met a fine young man while we were on the cruise."

"Oh no!" Joy jerked her hands away. "You *are not* about to set me up on a blind date." *First Granny, now Mom!* "I knew you wanting to have a dinner the day you returned was suspicious."

"Is this your version of hearing me out?"

"I never agreed to hear anything out. Especially you hooking me up with some stranger you met on a boat."

"He's not a stranger—"

"Do I know him?"

"Your father and I do."

"That makes him a stranger to me."

"You should be a lawyer. We'll pay your tuition and living expenses while you attend law school."

"Ha, ha very funny," Joy said dryly.

"Have I *ever* tried to 'hook you up?' "

"No, and let's keep it that way. I'm happy with my way of life."

Emily motioned toward Bertha's computer, which was always left on. "By plastering naked men all over your desktop?"

"As long as the naked men aren't family members, I don't see the problem," Joy easily covered for her granny, as usual, then glanced at her own laptop to ensure she'd logged off the chat room. She wondered if Angry White Man was still online and if he were as handsome as the men her grandmother had picked out for her. Already attracted to his mind, she couldn't envision him being unattractive.

"Reasoning with you is impossible." Emily took her cell phone out of the side pocket of her purse. "I'm about to call your father. Edward is a good man. A little older than you, but you need someone who is more settled and can handle your…" She waved the phone in the air.

"Stubbornness," Joy supplied for her mother. "So you plan on hooking me up with some controlling, old coot."

"Not controlling. You need guidance, darling. One date. That's all I'm asking."

"You have to promise to never, ever, ever arrange another date for me again if I do this."

A radiant smile overtook Emily's lovely face. "That's my girl. Now go on and clean yourself up and do something with that mop you call hair. I'll have your father bring Edward in."

Joy *tsked* and rolled her eyes. "You brought him here? Now? No." She glanced at her baggy jean shirt and denims. She'd barely had time to change out of her work clothes before Bertha had called her into the living room to chat. "And I look fine."

"He followed us here to meet you. Now stop being so difficult."

"You are wrong for this, and I'm not changing until it's time for bed. Come to think of it, you didn't say he wasn't an old coot. Do I need to break out the pain patches? I just bought Granny a new box."

"Don't be mean. He's only fifty." She tapped a few buttons on her phone.

"Fifty!" Joy pretended to choke on the thought. Wait until she told Angry White Man about this. He'd laugh so hard, he wouldn't be angry any longer. "When you are seventy-six it's only fifty, but to someone on my spot on the timeline, that's way past only. He's old enough to be my—"

"Brother," Emily cut in. "Now stop all the performing." She placed the cell phone to her ear. "Yes I'm here, honey. Bring him in." She narrowed her eyes on Joy. "But let me warn you, your daughter is in rare form tonight." She disconnected, crossed over to Bertha's computer and set it on STANDBY.

"You're almost as bad as your mother," Joy grumbled. At least Emily hadn't hired any gigolos—make that she hoped she hadn't. "What is his profession?"

"Edward is a doctor. He specializes in caring for the more mature."

"Oh cool, a gerontologist. Things are looking up."

"I knew you'd like that."

A few moments later, her father introduced her to Edward, an attractive man with a stocky build and full head of dark hair. To Joy's surprise, Edward wasn't a total dud. He talked politics, seemed genuinely interested in her and commended her for her choice of career fields. Time passed quickly, but not fast enough for Joy. She still had to book their flight and hotel room and write the children's lesson plan for the following week.

Emily covered her mouth with her hand and yawned louder than Joy had ever heard her yawn before. "Whew, it's getting late, Ben." She nudged her husband, the former judge.

"Yes it's getting late," Ben reluctantly said, kissed his daughter on the cheek, then shook Edward's hand. "This is my wife's idea, not mine."

Joy had to give it to her father. Though one year shy of eighty, he was still an imposing man, and usually took her side on issues. Emily had refused to pay Joy's tuition for college in order to force her to enter a more "aggressive program," then Benjamin gave his baby girl a very generous high school graduation gift. Between the gift, scholarship money and a part-time job, Joy could afford to obtain a master's degree in elementary education.

She hugged her mother and whispered into her ear, "I hope you don't think you're fooling anyone, Bertha Junior."

"What?" Emily asked innocently, eliciting a smile from Joy.

"Good night, Mom." She walked her parents to the front door and noticed a BMW parked out front. "Love you." She waved good-bye to her parents as they walked toward the limo, then returned her attention to Edward. "Is that your car out front?"

"Yes, ma'am," Edward said. "So tell me, why you aren't married?"

"Why aren't you married?"

He stood and held his hands out to her. "I haven't found the right one yet."

She didn't know what to do with his outstretched hands. "That makes two of us." She shifted her weight from one foot to the other and chewed on her inner jaw. "Would you like another soda?"

"I'd like you to lower your guard for a little while so you can get to know me. What are you afraid of?" He stepped closer, and she fought the urge to back away. She didn't know what was wrong. Everything about Edward appeared perfect, yet something didn't feel right. There were too many things wrong with Angry White Man, yet her mind continued to wander back to him.

"I can tell you're uncomfortable, so I'll call it a night also." He caressed her cheek, which sent a nauseating chill along her spine. "You are more than I expected."

She gazed into the soft brown eyes of this handsome man who had the same interests as her, and decided her parents and granny were correct; there was something seriously wrong with her—why wasn't she attracted to him? Why was she more interested in the Angry White Man she would never meet than a real live man?

"We're a perfect match, you'll see. What time should I pick you up tomorrow?"

"Any time after four works for me."

"Then we have a date. Five o'clock. Dress casual." He took her by the hand and led her to the door, which was way too intimate for her, but she didn't jerk her hand away. He stopped in the doorway and faced her. "I know your family has been very protective."

"Overprotective," she corrected with a smile.

"Yes, overprotective of you. I'm a patient man. We'll take this one step at a time."

She nibbled on her lower lip. "Granny needs me."

"You're right. She does," he said, shocking the heck out of her. "I admire the way you care for her, but you have needs, too. You don't have to deny yourself to care for her. At least with me you don't have to."

"I don't know what my mom told you, but I'm not looking for a relationship. You're a great guy, and we can be friends, but I don't want to lead you on."

"We're not getting married tomorrow, and believe it or not, this is just as crazy to me. I can't tell you how many women have tried to fix me up with their daughters."

"Being a single doctor, I'll bet you get that a lot."

"I've never met one of the daughters, but the more your mother talked about you, the more I knew I had to meet you. We're both in unfamiliar territory here. So, my friend, I'll see you tomorrow." He took out his business card and wrote his cell number on the back. "Call me anytime."

Chapter Three

Joy waited for Edward to ease into his car and pull away, and then she headed in to take a shower. She felt like a complete jerk. She'd set in her mind not to like Edward, then he turned out to be a nice guy. Granted, she wasn't attracted to him and didn't want to be anything more than friends, but she'd automatically dismissed him because of the source.

She showered, readied for bed, flicked off the lights and slid between the satin sheets with her laptop. She still needed to book their flight and hotel room and had to get her lesson plan together. She knew her grandmother's credit card information by heart, so booking their travel arrangements went smoothly. She'd also had her class plans mapped out, so typing them up for the substitute only took a few minutes.

I wonder if he's online? She glanced at the time—11:30 P.M. It would only be 8:30 for him. She moved the cursor over to the community shortcut. As soon as she entered chat room thirteen, other members began asking her what she'd done to Angry White Man. He had apparently come in a few times without his usual ranting. Instead, he had lurked a few minutes and left.

Sweet Thang: LOL. It wasn't me, I swear.

XQQQME: All times of day and night, for months, Angry White Man has been coming in here bashing women, then leaving. I'm homebound and stay online most of the day. I always see him cutting up.

Baby Girl: Yep. That man has serious issues, but he was in here a bit ago and didn't say a word. Tell us your secret. SMILE

Joy laughed. This was too funny.

Sweet Thang: I didn't do anything. Really.

Easy Money: Well, whatever you *didn't do,* keep not doing it because his ass was chasing the women away. This room has the hottest honeys out there. Hey, Baby Girl, you wanna hook up tomorrow?

... Angry White Man has entered community room thirteen

Joy loved the way the main window showed when someone entered or left.

... Too Lovely has left community room thirteen
... Twinkle has left community room thirteen

21

... Cherry Delight has left community room thirteen

Easy Money: Oh hell, here comes trouble, and there go the women.

... Sunshine has left community room thirteen

Sweet Thang: Whew howdy, Angry White Man. You *really* know how to clear a room!

Easy Money: Don't get him started.

... Ebony Jewel has left community room thirteen

Angry White Man: They just can't handle the truth.

Sweet Thang: Umm hmm

... Angry White Man has invited you to a private chat session

Chuckling, Joy accepted his invitation before the entire community evacuated. Hopefully, people would notice the private chat icon beside his moniker and not run.

Sweet Thang: How do you have so much time to be online?

Angry White Man: I do a lot of work on my laptop, so I pop in every so often to spread the word, and then get back to work.

Sweet Thang: Spread the word, huh. LOL. Okay, Rev. Angry White Man. So what word are you spreading tonight?

Angry White Man: I'm giving the masses a break tonight to give a little personal attention to one of my flock. Someone I believe can be saved before she goes down that same destructive, lying, conniving path many of the sisters before her have gone.

Joy burst out in laughter. Smart and funny, she knew her granny would like him.

Sweet Thang: You are a nut. But I like it in you.

Angry White Man: Are you flirting with me?

Sweet Thang: You're the expert on women. You tell me.

Angry White Man: I'll leave it alone—for now. So how did it go with your folks?

Sweet Thang: LOL Chicken. Let me see. After my mom told me what a failure I am, she set me up on a date with an older gentleman because she thinks I need someone to "guide" me.

Angry White Man: From what I can tell, you aren't a failure at all, but damn. LMAO Are you actually going out with an old man?

Sweet Thang: This will take a bit for me to type. I'm chat room ignorant. Explain what LMAO means while I do this.

Angry White Man: LMAO = Laugh My Ass Off.

Sweet Thang: I knew you'd get a kick out of that. I told my mom I'd go out with him once if she never Ever EVER set me up again. Did I tell you Granny tried to hire a gigolo for me to lose my virginity to when I get to Los Angeles? My life is so crazy it's funny but not funny at the same time. And this guy Mom hooked me up with—he's actually a nice guy, but we just didn't click. Now Mom will thin

Joy stared at the screen for a few seconds. Part of her message didn't show.

Angry White Man: Slow your roll, Sweet. Your messages are too long to transmit entirely. After a few lines just type … when you want to continue without comment.

Sweet Thang: Cool, thanks…

She waited a few seconds to see if he would comment.

Sweet Thang: Wow, this really works. Whenever I want you to be quiet, all I have to do is type … Okay, let me finish this rant…

Angry White Man: Don't abuse the power, baby.

Joy glanced up to see where her message had been cut off, then relayed to Angry White Man everything that had happened. He offered a few comments, and if she didn't know better, she would have thought he were a little jealous of Edward. Reading someone's emotions through a computer screen was impossible, she told herself. Angry White Man had no reason to be jealous. She knew she was the one projecting now. As wild as it seemed, she was falling for this man on the Internet and wanted him to tell her not to go out with Edward.

Oh man I need some help. One day on the chat lines, and I'm already tripping. These things are dangerous.

… *Big Thick Dick has invited you to a private chat session*

Joy declined the invitation and continued chatting with Angry White Man. A few moments later, a second private message window popped up on her screen from Big Thick Dick. Proper protocol was to invite someone to a private chat, but if you wished to just send a single private message, that was acceptable.

Big Thick Dick: I know you aren't wasting your time with

23

Angry White Man when you could be enjoying your time with me. This Big Thick Dick is waiting to find its home in your hot, wet pussy.

Sweet Thang: Thanks, but no thanks. And please do not message me privately.

She returned to her conversation with Angry White Man, but Big Thick Dick continued sending her vulgar private messages.

Sweet Thang: How do I put someone on ignore?

Angry White Man: Why, are you trying to ignore me? LOL

Sweet Thang: Never that SMILE. This Big Thick Dick of a jerk keeps harassing me. I told him I don't want to go private with him, but he won't take no for an answer.

Angry White Man: BRB, which means be right back, my little cybervirgin LOL.

Joy tried to figure out how to put Big Thick Dick on ignore while she waited on Angry White Man. A short time later, Big Thick Dick complained to her for siccing Angry White Man on him.

Excitement rushed through her at the thought of Angry White Man defending her. She began to laugh uncontrollably. This had been the most outrageous day of her life! First, her granny hired a gigolo, then her mother set her up with a more mature, settled man, now she had a cyber-boyfriend. She wiped the laughter tears from her face.

Angry White Man: I'm back.

Sweet Thang: Thank you.

Angry White Man: For what? I haven't done anything.

Sweet Thang: Sure you didn't. Where were we?

Angry White Man: Have you ever kissed? I mean with some tongue, not some chaste kiss on the cheek or something.

Sweet Thang: Plan on acting like you didn't see my question, huh? Okay, I'll play along. Yes, but I'm not into slob. Why?

She'd tried kissing many times, but the men she'd been with seemed to want to suck her whole face off. Kissing equaled nasty and sloppy in her mind. Why people loved it was beyond her, yet she found herself wondering how Angry White Man would kiss her. He was always on point, so she couldn't see him being a sloppy kisser. He'd be meticulous, careful and attentive to her needs. She licked her lips.

Angry White Man: Just curious. And if he slobbered all over you, he didn't know what he was doing.

Sweet Thang: I've read in several novels where folks' lips tingled and stuff while kissing. Is that true? I mean, if it's done right.

Angry White Man: If we kissed, you'd definitely be tingling.

Fingers hovering above the keys, she nervously nibbled her lower lip. Was this territory she wanted to enter into—hell yea—but should she?

Sweet Thang: Promises, promises.

Angry White Man: What about oral sex? Have you indulged?

No man had ever touched her most private area. Not even her doctor. And the man she wanted could be a psycho for all she knew. Yet she still wanted him. She touched her bottom lip with the tip of her finger. She wanted him to make her tingle. The juncture between her legs heated in response to her admission.

Sweet Thang: Man, you're all up in my business today. What are you, a reporter or something? Are you working on a feature article about virgins?

Angry White Man: As a matter of fact, I'm an investigative reporter, and writing an article about virgins over thirty is an excellent idea. Thanks. Do you masturbate? I'll answer that one first. One of my favorite pastimes.

Just when she thought her life couldn't get any more outrageous, it did. There was no turning back now. She was grown, and they weren't hurting anyone, she justified in her mind.

Sweet Thang: Yes.

Angry White Man: How about cybersex?

Sweet Thang: No.

Angry White Man: Your answers are so short. Have I angered, embarrassed or scared you?

Sweet Thang: I'm embarrassed and a little scared, but I don't know why. I guess I'm afraid to explore. This day has been overwhelming is all.

Angry White Man: Explore what? Your sexuality?

Sweet Thang: I guess so. Which is silly when you think

about it. I mean, what could happen? But the fear is still there. I can't figure out where the fear comes from. I wasn't abused as a child. My family is extremely protective, but what's the deal? And there is also this shame. Like wanting to feel good is wrong. It's crazy. Don't laugh at me, but I'm sitting here all hot and horny wanting you to

Angry White Man: To do what? Your message was too long.

Completely embarrassed, she flushed.

Sweet Thang: Thank goodness. The Internet is dangerous. I was about to make a fool of myself.

Angry White Man: I doubt that. Since you won't tell me what you wanted me to do, I guess I'll have to make it up. I write for a living you know.

Sweet Thang: So I'm told. Giggle

Angry White Man: Just sit back and relax. Allow me to read your mind. Tell me if I'm close.

Worried what he would type next, yet intrigued, Joy leaned against the headboard and resituated the laptop. In the battle between "what she wanted to do" and "what she should do," her wants beat out her shoulds. She wanted to explore possibilities with Angry White Man. She pulled her lip into her mouth.

Angry White Man: You want me to kiss you as you've never been before, taking the sensitive flesh of your lower lip into my mouth, nibbling, teasing until you tingle.

She could see the whole scene playing out in her mind. Her lips began to tingle and moisture joined the heat between her legs. Even her clit began to twitch.

Sweet Thang: You were more than close. You were right on target. I didn't expect to actually feel anything.

Angry White Man: Do you have an earpiece for your laptop? If so, let's switch over to audio.

Sweet Thang: Okay, give me a second.

Without thinking, she reached into her nightstand for her Bluetooth, then readied her computer and set it on the nightstand.

"Are you there?" She turned away from the glow of the computer and placed a pillow beneath her head.

"I'm here, baby."

She sighed wistfully. *That voice*. Deep without digging too deep, hoarse without sounding harsh, smooth without appearing slick—perfect. Edward's voice wasn't even half as nice.

"What are you thinking?" he asked.

"About voices."

"Any voice in particular?"

"I plead the fifth. I can't believe I'm doing this. My lips still... Never mind." She ran her index finger over her lips

"No never mind, tell me. There's no need to be shy or embarrassed with me."

"They actually tingle," she said quietly.

"That's it, baby. This is our world. There's nothing to fear or be ashamed of here. Have you ever touched yourself?"

Blood rushed to her face. "I told you I've masturbated..." In the midst of anxiety overload, she released a nervous giggle. "I can't believe I'm doing this."

"I mean really touched yourself. Where are you at?"

Second thoughts abundant, she looked about the dark room. "I'm in bed."

She heard him draw in a deep breath, then say, "That's perfect, baby. You're perfect."

No matter how much she told herself he was saying what he thought she wanted to hear, she loved hearing what he had to say. She didn't have a need to be perfect, but acceptable to her parents would be nice. Past tired of the disappointment in her parents' eyes, she sighed. Yes her father usually took her side, but she knew even he wanted "more" from her. He was just taking care of his lost baby girl.

"You still with me, Sweet Thang?"

"I'm here."

"What's wrong?"

"What makes you think something's wrong?" She hugged the extra pillow close to her body.

"I can hear it in your voice. We're friends before anything else. You can confide in me."

"Where have you been my whole life?"

"Waiting for you to find me."

"Awww, you are such a... *playa*. You need to stop." She laughed.

"But I was smooth, wasn't I?" He chuckled.

Avoiding what both of them wanted had become awkward. She knew he wouldn't force the issue, which she liked in him.

They'd go at her pace. Again, what she "wanted to do" and "what she should do" battled ferociously within her.

"Why shouldn't I?" she asked.

"Why shouldn't you what?"

She covered her mouth with her hands. "I didn't mean to say that aloud, but…"

"But what?"

Eyes closed tight, she lowered her hands. "I want you to make me tingle in other places," she rushed out before she lost her nerve.

"I'll need you to speak to me. I love your voice. If you could see what you've done to me… What are you wearing?"

"Sorry to break the mood, but nothing sexy. A T-shirt and panties."

"Seeing you in one of my T-shirts would be sexy as hell. Are you sure you want to do this, baby girl."

Oh how she wished she could see him, feel him. Her clit twitched again. "Yes, I'm sure."

Chapter Four

Everything has to be perfect. Sherri rushed about Edward's house to straighten up and set the mood. After ten years of being Edward's lover, there was no way she'd give him up to some wet-behind-the-ears woman-child. She couldn't give him the children he wanted, and the way they'd met wasn't under the best of circumstances, but she'd given him so much over the years and had so much more to offer. When honest with herself, her time invested in their relationship wasn't what had her preparing to seduce him into a marriage proposal. She was in love with him—had been since he'd saved her—and wished she'd told him her real feelings years ago instead of continuing with their arrangement so long.

She lit a few unscented tea light candles and spread them throughout the living room, master bedroom and bathrooms, then for a hint of scent, she placed a cinnamon spice votive candle in the main hallway.

Why she'd allowed their arrangement to go on so long was beyond her. By allowing it, he must have assumed she wasn't interested in more than being lovers. She'd gotten comfortable, complacent, and now some virgin who didn't know a condom from a balloon was primed to become Mrs. Edward Knox.

She placed the lighter on top of the refrigerator, then headed for the guest bedroom to change into something "more comfortable." Waiting for Edward to realize she was everything he needed hadn't worked. Time to turn up the heat so high any thoughts of this little girl would be burned right out of his mind.

Just as she made the finishing touches to her hair, she heard Edward's car pull into the driveway. She quickly ran the flat iron through the last section of her hair. Her long, naturally blonde hair was the envy of many and her favorite feature. Forty-seven years old and she had yet to find a gray strand of hair. She set the flat iron down and checked her watch. It was early, so she figured Little Miss Virgin must still be a virgin. That Edward hadn't slept with another woman since they'd become a "couple" so many years ago showed her he cared about her more than he let on. It was just this baby thing getting in their way. She shrugged off her uneasy feelings. They'd work it out. She would convince him he could love a child not of his own blood and to look into adoption, but first she had to get rid of Little Miss Virgin.

She buckled the strap of her high-heeled, red pumps, then stood and checked her entire look in the mirror. The black lace trim of her satin flyaway baby-doll nightie rounded her slender neck and continued to the crevice between her breasts where a dainty bow awaited Edward's fingers to untie his welcome home gift. Her heart warmed and pussy clenched in anticipation of Edward's return.

She applied a coat of deep raspberry lipstick, then rushed into the living room and waited patiently beside the sofa. Within seconds, Edward entered and stood in the doorway with his eyes and mouth wide open.

"Sherri." The shock displayed on his face quickly transformed to lust. "You're looking…" He cleared his throat and set his suitcases to the side, then took off his loafers and shut the door. "I didn't expect to see you."

"I could leave, if you'd like," she teased and headed toward the guest room. She heard him approach, but she continued to sashay slowly along the hallway. "It won't take long for me to change."

From behind, he wrapped an arm around her waist, drew her close, and ground his dick between her buttocks. He smoothed her hair away from her left ear and nibbled on the lobe, whispering, "A month is much too long."

"Yes," she purred, her juices flowing, "entirely too long." Confident his little virgin didn't have what it took to catch a real man, she glanced over her shoulder into his lust-filled eyes. "So what are you going to do about it?"

"I'll think of something." He suckled along her neck.

"As long as that something involves you entering me soon—"

Her words were cut off as he picked her up and carried her into the master bedroom.

She squealed in sheer delight. *Oh yes, he's mine. All mine.*

He dropped her onto the bed. She watched him quickly disrobe and roll a condom on. He took off her shoes, then kissed each of her freshly polished toenails while caressing her calves. With each touch of his lips, tiny shards of pleasure raced along her leg to her crotch. Over the years, he'd located and learned how to stimulate each of her erogenous zones.

He suckled the soft flesh between her toes, and she thought she'd go mad. Only a man in love took the time to learn his lover's needs and strove to fulfill them. Edward knew her well and always pleased her.

He crawled between her legs and feasted on her inner thighs. It took all of her willpower not to scoot down so his mouth would meet her waiting, wanting clitoris. She gripped the spread and allowed him to continue doing things his way. In the end, she was always rewarded.

He fingered her thong to the side, slipped two fingers into her moist pussy and gently suckled her clit.

She moaned and wrapped her hands around his head. "So good," she breathed out. As he continued to stimulate the engorged nub between her legs with his thumb, he replaced his playful fingers with his tongue and eagerly swallowed every drop of her juices. She held his head and pumped his tongue until an orgasm threatened to rip through her body.

"Edward…" she cried and tried to swallow his tongue with her pussy. This was too good, too powerful. She didn't want to come like this. "I need more. Please. I need you."

The tea lights spread throughout the room provided just enough light for her to see the desire in his dark eyes as he lifted himself, then plunged into her.

"Oh God yes!" She gripped onto his butt and met him stroke for stroke. A month was definitely too long for her to go without this good loving! She knew she should have insisted he take her on the cruise with her. Things would change once they were married.

He pulled out. "Roll over," he demanded.

Happy to oblige, she rolled over and eagerly waited for him to re-enter. With his first thrust, she almost lost it. He continued pounding from behind while he wrapped his hand around and fondled her breasts. She wasn't sure she could hold her orgasm at bay any longer.

"I want on top," she panted, in an attempt to stall her impending sexual explosion. She was supposed to be the one rocking his world, not the other way around. She needed time to regroup and take control of the situation.

Without missing a beat, he lay on his back, then grabbed her by the waist and sat her on his erection. She'd thought by her being on top she'd be the one in control, but he held her hips and guided the force and depth of each stroke. It felt so exquisite she didn't fight it. She no longer cared about rocking his world. She just pressed her pelvis into him harder and took every inch of him into her body.

"Umm, that's it, baby," he groaned. "Take it all. Take it all."

The orgasm she'd been avoiding refused to be put off any longer. "Oh sheee…"

Without pulling out, he quickly flipped them and lifted her leg over his shoulder and continued to pump.

"That's my spot!" she cried. "Hell yeah, that's my spot." Within seconds, an orgasm the likes she'd never experienced took hold of her and wouldn't let go. Her breathing became ragged, vision blurred and hearing muffled. She thought she heard Edward saying something, but she was too far-gone.

* * *

Showered and sated, Sherri kissed Edward on his chest, then lay in the bed and faced him. What they'd just shared was incredible. He'd obviously changed his mind about pursuing the virgin, but she couldn't allow things to go back to how they were. It was time for her to take charge in their relationship and move it to the next level.

She slowly ran her index finger over his nipple. Eyes closed, she reaffirmed that the time had come for her to stake her claim. He loved her; she just needed to be more aggressive and reach for what she wanted. "I'm ready." She opened her eyes. "We're ready to move to the next step. I want marriage."

"Stop playing around." He chuckled.

Her pain from his laughter quickly turned to anger. "I'm serious." She sat up.

He scooted up and leaned against the headboard. "But…" His brows dipped into confusion. "You've been fine with our arrangement."

"Well, I'm not anymore." She reached for his hand. "What we have is special. Okay, we don't have to marry, but I won't tolerate your chasing after that little girl."

"Who the hell do you think you're speaking to?" he said with a threatening tone she hadn't heard in years. "You have got to be kidding me. You knew from the start I had no intentions on ever marrying you."

She drew in a deep breath and stood her ground. "Initially,

yes, but things have changed for us. We can adopt."

"I want," he drew his hand to his chest, "I deserve someone worthy of me. I only want the best—a real family with my real children. Not some child whose parents didn't even want him."

The best… the best… always the best. She was the best, and because she'd been so lax in taking what was rightfully hers, he didn't appreciate all she was to him. But her love would get them through this rough spot. She wouldn't allow him to lose a good thing. If she could just have his child… A plan quickly formed in her mind to fake pregnancy, then just as quickly dissipated. *I watch too many soaps.*

"I am worthy. I'd do anything for you. I've been at your beck and call for years."

"How do you figure you're good enough? Yes you've been at my beck and call, but that is why I paid for your condo, your car, pay your bills, give you money every month. You want for nothing. I even hired a maid to clean your place twice a week. You're nothing but a high-priced whore." He exited the bed and snatched his robe off the end of the bed.

She wrapped the thin summer comforter around herself and rushed over to him. He'd saved her life, literally, and treated her as she should be treated. He had to be in love with her. She just had to make him see it before he ruined everything with that, that, that virgin. "Our relationship has grown past that."

"I only want the best. I only accept the best."

"I am the best. Admit it, Edward. We belong together."

He slipped into his robe and yanked it closed. "I've been waiting my entire life for someone worthy of me. I'd given up, then you came along—"

"And I fulfilled your every need," she cut in and eased toward him, but he stepped back.

"No. You fulfill my sexual urges."

"Give me a break." She held the comforter closed with one hand and rested the other on her narrow hip. "I know what I have between my legs is good, but no pussy is that damn good. The reason you treat me so well is because you care for me."

He ran his hands over his mane of thick black hair. She wished he'd cut it, but he loved it so she didn't bother him about its length. "Of course I care for you. I'm not some unfeeling ass. I killed your fucking pimp and took responsibility for you. But I want what I want. I've waited patiently for the right woman to come along. You know me. I never settle. I deserve the best. I'll be honest. I thought she may never come, but that was a chance I was willing to take. Now you want me to throw away this once-in-a-lifetime opportunity for a whore."

Tears streamed down her face. "You don't mean that, Edward. You can't just turn your feelings for me off." His want of a child had clouded his judgment, but she'd stay strong for both of them. He'd been loving and attentive for years, she wouldn't give up on him easily. "You're going to regret what you've said, but I forgive you."

An eerie laugh ripped from his gut. "Don't play me for stupid. The only reason you're talking marriage and love now is because you think your job security is being threatened. Allow me to alleviate your fears. Even after I marry Joy, I'll still have sexual urges only you can fill. Our relationship doesn't have to change. I'll even deposit a hundred grand in your savings account so you won't be dependent on me. "

"No." She reached for him again, and again he backed away. "I'm not running some game on you. I want to be Mrs. Edward Knox. I've given you my heart, body and soul. I love you."

"You're not in love with me. You're in love with the security of being a doctor's wife."

"That's not true.

"You're not even what I want in a wife. Hell, do you remember how I used to suggest you take a few college courses, maybe get a job to fill your time?"

She remembered very well. She'd thought he was kidding. She was too damn old to be returning to school. And what for? He provided her with everything she needed. Same went for a job.

"I deserve someone who wants more out of life than to be a good lay. I gave you options, but you're nothing but a high-priced whore—by choice."

She sniffed and wiped the tears from her face. "My full-time job was taking care of you. I don't have time for school or a second job."

"We have separate domiciles. I work six days a week, ten hours a day. I see you maybe twice a week. What do you do all day besides shop, hang out at the athletic club and watch television?"

"I have to look good when we go out, and I stay in shape for you also."

"Bull. It's this simple. This is not *Pretty Woman*. I am not marrying a whore."

Every time he said the word "whore" was like a flaming knife being plunged into her heart. Now her mistakes were clear. He'd been trying to get her to change into the woman he wanted, and she'd dismissed him.

"Get dressed and leave my key behind on your way out."

"Edward, no!" She latched onto his arm. "You can't do this."

He wrapped his hands around her throat and squeezed. The comforter fell from her naked body as she tried to pry his fingers away.

"You think I'd give my family up for you?" She looked into his enraged eyes and saw loathing. He shoved her away. "Now look what you've made me do."

She drew in several deep breaths. "I'm sorry," she eked out. "I'm sorry." She knew Edward's history. How he'd watched his father beat his mother to death. How he'd been put in foster care. How he'd run away when he was fourteen. How he'd missed too many meals to count. She chastised herself for taking Edward's needs for granted. He had done without for far too long. He did deserve the best, and she would do what she had to, to become what he wanted.

"I don't want to be this type of man. Why do you make me hurt you?"

"I'm so sorry, Edward. Please forgive me."

He sat on the bed and lowered his face into his palms. "I'm marrying Joy. I can see our arrangement is too much for you. I'm not a monster. I'm not my adoptive father. I'll put a hundred grand in your account."

She knelt before him. "Don't put me out of your life. We'll remain lovers." She laid her head in his lap. His little virgin wouldn't last long. After Edward had a child of his own bloodline, he'd lose interest in her. In the meantime, Sherri planned to find a job, enroll in college and continue being Edward's sexual fantasy.

He weaved his fingers through her hair to her scalp and massaged. "Are you sure? You'll be my lover, but we can't be seen out together anymore."

"I understand."

"I still need the key to my place back. I want all traces of you out of this house by tomorrow. I'll come to your condo from now on."

She refused to cry. "That makes perfect sense."

He combed her hair with his fingers. "I also want you to cut your hair."

She sat straight up and finger-combed her hair. "What? But why?"

He caressed her face. "You're so beautiful. Your hair is a distraction, not an enhancement. Don't you think it's time for a new style? And how about dying it darker. I'd like to see what you look like as a brunette."

This didn't make sense. He'd always loved the way her hair brushed against his chest when they fucked. No, he knew how much she loved her hair. This must be his way of punishing her for upsetting him. And she didn't blame him. She deserved to be punished for being so stupid. He'd given her hint after hint about the type of woman he wanted her to become so they could marry, but she'd ignored them.

"It's your choice," he continued.

* * *

Joy hugged the pillow close to her tingling body. "I can't believe we did that," she said lazily and adjusted her earpiece. "That was great." They'd switched from Internet to cell phones earlier for a clearer connection.

"If I smoked, I'd be lighting up right now. Damn, woman, you learn fast."

"Why thank you." She giggled. "Must be the teacher in me."

"Are you actually a teacher?"

She crinkled the end of the pillow between her fingers. "Fourth grade," she said tentatively.

"Cool. My mom's a teacher. Is something wrong?"

"No, no. I'm just feeling a little insecure tonight. Don't pay any attention to me. My mother has that effect on me."

"You didn't seem too insecure a few minutes ago," he teased.

Excitement welled up in her. "I still can't believe we did that. What's your real name? I'm Joy."

"Sean."

"Pleased to meet you, Sean. I can hardly wait to get to California for a live performance."

"Oh no you don't. I don't touch virgins. I already have enough going against me."

"Chicken."

"Reverse psychology doesn't work on me. To remove any temptation, I'm booking a flight for D.C. as soon as we get off the phone."

"Scary cat."

"Who you calling scared? Didn't you tell me you haven't even been in a sex shop before, cybervirgin?"

"Ex-virgin." She rested her head on the pillow fully. "And the sex shop not being a part of my life has nothing to do with fear. I don't know where any are and my curiosity hasn't been so great to find one." She yawned.

"Yeah right. Look, Joy, you're tired and I have a flight to book. We'll talk tomorrow. Good night, baby girl."

"Goodnight, Sean." She disconnected, saved his number, then headed for the shower. He had given her his phone number and insisted she call him by blocking her number. *Such a gentleman.* He'd said he wanted it this way to help her feel more secure, but for some unknown reason, she already felt secure with him, as if she'd known him her entire life. To make him happy, she'd gone ahead and blocked her number, but next time, who knew.

She turned on the shower and began stripping. Tomorrow was one long day she didn't look forward to. Mainly the end of the day—her date with Edward. *One date. I can make it through one date.*

Chapter Five

Joy stayed after school a little longer than usual to handpick who the substitute would be for her next week. She couldn't just leave her babies with anybody. Plus, she was stalling. By choice she hadn't been on a date in years and wasn't looking forward to this one. Over her lunch break she'd spoken at length with Sean about her date. He suggested something probably happened to her when she was young to make her shy away from men. Well, whatever the problem was, she definitely didn't want some repressed memories surfacing. Minus the meddling family, she liked her life as it was and didn't see a reason to change. After she left the school, she stopped at the beauty salon for an appointment Bertha had set up. She looked in the rearview mirror. The bobbed cut framed her face nicely, if she did say so herself.

Glad her mother's car was nowhere in sight, she closed the door to her Altima and strolled along the walkway to the porch. She'd half-expected Emily to be there—actually, she'd fully expected her mother to be there "coaching" her on what to wear and how to "behave" on this date from hell. She stopped her train of thought. Categorizing this evening as the date from hell wasn't fair to Edward. He was a nice man and deserved a fair chance.

She lazily stepped into the house.

"Run, Joy, run," called Bertha from her room. Helen, one of the twins, rushed out of the room.

Without a second thought, Joy ran back outside for her car. Her sisters were as meddlesome as her mother—maybe even worse. Heather, the other half of double trouble, was standing in front of the Altima with one hand on her hip. "What the hell have you done to your hair? Get back in there now."

Joy resisted the urge to pout. First her mother railroaded her into this date, now her too bossy sisters were about to make her look like Little Orphan Annie. Her sisters had given her at least ten versions of the orphan's red dress with white collar.

"Cut it. You're not my mother. You can't tell me what to do."

"Joy," Emily snapped, "get your behind in this house and stop sassing your sister."

Startled, Joy swung around and saw her mother. "Eeewwwww, I can't believe my life." She walked past her mother to her grandmother's room.

"I'm sorry, baby. I tried to call and warn you." Bertha nodded toward the door where Emily and her partners in crime stood. "But *they* took my cell phone and sent Nancy on an errand," she said, referring to her caregiver.

"Don't worry about it." She gently hugged her granny who was sitting against the headboard of the bed. "How was your day today?"

"Fantastic until you know who showed up." She fingered Joy's short hair. "I love this cut. Don't listen to anything they say. You are perfect just the way you are."

Joy barely got out a "Thanks, Granny," before her sisters fully entered the room.

"Stop coddling her," Heather began.

"That's her problem now," Helen finished and pulled Joy from the bed.

"If you two look at each other, you'd see exactly what my *problem* is. Make that *who*."

"Stop acting childish, Joy," her mother chastised.

"Then stop treating me like a child." She pulled away from her sisters. "I'm thirty-three years old, Mom. Do you know how humiliating and demoralizing this treatment is?"

"Oh God," Heather drawled, "she's broken out the college words."

"We've been shopping all day and have found the perfect outfit for you to wear tonight," Helen said with entirely too much sweetness in her voice for Joy. "Come on to your room and see."

"I'm not wearing anything red. Granny, do you want to come see?"

"No thanks. I need to rest up a bit."

Joy hugged her granny, then walked to her bedroom with her mother and sisters close behind. There was no use in fighting them. They'd just make her life more miserable.

"I was serious about not wearing red. I hope you didn't waste your time."

"Stop being difficult, Joy," her mother said.

"Red is your color," Heather added.

"You should wear it every chance you get," Helen finished.

Joy entered her room and was shocked to see Anna, her niece who happened to be two months her senior, sitting on the bed with her arms folded over her chest and a scowl on her face.

"They made me do it," Anna said. "I told them to step out of your business, but you know how they are. The walls listen better than them."

"You are not too old to turn over my knee," Helen, Anna's mother, warned.

"Straighten your face, girl," Heather added.

Joy hugged Anna. She felt sorry for her niece. At least Joy had Bertha as a buffer from the overbearing women in the family, poor Anna had no one. "I'm sorry you're mixed up in this mess."

"It's not your fault, and you know I've got your back." Anna motioned toward the bed where several dresses and a nice pants outfit were displayed. "As you see, we've been shopping. You know I threw a fit until they put back *all* of the red dresses except this one."

Anna picked up a simple, sleeveless red dress with medium-sized white polka dots and a small white collar that Joy had to admit was cute. Instead of Little Orphan Annie, this dress resembled something Minnie Mouse would wear. Jokingly, she looked around the room for a red bow to put in her hair. The other dresses actually appealed to Joy also, so she knew her sisters hadn't chosen them.

Joy picked up the pink slacks and white blouse. "This is a casual date. This stuff is all too fancy."

The twins smiled at each other. "Excellent, now shoes," Heather said as if Joy had chosen to wear the pants outfit.

"I bought the perfect shoes for those slacks." Her mother sorted through a stack of boxes near the closet. She selected three boxes and set them on the bed, which the twins had cleared of the other outfits. "But I know how you like choices, so I bought three nice pairs of shoes." She opened all three boxes.

"Thanks, Mom." Joy took out the strappy pair she knew her mother would like most. "These are nice," she said honestly. "The clothes are all nice, but this is a casual dinner. I should be wearing jeans and a nice blouse, not dress slacks, high-heeled pumps and Lord knows what else you all have up your sleeves."

Heather broke in with, "Look at the earrings I picked up

for you." She opened the jewelry box and displayed the most gorgeous pair of diamond teardrop earrings Joy had ever seen.

"I... I..." Joy stammered. "I can't wear these. They're too... too..." She guessed the earrings cost more than she would make in a year. She loved her family, but hated the way they wasted money. Most of her students came from low-income families and much of her salary went to ensure they had supplies, proper clothing, healthy snacks...

Heather beamed. "I'll take that as you like them, and of course you're going to wear them. Edward has money. This will show him you don't need his financial backing. You're with him because you want to be, not because you need to be."

"I'm not into playing games, and these are too expensive. It's not even my birthday."

"These aren't too expensive. If you'd quit playing around with the 'Little Rascals' and get a real job, you'd know that."

Joy's siblings made more in a month than she did in a year, but she loved working with the children and had a comfortable life. "I have a real job."

Heather fingered her baby sister's hair. "I don't know what we'll do with your hair. What possessed you to cut it off?"

"There's nothing wrong with my hair." Joy stepped away from her sister.

"You look like a little boy," Helen added. "Do you have any clothes that actually fit?"

"And then you two wonder why I don't like you."

"Joy," snapped her mother.

"Well, it's true. I love them, but can't stand them." Most of the time she felt the same way about her mother, but decided to keep that little fact to herself.

"I love your hair," Anna said honestly. "Anything past the shoulders is just a waste." She turned toward her mother. "Why don't you all keep Granny company while I try to tone down some of Joy's beauty. We don't want to give Edward a heart attack." She winked at Joy.

The three older ladies hesitated, but left Joy alone with her niece.

After closing the door, Anna went over to the walk-in closet. "They didn't tell me this was a casual dinner, and you know I asked."

She joined her niece in the closet. "I love the outfits you

picked, though. And those earrings are gorgeous!"

"Who you telling?" Anna giggled. "You know I guilted Auntie Heather into purchasing me a pair also." She pulled out a pair of pastel yellow gauchos, a matching light-weight, V-neck tunic and a pair of sandals. "This will be perfect."

"Ooooo, you're going to be in trouble," Joy teased.

"Huh-uh, I'm telling them you refused to dress in the clothes they bought. You know they'll believe me."

After a quick shower and dressing, Joy sat at the mirror and allowed Anna to bump her hair with the curling iron.

"Have you ever been in a sex shop?" she asked her niece.

Anna stared into the mirror at her aunt. "Of course, why?" she slowly asked.

Joy hunched her shoulders. "I don't know. I've just been a little curious is all."

"All right now!" Anna squealed. "Baby girl is *finally* hot in the pants. What's his name?"

Sean came to mind. "Remember, I don't have anyone. That's what this date is supposed to solve."

"Liar." She set the curling iron on the dressing table and began finger-combing Joy's hair. "Sheeeeeet, if I'd of known better, I wouldn't have let Mom know jack about Elliot. She almost ruined our relationship. So how long have you been with your mystery man?"

"Not long. We clicked instantly, but... well... He's just gotten out of a bad relationship and isn't ready to start a new one."

Anna snatched the curling iron up. "Listen to him. If he says he's not ready, believe him."

"Yeah, I know. We're just friends."

"But you're hoping for more."

Joy smiled at her niece who was more like a sister. "I'm listening to him. He's not ready."

"Guuuurl please. You're as hardheaded as the rest of the Warren women. You don't give a damn what that man says, you're planning on showing him he doesn't know what he's talking about. That's why you have a sudden interest in the sex shop."

"Of course I care what he thinks."

"All I'm saying is be careful. If he shows signs or says he isn't ready for a relationship, then he isn't ready. And I'm not so sure it's wise to have a 'friendship' with a man you're interested in romantically. It rarely works out."

"I know, I know, I just… I don't know. I enjoy his company."

"Just be careful." She pointed the curling iron at Joy's reflection. "And if he's willing to have a sexual relationship with you, but not an emotional one, then he isn't worth your time."

"Agreed. Now tell me about the sex shop."

Anna's lips curled into a devilish grin. "I'll do you one better. I'll pick you up in the morning. I'm about to bust your sex shop cherry." Both women laughed.

"You are too foolish. And I took tomorrow off to go shopping with Granny."

"Can you imagine Granny in a sex shop?" Anna laughed so hard, tears rolled from her eyes. "We have *got* to take her with us."

Joy wiped her own batch of laughter tears from her eyes. "You're a troublemaker."

"Hell yeah. Do we have a date?"

"Hell yeah."

* * *

Joy placed the folded blanket in the BMW trunk next to the picnic basket. She hadn't been on a picnic in—forever—and was reminded of her childhood when Bertha, she and her grandfather practically lived in the park.

Grateful she and Anna had held their ground on what she should wear on this date, she smiled.

"Thanks, Edward, this was really nice." Though it was near ten and the park was practically deserted, she'd honestly had a great time. She stepped back as he closed the trunk.

"I think the art of the picnic has been lost. I'm glad you're enjoying yourself." He wrapped his hands loosely about her waist before she had time to think about objecting. "I don't want to, but I believe it's time for me to take you home."

They'd joked and talked politics and about her childhood, but she still didn't have that "zing" for him. Several times throughout their time together, she'd mentally compared him to Sean, and Edward fell short each time. She didn't know what it was about Sean, but she needed to get over whatever it was. The man obviously didn't want a relationship. Hell, he didn't even want to have sex with her. What kind of single man declined the chance to have sex with an of-age virgin? And worse yet, what was wrong with her? She shook it off and swore to give Edward a fair chance. This silliness with Sean was just that—silliness. *I'm using Sean as an excuse not to give Edward a chance. No more excuses.*

"The night's still young. How about a movie?"

Edward's eyes lit up. "Are you sure?"

"Positive."

By the time the movie ended, Joy was past exhausted. She'd stayed up too late the previous night on the phone with Sean and was used to being in bed by ten. On the drive home, Edward began talking about the cultures in the different places around the world he'd visited. Normally, she would have been interested. Tonight, she was just ready for sleep.

Her mind drifted to thoughts of the girls' day out she had planned with Bertha and Anna. Their first stop would be to have pictures taken and breakfast, then the sex shop, and if Bertha wasn't too tired, a movie. Pictures was Anna's idea. She knew Bertha would get a kick out of it. Joy yawned.

"… a virgin," Edward commented as he stopped his BMW at the intersection close to her home. "I just love an old-fashioned gal."

"I'm sorry, I missed part of what you said."

He looked over at her. "Oh no. I shouldn't have kept you out so late. You can barely keep your eyes open. Next time we start our date earlier."

She could have sworn he said something about being a virgin. "It was my suggestion to go to the movie. Thanks again for the great evening."

"Thank you for being so sweet. I love an old-fashioned gal." He winked at her.

"I'm not old fashioned."

He turned onto her street. "That's a compliment. Things have changed so much in our culture. We could use a turning back in time on many issues. I'm lucky to be in the presence of such a smart, driven, beautiful woman."

Heat of embarrassment rushed to her face. "Thank you," she said softly.

"And that you're actually a virgin. You should be commended."

"Hold up! Who said I'm a virgin?"

Edward looked as if he wanted to suck his words back into

his mouth. "There's nothing to be ashamed of." He pulled the car into her driveway.

Joy had never been so humiliated, outraged and downright pissed off in her life. Tears welled up in her eyes.

Edward weaved his fingers through her hair. "I'm sorry. I'm just completely taken by you. That was insensitive of me."

"How could she?" Joy turned from his touch. "I'm sorry, but…" She lowered her face into her palms. Why she'd even considered giving someone her mother selected a chance was beyond her. "This is so embarrassing."

"You have nothing to be embarrassed about." His heavy hand rested on her back. "Absolutely nothing. I'm the one who should be embarrassed, and I'm ashamed. I wasn't thinking. Please forgive me."

"It's not your fault I'm a freak."

"You're not a freak."

She opened the door and stepped out of the car, ignoring his soft calls for her. "Thanks again for taking me out."

"I'll come by tomorrow afternoon. We'll do whatever you want. Even stay in if you'd like."

Not only did he know all of her business, but she'd cried in front of him like a big baby. "I don't think that's such a good idea." Afraid to see the pity in his eyes, she couldn't even look at him. "I'm sorry." She rushed into the house.

Once inside, Joy sucked in her remaining tears.

"So how was your date?" Nancy, the nurse's aide, asked from the sofa, then concern marred her face. "Oh my goodness, baby." She opened her arms to Joy. "What happened?"

Joy was so upset she didn't remember walking across the room and falling into Nancy's arms in a heap of tears. "How could she?" Joy mumbled.

"What's going on out there?" Bertha yelled from her room. "Is that the baby? Did that bastard hurt my baby? Get me the hell out of this damn bed!"

Nancy went to Bertha. A few minutes later, she wheeled Bertha into the living room.

"I'll kick his ass." Bertha raised her fist into the air. "Where the hell is he?"

"Calm down, Bertha." Nancy wheeled her over to Joy who was curled up in the plush armchair. "You'll get your pressure up."

Joy burst into nervous laughter. She could imagine her granny going after Edward. She hugged Bertha. "Oh, Granny, I love you so much. Can we run away and never come back."

"I'm just about all packed. Let's go!"

Nancy chuckled. "Don't encourage her."

"She started it," Joy and Bertha said in unison.

"You are both too bad for words. Tell us what happened before Bertha puts a hit out on Edward."

"It's not Edward. Mom…" Joy still hadn't wrapped her mind around what her mother had done. "I feel so betrayed." She wiped more tears from her cheeks. "She told Edward I'm a virgin."

"What the?" Bertha pointed to the house phone. "Oh no she did not!"

"Please, Granny, I don't want to speak with her."

"You don't have to say a damn thing, baby. Dial the number, Nancy."

Nancy dialed, then handed the phone over.

"Granny, please, don't do this." Joy wished she had kept this one to herself. She didn't want a big fight. All she wanted was to hide.

"Benjamin, wake that wife of yours up… Hell no Joy isn't okay. Thirty-five minutes. I expect to see Emily, Heather and Helen here in thirty-five minutes, not a second more." She tossed the receiver behind her. "This is it, the final damn straw. Nancy, call the vet. The damn camel's back is broke."

Worried her granny would have a heart attack, Joy lied, saying, "It's no big deal. I was embarrassed at first, but now that the shock is over, I'm good. Really. Please, Granny, let it go."

"No more letting go. Who does she think she is?"

"Calm down," Nancy said. "I'm sure your blood pressure is skyrocketing." She went for her medical bag.

"We'll I'm about to die in a blaze of glory, because no one disrespects—" Her tirade was cut off by Joy's cell phone ringing. "Hand me that thing."

Joy reluctantly handed over the phone. Bertha glanced at the LED screen, then answered, "Thirty-four damn minutes left. You planning on wasting them blowing up this damn phone?" She hung up.

"No more MTV for you, Granny," Joy said in an attempt to calm her down.

"My sweet little thing, I love you, but sit your butt over on that there couch and be quiet. I know what you're trying to do, but I'm too angry to let this continue. It has to stop and stop now."

Thirty-two minutes later, Benjamin rushed into the house and ran to his baby. "What happened?" He swooped her into his arms. Joy felt secure in his arms and rested her head on his chest.

"Oh, Daddy, I'm so glad you're here."

"Where the hell are Emily, Heather and Helen?"

He didn't look away from his baby. "They're right behind—"

"What happened?" Emily interrupted as she and the twins rushed into the house.

"I never thought the day would come that I couldn't stand the sight of my own child, but," Bertha shook her head, "it's obviously a new day."

Joy saw the worry on Emily's face turn to pain. "What? What happened?"

"Joy is thirty-three years old. If she decides to date or not date is none of your damn concern, and it sure as hell isn't your place to tell any damn body she's a virgin!"

"What!" Benjamin snapped. "You didn't."

"Mom, how could you?" the twins blurted out.

"I swear I didn't intend on telling him. It just slipped out. I swear."

"Don't you two pretend like you're so outraged," Bertha scolded.

"Granny, we had nothing to do with this. We'd never."

"The hell you wouldn't. You two pitched a fit because this grown-ass woman wanted to pick out her own clothes to wear and had her hair cut. You are going to stop interfering in this *woman's* life. Do you hear me?"

Emily stepped up to her mother's wheelchair. "I made a mistake. I'm sorry. I'm not perfect, but there is no way you can keep me from *my* child."

"Would you like to bet on that, missy?"

The argument continued for what seemed like an eternity to Joy. "Stop! Everyone just stop!" She walked over to her granny and placed her hand over hers. "Thank you for always being my greatest protector, but like you said, I'm a grown-ass woman." She smiled. "I'm angry and hurt, but I'll survive."

"Baby." Emily reached for Joy, but Joy moved away.

"Please, just leave me alone. Don't come over, don't call, don't send a bunch of emails, don't send people to check on me. I'll be fine as long as you leave me alone. I need time. That includes you two also." She nodded at the twins.

"That's ridiculous." Emily rested her hands on her hips. "I understand you're angry. You should be, but—"

"But what? I should allow you to continue disrespecting my wishes, treating me like a child, like there's something wrong with me, like I'm some sort of freak?"

"I'm looking out for your best interest. If you weren't so hardheaded, you'd realize I've been around a little longer than you have. I might actually know a little something."

"So telling a complete stranger I'm a virgin was in my best interest. Thanks, but no thanks. You've humiliated me, yet again, and I'm sick of it. Last time I checked, Granny has been around a little longer than you have. If you weren't so hardheaded, you'd admit she might actually know something. Now leave me alone." She turned and bumped into her father.

"Look at you. All grown up. You've made me proud." Benjamin hugged his youngest child. "I'll do my best to ensure they give you the space—and time—you need."

* * *

"What's wrong?" Lights out, Sean adjusted his earpiece and leaned back in his easy chair. Joy had called him without blocking her number, then barely spoke. He didn't know what was wrong, but if that Edward dude hurt her, Sean was ready to catch a flight to Atlanta to dispense his own pain. How he'd become so protective of Joy so quickly was scary to him. He could see he was falling for her fast and couldn't see how to stop it.

"What isn't wrong would be an easier one to answer. Somewhere along the line... I don't know. I mean I've always thought myself better than my siblings because I stood up to my mom and became what I wanted to be, but I'm just as bad, maybe even worse. I love my family so much, but I feel miserable whenever we actually spend time together."

"Then maybe you should move away from your family." For a fleeting moment, he considered suggesting she move to Los Angeles, but came to his senses. "Distance saved my relationship with my mother. She wanted me to be a lawyer or doctor. And then there's marriage. According to my mother, I'm denying her grandchildren." With all the issues he had with his mother, the main one he'd never reveal—her staying married to his father so long.

Most children wanted their parents to stay together. Deep down inside, Sean wanted the same for his parents, but not as things were. He couldn't stand to see his mother's pain from his father's straying. His resentment toward both of his parents had grown to the point he couldn't stand to be around either of them—his mother for choosing to be a victim and his father for victimizing.

"Boy, can I relate," Joy said. "My mom has tons of grandchildren, including greats, yet I'm somehow denying her grandchildren. And don't get me started on being a lowly grade school teacher for 'trailer trash.' " He heard her blow out a long breath of air. "I would leave now if I could, but I can't."

"Your granny?"

"Exactly. There's no way I'd leave her. Don't get me wrong. I know she'd come with me, but the family needs her more than they realize. Especially Mom. I can't take granny from her."

Longing to lift her mood and forget about his own family woes, he asked, "So what's on your agenda for tomorrow? Shopping for your trip?"

"In a way." She giggled. "I'm exploring a sex shop with my niece in the morning. We've planned a girls' day out. Granny's even coming!"

"You can't take a kid into a sex shop. And your granny? Baby girl, I know you're a little naïve about certain things, but—" Her laughter stopped him flat. "What?"

"Granny tried to hire several gigolos to do what you refuse, and my niece is my age. I see I've forgotten to inform you that my granny is a tad bit eccentric and my siblings are all old enough to be my parents."

"That explains a lot! No wonder they baby you so much. You're a boatload of feature articles. First 'Virgins Over Thirty,' now 'Children With Siblings Old Enough To Be Their Parents,' and my personal favorite: 'Grannies Who Hire Gigolos.' "

"Don't forget 'Breaking Your Sex Toy Cherry.' "

Her laugh came though the line loud and clear. The occasional snort here and there was the cutest little thing to him.

They continued to joke around for hours. The more she came out of her funk, the more his heart sang. Heart singing? He'd never thought such flowery language would fit him, but damn, here he was whipped by a virgin he'd never even seen.

How the hell did this happen to me? He looked down at his engorged dick. *This woman is trouble.*

"… and I just wanted to thank you," Joy said softly.

"For what?"

"For being the first person I can be completely honest with. For arguing the losing side of debates."

"Hey." He chuckled. "I kicked your butt."

"Yeah right. As I was saying. For arguing the *losing* side of debates. For being you."

Her heartfelt words made love to his soul. What it was about her, he couldn't explain. And the feelings he was developing terrified him, they went beyond the physical.

"For helping me explore my sexuality without making me feel like some sort of freak."

"And what a pleasure it has been."

"Oh yeah, it's been nice." She lowered her voice. "Even though you won't make love to me, you sure know how to make me feel good."

He sucked his lower lip into his mouth to keep from telling her he'd catch the next flight to Georgia and give her exactly what they both wanted.

"Are you sure you want to go all the way to D.C. instead of showing me…? Well, you know."

"And you know what you're doing to me." He wrapped his hand around his hardness and stroked gently.

"Umm, hmm. I'm sure you'd feel better than anything I can buy at that stupid shop. Just thinking about you entering me has me hot and wet."

"Damn, baby, you learn fast."

"I have the best teacher. When you stop all of this staying away from me nonsense, I want you to teach me how to straddle you."

He could see her there with him, straddling him, his hands on her waist as she lowered herself. "You'd have to take it slow."

"Slow, I can do."

He could feel her. Timid at first with the depth she took in. Her inquisitive hands would caress his chest, and her mouth—

he'd taste every succulent inch.

Her soft moan increased the grip and speed of his hand. When she was finally ready to come, her body would tighten around him and pull him into heaven with her. "Umph." He sucked in, making a hissing sound between his teeth with his release. He wanted to hold onto this feeling, stay in this zone forever, but the feeling faded.

"You with me, baby?" he finally asked.

"I'm sorry."

Concern quickly pushed out the remainder of his euphoria away. "What's wrong?"

"I'm just... Now this is embarrassing."

"What?"

"I wasn't trying to be rude. It's just all of these images of us making love filled my head, and the next thing you know, my fingers had joined in on the fun and I climaxed. I started us out, then slipped into my own world."

A smile stretched clean across his face. "Joy, I'm sitting here with cum all over my chest."

"Eeewwww nasty."

"Exactly." He snatched his cell phone off the table so he wouldn't lose the connection and went into the bathroom to clean himself. "Wait until we break in your sex toys. Make sure you get a dildo that vibrates."

"We? Are you saying you aren't running away to D.C.?"

The excitement in her voice had him firming up again, but he couldn't meet her. He knew they'd both want more than a sexual relationship. His two previous relationships ended because of cheating. He wouldn't chance his heart, especially on a long-distance relationship, that was just asking for trouble. "Sorry, but I'm not crazy. I'm headed to D.C."

"Chicken."

Chapter Six

"Anna, Joy, look at this!" Bertha laughed.

Joy turned away from the DVDs just in time to see her granny lean forward in her wheelchair and reach for the eighteen-inch dildo on display. "Oh—my—God! That thing is huuuuuuuuge." Laughing, Joy took the dildo off the hook and handed it to her granny. "I should get two—one for Heather and one for Helen."

Bertha set the dildo across her lap and poked it with her fingertips. "Anna, please tell me you young folk aren't sticking these things in your vaginas. You'll stretch everything out!"

"I can't speak for anyone but myself—Hell no!"

A few of the other patrons in the store joined in the laughter. One of the young, perky clerks approached with a broad smile on her face. "Hello, ladies, you all look so lovely today."

"Why thank you," Joy jokingly curtsied in her brand new red dress with the medium-sized polka dots.

Bertha tapped Anna's leg. "Did you bring in the pictures?" She turned toward the clerk. "We had our photos taken this morning before we came here. The nice young woman at the studio had our package ready before we finished eating breakfast. Everything's so fast nowadays. I sure pray men haven't gotten faster in bed." She turned to Joy. "I'll bet that's why these stores have become so popular with women. Show her one of the wallet pictures, Anna."

"Sorry, Granny, they're in the car." Anna reached for a slender violet vibrator. "I'll bet this one glows in the dark or lights up somehow."

"Did y'all see that swing over there?" Joy thumbed toward the seat. "I couldn't even figure how to sit in it."

"That's the bondage area," explained the clerk.

Anna returned her attention to the selection of dildos and vibrators displayed. "Oh, here you go. The Rabbit Pearl will be perfect for you. I love mine. I want penetration and clit stimulation simultaneously."

Joy picked up the display Rabbit Pearl and fingered the smaller extension on it. "So that's what the extra piece is for. Cool." She returned the display and tossed a packaged Rabbit

Pearl from the rack into her basket. Her cell rang. She didn't recognize the number, but answered anyway. "Hello."

"Honey, we need to talk."

Joy's mood sunk. "Mom, I asked you not to contact me unless there's an emergency. I need time." She held the phone to her ear and headed for the checkout. She couldn't believe her mother would call from a strange phone, but then again, she'd told a complete stranger her daughter was a virgin.

"I'm sorry about telling Edward you're a virgin. I shouldn't have said anything."

"It's about more than your telling my business. You consistently disrespect me—"

"That's not true," Emily cut in.

"You won't even allow me to finish a sentence. All I asked for is a little time, but could you give it to me? No. You don't care what I want or need."

Anna wheeled Bertha into the line beside Joy.

"Don't be like this, Joy."

"Like what, Mom?" She began taking items out of the basket and setting them onto the counter. She had planned on finishing her girls' day out, but now the mood was ruined and all she wanted was to call Sean. Hell, if she got lucky, he may want to help her break in her new toys.

"I apologized. Not talking to someone because you're angry is plain old childish."

"I'm not talking to you because I don't want to say something out of anger. And so what, you apologized. Whoop-di-do. Those are only words that don't change the fact that you continually disrespect me." They moved up in line. Joy spoke softly, but didn't care who heard their argument. She was just being polite.

"That's not true."

"Then why are we having this conversation now? I asked you to give me some time, but you couldn't even give me twenty-four hours before you force yourself in where you aren't wanted. That is not respect. Do not call, email, or contact me in any other way unless there is an emergency. Good-bye, Mom." She disconnected and turned off her phone.

* * *

Joy didn't want to be a spoilsport and had insisted they continue with their plans, but Bertha and Anna weren't hearing

53

it. Instead, Anna dropped Joy and Bertha off at their home and called it a day.

Joy took her new toys into the basement—her sanctuary— and dumped them onto the pool table. She wanted to call Sean and tell him about her argument with her mother, but didn't want to sound like all she did was complain. She drug herself back upstairs and cuddled on the bed with Bertha to watch an old Doris Day movie. Within a few minutes, Bertha fell asleep.

Near the end of the movie, the doorbell rang. She didn't expect anyone and prayed it wasn't her mother or sisters imposing themselves on her. She stilled her nerves and prepared herself for who may be on the other side of the door.

She opened the door and was stunned. "Edward? I mean…" she stepped back, "come in."

"You forgot about our date?" He entered carrying a bag of groceries. "I'm wounded."

Mouth and eyes wide open, she said, "I feel like a total jerk. I completely forgot." She closed the door and followed him into the kitchen. Yes she was distraught last night, but she didn't think she was so distraught she had agreed to another date. "What in the world is wrong with me?"

He chuckled lightly. "I was playing. You didn't forget." He set the bag on the large island in the center of the kitchen. "Last night when I mentioned coming over today, you were a little pre-occupied, so I decided to chance it." His eyes roamed over her body. Barefoot and in a wrinkled Minnie Mouse dress, she knew she must be a sight. "You look beautiful."

The sincerity in his voice brought heat to her cheeks. "Thank you." Used to her mother and siblings putting her down, compliments made her feel awkward. Thoughts of Sean flowed through her mind and guilt began stirring in her. *What's wrong with me?*

"Edward, umm, you're a really nice guy but…"

He looked up from the bag into her eyes. "Oh no, not the 'but' speech," he said teasingly.

"I don't want to lead you on. You're looking for a wife, and I'm not looking for a husband. I don't know what my mom told you about me," she smiled, "besides my virgin status, but I don't want a relationship. And I know this will sound horrible, but to be honest, even if I were looking for a relationship, I couldn't pursue one with you. There's no way I'd seriously consider anyone my mom picked out for me."

He took a small package of sliced Portobello mushrooms out of the bag. "Did you enjoy yourself last night?"

"Yes, but—"

"Do you find me attractive?" he cut in.

She laughed. "I can't believe you asked if I find you attractive."

"Do you?" He took out yellow bell peppers and zucchini. "I know I have a few years on you, but I'm in excellent shape. Now be honest. Do you find me attractive?"

"I think you are a very handsome man," she answered honestly. "But—"

"Do I make you laugh?" he cut in.

"You did a few seconds ago."

"How about conversation?" He pulled out a stick of butter and Italian seasoning. "Does our conversation flow easily or feel forced?"

"Easily. What are you making?"

"A grilled sandwich I made up. Now sit on the stool. Has a man ever cooked for you?"

"My dad and brothers have."

She washed her hands at the sink, took out the cutting board, two sharp knives and two plates, then set them on the island and took her seat. She was hungry and the ingredients for the sandwich looked delicious.

As he asked question after question, he finished emptying the contents of the grocery bag. Whenever she'd try to expand on her answers, he'd cut her off with the next question.

He washed his hands and joined her at the island. "Okay, time for the most important question." He took her hands into his and gazed into her eyes. "Does my breath stink?"

She practically fell off the stool in laughter. "You are too foolish!"

He helped her sit up. "I'm just enjoying an afternoon with my friend. Are you enjoying your afternoon?"

"Yes."

"Then why would you throw away our friendship because your mother introduced us? Why do you allow her to have so much influence over your life?" He began slicing tomatoes.

"I have no idea." She grabbed the zucchini and sliced it lengthwise into several pieces. "In this case it's a damned if you do and damned if you don't scenario. I love my mother, but she's driving me crazy. Even if our friendship is platonic, it's like giving her permission to interfere in my life."

"If your mother hadn't introduced us, would you want to continue being friends?"

Technically, if not for her mother, she wouldn't have given him a chance, but that was a different discussion. "Friends, yes, but nothing more. I'm serious. I'm not ready for more, and I just don't see us like that."

"Then, again, I ask. Why would you throw away our friendship because your mother introduced us?"

"You're right. Good friends are hard to come by." She held out her hand. "Hello, I'm Joy Warren."

He smiled and shook her hand. "Pleased to meet you. I'm Edward Knox."

After lunch, Joy looked in on Bertha, who was still asleep. Seemed of late that Bertha had been sleeping most of the day away.

"You're relationship with your grandmother is beautiful," Edward whispered from the doorway.

"She's my best friend." She kissed Bertha on the cheek, then returned to the kitchen. "I wish she'd wake and eat a little. She hasn't eaten since breakfast, not even a snack."

"Try not to worry. As she ages, she'll need more sleep than food. This is normal."

His words actually comforted her. "You're a good man, Edward."

This time he was the one who looked embarrassed. He took a few DVDs out of the grocery bag he had brought in earlier. "Are you in the mood for a comedy?"

"Sure. But we'll have to watch it downstairs. The DVD player in the living room is broken. You can go down and set up the movie." She motioned toward the basement door at the back of the kitchen. "I need to turn on the monitor so I can hear Granny if she needs me. I'll be down in a second."

To Joy's delight, Bertha was awake and ready to eat a little chicken stewed in carrots and celery with a touch of garlic. Bertha wasn't in the mood for guests, so when Joy suggested they all watch a movie in Bertha's room, Bertha said no thanks. She just wanted to eat and rest up for their trip.

After caring for her grandmother, Joy cleaned the few

dishes and rushed down the stairs to Edward. "I'm sorry it took so long. I had to feed Granny."

"It's okay," he said from the lounge area. "I've selected one of your movies for us to watch."

She curled up on the opposite end of the couch from him. "Sounds good to me."

He pointed the universal remote at the television and switched the set to AV, then lowered the remote into his lap and turned toward her.

"Is something wrong?" she asked.

"No," he said softly. "I was just trying to figure out a way to bring something up without angering or embarrassing you."

"This sounds serious. What's going on?"

"I didn't mean to pry, it's just..." He started the DVD.

Death would have been better than the sound of the pornographic movie that played. She'd completely forgotten about the trip to the sex shop they'd made and that she'd left her purchases out in the open.

She spun around toward the pool table—the items were gone. All she could do was close her eyes and laugh. She didn't know what it was, but somehow Edward had been present for her most embarrassing moments in life.

"I know you're curious." He pulled the boxed rabbit vibrator from under the couch. "But don't use this." He set the vibrator on the coffee table, muted the sound on the television and moved closer to her. "I'm not saying don't masturbate. Masturbation is healthy and normal, but don't use vibrators or dildos until after you've lost your virginity."

She knew he was a doctor and all, but the way he spoke with such a straight face was funny as hell to her. She also ranked his little sex education class right up there with her other most embarrassing life's moments, but she found it funny this time.

"I'm sorry." She placed her hand on her chest. "I'm not usually so rude. I know certain things are supposed to be private. My mom and I had another fight this morning, and I forgot all about our trip to the sex shop."

"Your mom went to the sex shop with you?" He edged closer to her.

Joy giggled. "Nooooo, not my mom. Granny and my niece."

"You took your grandmother into a sex shop!"

"Oh my goodness." She fanned her tears of laughter. "This has gone from bad to worse. I do not drag Granny around sex shops. She would have killed us had we gone without her." She blew out a long breath and tried to shake off her giggles. "Whew, howdy, this has been some day." She glanced toward the television and saw a woman going down on a man and was shocked she wasn't embarrassed. "Thank you," she said softly and faced Edward.

"For what, being nosey?" He eased closer.

His mischievous grin played well with her own mischievous streak, and she found that he hadn't dyed his light sprinkling of gray hairs sexy. She'd noticed how attractive he was when they first met, but looks weren't everything—especially since he came from her mother's recommendation. Spending this extra time with him had allowed her to see the real Edward instead of the man Emily wanted to control her out-of-control daughter.

"As Granny would say, 'You're good people.' Thank you for not making me feel like some sort of sex-crazed, freaky virgin." She flashed a smile. "That's if you can be a virgin and sex-crazed at the same time."

"And thank you for letting down your guard and giving me a chance."

Sudden movement on the television screen caught her eye. The man grasped his penis and came all over the woman's lips. The woman lapped up the cum as if she'd been starving. Joy became transfixed on the porn flick. She knew about a male's orgasm and had read about them countless number of times, but to actually see a man come—her heartrate increased.

"You've never seen an X-rated movie, have you?" Edward asked softly.

"No, not really. I obviously don't have anything against them. They've just never been part of my reality." The man on the DVD knelt in front of the woman who was sitting on the edge of the couch. He stuck his dick inside of her vagina and pumped like there was no tomorrow. The part that really amazed Joy was she found herself getting horny. The woman on screen pinched her nipples. Joy felt a tight sensation in her own breasts and looked down. Sure enough, her nipples had become hard and tented the front of her dress. She returned to watching the couple when a thought hit her out of nowhere.

"Wait a cotton-picking minute. He just came." She turned toward Edward. "Men aren't ready to go again that quickly, are they?" Her eyes grew wide. "Oh, I'm soooo sorry. Mom always says I am too curious for my own good. Don't answer that. I was the student who always asked too many questions. My classmates hated me." She looked at the screen. "They must have cut a few hours out."

"I love your curiosity." His voice had become more husky. She didn't know if the change was real or if her imagination was working overtime, but she liked it. He set his hand on top of hers, and unlike usual, she didn't want to pull away. "Can I ask you a personal question?"

Nervous from anticipation for what she wanted to come next, she jokingly said, "You know I'm a virgin, you've seen my sex toys and we're sitting here watching a porn flick together. Is it more personal than that?"

He smiled. "I guess not."

"Then ask away." The man pulled out of the woman and fondled her clit with two fingers. Soon, the woman squirted as if she were having a male orgasm. "No way!" Joy faced Edward. "I swear I'm going to let you ask a question, but that's not real, is it? I've never read anything about a woman squirting like that."

"A woman squirting is rare, but real." As he twisted a loc of her short hair between his fingers, her overactive imagination took over. In her mind's eye, she saw him fingering her as the man had the woman in the DVD.

Warmth flowed through her body and knocked out any interest she had in asking or hearing questions. Edward leaned in and brushed his lips over hers. She loved the softness of his touch.

"Have you ever seen a man before?" he whispered and gently kissed her lips.

Nervous as all get out, yet ready to taste him, feel him, be with him, she answered, "There's a man right there on the screen."

"You know what I mean." He took off his sweatshirt and dropped it to the floor.

All Joy could do was stare and pray she wasn't drooling. Edward was a great height—around 5'10"—but she'd thought his medium build was a little chunky for her taste. Under his too-baggy sweatshirt lay a body to die for. This man was ripped! She wanted to touch the creamy goodness of his well-defined shoulders and work her way down his broad chest to his well-developed abdomen.

She forced herself to look away. "I'm sorry. I didn't mean to be rude."

He gently stroked her cheek. "I want you to look." He placed her shaky hands on his shoulders. "And touch."

Solid—too solid to be considered cream. She withdrew her hands. "I... I'm not ready to make love."

He placed her hands on either side of his waist, leaned in and suckled along her neck. "Neither of us is ready to make love today," he breathed more than said. "But there are other things we can do." He slowly unbuttoned the front of her dress.

She'd never imagined the phrase "other things" sounding sexy, but there she sat with her panties soaked from moisture building between her legs, her nipples hard and her wishing she were engaged in "other things" right now.

"You didn't answer my question." He slipped one of his large hands into her dress and caressed her breast. The touching made her ache, but in a good way.

"Question? Oh, no, I haven't seen a man." Her gaze traveled downward to the bulge trapped in his jeans. She wanted to do a lot more than see him.

He unzipped and lowered his pants below his hips, then freed himself from his briefs. "Some things you don't have to remain curious about."

Her curiosity kicked out the last bits of shame and shyness she held. He was much thicker than the vibrator she'd purchased. She wondered what it would feel like to have him in her. With his size, maybe they could just try the tip for now. The mere thought of him in her had her hot and wet.

He took her by the hand and molded it around his hardened girth. "It's okay to touch."

Hand wrapped firmly around him, she liked the throb of him between her fingers. She throbbed also—between her legs. Now that she had an up close and personal view, she could see the appeal of taking a man into her mouth. She looked into his eyes and slowly stroked him from base to tip, tip to base, base to tip.

He drew in a sharp intake of air and pulled himself free of

her.

"I'm sorry, did I hurt you?"

"Oh no, baby." He cupped her face and nibbled along her earlobe. "When I leave here today, you will still be a virgin," he whispered. "If you had continued, well…"

As his hot mouth traveled along her neck, she no longer cared about virginity or his want of a wife. Her body needed what he had to offer. "What if I don't want you to leave here today with me being a virgin?"

"Then I will satisfy your needs in other ways until we're married." He hooked his finger into her satin bra and freed her breasts.

Logically, she knew her breasts weren't physically connected to her clit, but somehow his caressing and suckling her breasts had her clit crying out for attention. He slipped his free hand into her panties and fondled the apex of her passion.

Moaning with pleasure, she arched her back and gyrated her hips.

"Undress for me." He nudged her dress off her shoulders.

Disappointed he'd stopped suckling and fondling, she followed his instruction and stood before him.

"Don't worry, baby, I have something you'll like." He pulled her to stand between his legs, held onto her waist and kissed her belly. "Straddle me." He slouched back on the couch.

"Don't you want to take off your pants?" His briefs had inched back up and covered half of his hardness.

"Trust me." He nudged his briefs back down and held onto her waist. "You'll like this."

She straddled him and allowed him to guide her hips to the base of his hardness.

He splayed one of his powerful hands across her butt, pressed down and rocked her forward and back. Simultaneously, he drew her close with his other hand and returned to suckling her breasts.

"Oh my." Joy swooned. This was way better than anything she'd ever tried. Her heart pounded so hard, she was sure he could feel it, and her breathing… staggered. She knew this feeling, knew what was coming next, but this was more intensified than before. She wanted to hold onto this forever.

"Let go, baby. Let it come."

Instead of following her will, her body followed his, and

she came.

Edward pulled her mouth down to his and practically swallowed her face—exactly what she hated about kissing. Next thing she knew, he'd laid her back on the couch and was on top of her, his dick pressing against her clit.

Instead of entering her, he lowered his forehead down to hers. "I'm sorry, baby, but I have to leave before I break my promise."

Glad for the reprieve from the slob, she teased, "What promise?"

"The one I made myself not to make love to you until we're married." He closed his eyes. "Leaving you here is the hardest thing I've ever had to do."

"Then stay." As long as he didn't kiss her again, she was sure they could work out the rest. "This virgin thing is highly overrated. Believe me. I know."

"Stop tempting me, woman." He nibbled her lower lip. "Oh God this is too hard." He sat up and pulled up his pants, but didn't zip them. "I'm sorry, baby. But I really need to leave."

"Chicken."

He chuckled. "You got that right." He donned his shirt and shoes. "I know you don't want to hear this, but..." He hugged her. "I'm in love with you, Joy."

Stunned silent, she couldn't say a word, move, react at all.

He kissed her lightly. "I hate to rush off, but I must go." He grabbed her vibrator on his way out. "You won't be needing this." He skipped up the steps and out.

Still stuck on his saying he was in love with her, she couldn't even compute his taking her vibrator into the equation.

Chapter Seven

Sherri slowly rolled the vibrator along her inner thigh.

"No foreplay tonight. Just be ready when I get there," was all Edward had said when he'd called.

Her day had been too perfect to allow his little virgin to ruin it. The girl obviously couldn't handle a man. She pushed thoughts of Joy out of her mind for more pleasant ones. Earlier in the day she'd interviewed for an administrative assistant position and bumped into a former client—Tony, the principal of Joy's school. She knew something odd was going on with this interview. She wasn't born yesterday. Grade schools weren't usually open on Saturdays. She'd forgotten it was the weekend and called to inquire about the ad in the newspaper. Tony had answered, but she hadn't recognized him. Intrigued with the position, she'd gone over to the school for the interview.

When she first saw him, she was in total shock. Tony had actually remembered her name after all of these years. She'd thought she was just another twenty-dollar blow job to him.

Back in the day, she'd rocked that man's world so many times she lost count, but today... Today he'd laid her back on the tacky-green upholstered sofa in his office, spread her legs and worked his tongue like nobody's business. Her legs had actually trembled with delight. Even now she could feel his soft, hot tongue dipping into her sweetness. His mouth suckling her tender flesh. This job would have definite perks.

Caught up in the memory of her early morning rendezvous, she hadn't even heard Edward enter her condo. She just looked up, and he was taking the vibrator out of her hand.

"That's my girl," was all he said before plunging into her.

Oh yes, this is what she'd needed. Her new sex toy—Tony—was a delightful appetizer, but she was ready for the entree. She'd been horny as hell all day, and only Edward could satisfy her craving for hot, sweaty, funky sex.

She wrapped her legs around his thighs and tilted her hips upward. He hit her sweet spot, and she just about screamed. Edward's size alone would rip that little virgin to shreds. He needed a real woman. Nearing the edge, she drew in a deep breath.

"Oh God," Edward cried out and gripped the sheets.

Sherri continued to pump beneath him. Soon... soon she'd come... so close... so close...

Edward rolled away from her onto his back.

She watched his chest rise and fall. "Umm, Edward, I didn't come yet." Since he was usually an attentive lover, she gave him the benefit of the doubt.

Staring at the ceiling, he continued breathing heavily. Once he calmed, he reached over and combed her hair over her shoulder. "I thought you were going to cut your hair?"

"The earliest appointment I could get is Tuesday," she lied, praying he would change his mind.

Grumbling, he ran his hands over his face, walked over to the bathroom and flushed the condom.

"What's the matter?" she asked from the doorway.

"I'm a fucking idiot." He turned on the shower. "A complete fucking idiot."

"What happened?"

"I just... I got carried away with Joy is all." He stepped into the shower and closed the stall door.

Glad the happy couple was none too happy, she gave him a few minutes alone with his misery, then entered the shower. "Do you want to talk?"

"You're not the one I should be talking to." He exited the shower and grabbed a towel off the rack.

* * *

Packed, showered and dressed for bed, Joy peeked into Bertha's room. "What are you doing up so late, young lady?" She slipped into bed beside her grandmother.

"I was trying to wait until your mother shows, but she's got me licked this time. She knows I go to bed early and after staying up late last night, I won't be able to stay up tonight also."

"After the way I lit into her, I doubt we'll be hearing from her tonight. Now tomorrow..."

"You don't know your mother very well then." She used the remote to turn down the television volume. "You all ready for our trip?"

"Oh yes. More than ready, actually. I need to make the great escape."

"From your mother or Edward?"

"Both." She leaned against the headboard. "Do you really think Mom will call?"

"Oh, she'll do more than call. She'll be paying a visit as soon as she thinks I'm asleep. She takes being hardheaded to a dangerous level. I remember when she was five, maybe six years old, and she decided she wanted to be like her brothers and wear pants to school. I talked until I was ten shades of blue, but she kept coming back with reasons she should be able to wear pants."

"Yep, hardheaded sounds like Mom."

"Since I wasn't giving her the answer she wanted to hear, one night after everyone had gone to sleep, she gathered up her dresses and put them all out in the trash."

Joy laughed. "And she says I'm bad."

"That's not the half of it. The next morning was trash pick-up day. The garbage man used to come around six A.M., so you know I was ready to tie a knot in someone's behind when I found out why she hadn't dressed for school."

"That's too funny."

Bertha smiled and shook her head. "Emily has always been a mess. She won't stop."

"I'm just as stubborn. Maybe more so."

"So what's the story with you and Edward?"

"I don't know. He's smart, funny, handsome, has the right political views, rich." She hunched her shoulders. "But I'm just not feeling him. I mean I don't want to use anyone."

"What do you mean?"

"Well, let's just say this afternoon I played virgin slut."

Bertha laughed. "Oh sweet Jesus this child is a hoot. Virgin slut." She shook her head. "You're more of a mess than your mother. Now what happened?"

"We didn't have sex, but not because I didn't want to."

"So he turned you down?"

"Not quite. It's just, I want him physically, I want friendship, but I don't want marriage with him. I don't want to use him."

"Oh I see, lust. There's nothing wrong with a little lust, darling. Lust is healthy."

"I'd agree if it were only lust for him also. But he wants more. He wants marriage. I can't see myself married to him."

"Have you told him how you feel?"

"Yes. I know he thinks I'll change my mind, but I won't."

Bertha studied Joy a few moments. "How do you know? I

65

hope you're not passing on Mr. Right because your mother introduced you."

"That was the main reason at first, but now that I've gotten to know him a little better... I don't know. I can't explain it. He just seems a little controlling to me." She chewed on her inner jaw. "He took my vibrator because he doesn't want me using it."

"Sounds a little uptight to me."

"And there's another issue I can't really be upset with him about. He says he's in love with me. A few days ago I would have said that's impossible, it's too soon, but now..." She peeked over to see Bertha's reaction.

"You've found someone, haven't you?"

"Kind of, sort of. I met him the other night on the Internet."

"See, I told you that's how young folks do it today. It's someone from the community I signed you up for."

"None other than Angry White Man.'"

"Oh Lord have mercy on my soul. Joy," she said calmly, "remember how you told me the Internet is full of psychos? He's one of them. He hates women."

"No he doesn't. He's hurt and acting out. We've become friends, and he's a good enough man to say he isn't ready for a relationship."

"You're just like your mother; you can't take no for an answer, but this time listen. Edward is looking better by the second. So is your angry white psycho here in Atlanta?"

"Stop being mean and no. He lives in Los Angeles."

"Don't bring any psycho babies home." Bertha giggled.

"You won't have to worry about that. He's flying to D.C. to avoid me. He says being in the same city would be too tempting."

"On second thought, I'm starting to like him."

"Once you break through his anger-enforced protective shell, he's the best. We talk for hours, and it seems like it's only seconds. I think about him all the time but, but it can't be. He's too wounded. I just don't know what to do. After Edward left, I actually felt guilty, like I'd cheated on Sean."

"Sean?"

"Angry White Man and I are on a first name basis."

"Honey, you shouldn't feel guilty or bad about being attracted to Edward. You don't have anything with this Sean.

You are free to explore both."

"I know I shouldn't, but it's how I felt."

The doorbell rang.

"That had better not be Mom." Joy exited the bed.

"It is. Who else would come this time of night unannounced?"

"This is ridiculous." The bell rang again. "I'll be right back."

"Leave the door cracked so I can hear."

Joy rushed to the door and opened it.

"What are you doing opening the door in your skimmies?" Emily pushed Joy into the house.

"First off, I knew it was you. Secondly, what are you doing here? I asked you to leave me alone."

"We need to talk without interference from Mother or your father."

"No we don't. What I need is a break from you. This is crazy. You're acting like some obsessed woman. Why can't you just leave me alone?"

"Because you're my baby, and I'm worried about you. I failed you once, and won't fail you again."

"You're making absolutely no sense. There is nothing wrong with me being a virgin. There is nothing wrong with my being a grade school teacher. There is nothing wrong with my living with my grandmother. I'm sorry I don't measure up to your expectations, but I'm not sorry for who I am or what I've become. You have not failed, and I am not a failure."

Emily reached out to Joy. "Oh no, darling. That's not what I meant." She shook her head. "This has gotten completely out of hand." She drew in and released a long, slow breath. "Honey, I'm truly sorry I told Edward you're a virgin. That was completely out of line, and I've regretted it from the moment it slipped from my loose lips, but shutting me out isn't the answer."

"Do you hear me, do you hear yourself? You have to stop this. This goes beyond your telling my business. I need you to recognize me as the intelligent adult that I am. I need you to respect me and my decisions, even if you don't agree with them."

"But I do."

"Then why are you here? Why am I repeating the same

conversation we had earlier. Please, just please leave me alone. Look, I can see this is going to be too difficult for you. I'm checking me and Granny into a hotel. Don't try to find us."

"But what about your job?"

"You've never cared about my job before. Please just leave me alone." She opened the door. "I'm turning off my phone and buying a disposable one until I'm ready to deal with you. I'll speak to Daddy daily."

"You're really checking into a hotel?"

"I'm standing in the doorway in my skimmies. Aren't you worried about me giving a peepshow to the neighborhood?"

"But for how long? You can't do this."

"I love you, but I can't be around you right now. Please leave."

Emily embraced her daughter. "Please forgive me, baby. I'm just trying to protect you. I know I can get carried away at times." She wiped tears from her eyes. "I'm truly sorry."

"I know you're sorry, but I need a break. I'll be fine."

"Okay…" She kissed her on the forehead. "I love you, baby."

"I love you, too."

"Let me go kiss Mother. I know she's listening."

* * *

After Emily left, Joy tucked Bertha in. "I love you."

"I love you, too." She smiled. "I like the way you covered for our trip. You're good."

"I learned from the best." She hugged her. "We have a long day tomorrow. We had both best get some rest. Good night." Just as she closed Bertha's door and headed for her bedroom, the doorbell rang. "That woman is out of her mind," she mumbled and opened the door. "Mom—" She hopped behind the door. "Edward!"

He stepped inside, closed the door and practically swallowed her face in the most gross, sloppy kiss she'd ever had. Oh no, she would never consider marrying him under these circumstances. She might drown.

She pulled away to get her robe. "I'm sorry. I thought you were my mom. I mean, I'll be right back."

"It's okay, baby." He wrapped his arms around her waist and molded his body onto hers as she walked toward her room. He was hard and the grind of him on her back had her heating up. "Just don't answer the door like that again." He held her still. "I didn't come here for this, but seeing you like… Stay still for me a few seconds while I gather myself."

She didn't like how her body reacted to his close proximity. She wanted more than just the physical. Eyes closed, she admitted her feelings for Edward went deeper than just the physical, but those feelings weren't deep enough to turn into the type of love he wanted to share with her and she wanted with Sean.

"Where's my vibrator?" she said in an attempt to push him away verbally.

He slipped one of his large hands under her tank top, fondled her breasts and slid his free hand into her boy shorts and massaged her clit. "You can't have it back," he whispered and suckled along her neck.

Being outraged would have to wait until after he stopped making her feel so good. She was quickly learning why people's judgment became skewed when sex was involved.

He swooped her into his arms, carried her into the bedroom and laid her on the bed. "Exquisite," he said with the moonlight reflecting off the need in his eyes.

Exquisite indeed. She watched him undress. "I want my vibrator back."

"I'm the only sex toy you need." He entered the bed. "Come and play with me." He took her hand, wrapped it around his hardness and guided her to stroke. "That's it, baby."

Fear gripped her from nowhere, and she tried to withdraw her hand.

"Not yet." He held her hand tighter and leaned in to kiss her.

Heart racing, she yanked her hand away. "I don't want to." She couldn't catch her breath and a dark presence tried to suffocate her.

As if doused by freezing water, Edward suddenly stopped and pulled Joy into his arms. "Oh my, God, baby, breathe."

Joy couldn't hear or see. All she could do was feel, feel the fear. "I don't want to," she repeated.

"It's okay, baby," Edward said softly and rubbed her back.

In her mind there was no Edward. She was trapped in the room with this presence, and it wouldn't let her go. She pushed and pushed, trying to make it let go of her.

* * *

Unsure what to do, Edward held Joy until she exhausted herself and finally calmed. "It's okay, baby." He rocked her. "Come on back to me."

After a few minutes, she relaxed and he knew she had come back from where her mind had taken her.

"What's wrong with me?" she mumbled.

He couldn't tell her what he suspected, wouldn't. "You're just not ready. I'm sorry. I was too aggressive."

"That was way past not ready, and I'm afraid to find out exactly what that was." She lay on the bed and hugged her pillow. "I'm sorry. As you see, I'm too messed up for anyone. Please, just go."

He lay across from her. "I'm not running, and I won't let you push me away."

"I'm not marrying you."

"I didn't ask you to marry me."

"Friends, that's all I can do."

"Friends." He could tell she wasn't ready to discuss what had just happened. "I saw bags packed. Are you going somewhere?"

Relief washed over her face. "Don't tell my parents, but Granny and I are headed to L.A. tomorrow morning. We'll be there for the week. I tried to convince Granny to wait until the school year was out, but she insists on going now."

"I'll take you to the airport."

"Oh no, that's not necessary."

"Of course it is. Plus, I want to meet Bertha." He kissed her forehead. "I know what just happened scared the hell out of you. I'm sorry I scared you. I'd never hurt you."

"I know," she said softly. "It's not you."

Her words and body language didn't match, which worried him. He had to determine if his suspicions were correct and devise a plan of action. Joy would be his.

* * *

"Please, Benjamin."

"No, you've gone too far this time." He turned away from his wife. "Too damn far."

"Me! She's planning on running off with Mother."

"You're stalking our child. Leave her alone or I swear to God—" The doorbell rang, interrupting his tirade. "Who in the

70

world?" He stomped across the marble tile to the front door.

"I'm not failing her again."

"Be quiet, Emily."

He opened the door and barely had time to step to the side before Edward burst in. "Who the hell molested Joy?"

A sucker punch to the gut would have had less effect than the punch Edward delivered to the Warrens.

Emily began crying, "Oh my God."

"Answer me."

"She remembers," Emily stammered. "She remembers." She lowered her face into her palms. "She remembers."

"So it's true! Damn," Edward bit out. "It was someone with a stocky build like me."

"Yes." Emily sniffed. "It was my uncle. My mother's brother. I didn't know. I swear I didn't know." She shook her head. "I failed my baby."

"Did the bastard penetrate her?"

"None of your damn business," Benjamin cut in before Emily had a chance to continue running her mouth. "This has gotten completely out of hand. I'm on my way to Joy's to see how much she remembers."

"She doesn't remember anything, but it's just below the surface," Edward grumbled. "I know you're trying to do what's best, but you're just making matters worse."

"How did you find out?" Emily asked.

"Joy isn't timid or shy in any way, but sometimes she backs away from me as if she's scared. It's hard to explain, then tonight, she sounded like a child. How could this happen to her and what did you do about it?"

"Take a seat." Benjamin motioned toward the living area.

"This is all my fault." Emily settled on the sofa next to her husband.

"What happened?"

"I didn't want Mother to know I'd gone back to work fulltime, and left Joy with my uncle." She wiped tears from her eyes

"It's not your fault, Emily." Benjamin stroked her back.

"How did you find out?" Edward cut in.

Eyes narrowed on Edward, Benjamin bit out, "You know, young man, you are incredibly rude. I believe it's time for you to leave."

"I'm sorry, it's just I'm concerned about Joy. She had a panic attack. She thought I would hurt her. Instead of seeing me, I think she sees this man."

"Oh, Edward." Emily reached for him. "I'm so sorry."

"No, I'm sorry. Mr. Warren is correct. It wasn't your fault."

Chapter Eight

"So what's up with you and the old man?" Sean asked.

"I don't think I'll have to worry about Edward anymore," Joy said into her earpiece as she slipped pain patches into Bertha's overstuffed suitcase.

"Why?"

"Last night someone dropped a dose of psycho in my lime-grape Kool-Aid is all I can say. I don't really want to talk about it. Are you still sneaking out of town on me?"

He laughed and all thoughts of her fiasco with Edward retreated. This is where she wanted to be. Away from the dark figure overtaking her.

"I'm visiting my parents. I haven't seen them since my dad had a heart attack two years ago."

"Oh my goodness, how is he?" She zipped the suitcase and took a seat on the couch. She would need to call a taxi soon.

"He's doing well. At least I guess he is. To tell the truth, I haven't really spoken to him since I visited."

"Are you two at odds?"

"It's just not a man's way to make phone calls and write."

"You call me all the time."

"That's completely different. I want to have sex with you. And like I said, I'll be visiting him while I'm there."

"I didn't miss your saying you want to have sex with me," she teased. "But I'm going to be nice and pretend like you didn't say that." She took the phonebook off the coffee table. "Your parents are divorced, right?"

"Yes, ma'am. The best thing that ever happened to my mom."

"How can you say that and say you and your dad aren't at odds? Most children want their parents to be together." She flipped to the taxi section.

"I love my dad. I really do, but forgiving him. It's just hard. I don't think he was ever faithful to my mom. Hell, I can't tell you how many half-siblings I have out there. Sometimes at night, I'd hear my mother crying. I knew the reason. Then my dad would come home a few days later, and she'd take him back again."

"Why did she keep taking him back?"

"Love makes you stupid."

"She finally divorced him, so maybe love didn't make her stupid."

"The final straw happened when I was in high school. She'd gotten pregnant. I'd never seen her so happy. Dad started hanging around the house more and saying this baby was just what my mom needed, but I knew what he meant. He meant she needed a baby to keep her mind off his wandering ways. She hadn't even started showing, and he was back to his old tricks. She went into labor early, and my good old dad was nowhere to be found."

"Oh no."

"My baby brother only survived two days. My dad came home a week later."

"And yet you say you two aren't at odds. Sounds like you have a legitimate reason to be at odds to me."

"Don't get me wrong. There is definite resentment there, but... I guess you're right. I saw him hurt my mother too many times."

"And you, too. His behavior had to hurt you also."

"I guess so."

"So how's your mom doing now?"

"She has a new man. One she's been wanting me to come home to meet. She's so happy. I'm glad she's finally found someone."

"Good for her." She heard a car pull into her driveway. It didn't sound like her parents' car. She walked over to the window and checked. "What's he doing here?" she mumbled.

"Who?"

"Edward."

"I guess your psycho-laced, lime-grape Kool-Aid didn't scare him off after all."

Laughing, she said, "You are too crazy. When does your flight leave?"

"Don't you want me to get off the phone so you can spend some time with grandpa, I mean your man?"

"Ha, ha, very funny," she said dryly. "He isn't my man and never will be. My future man is flying out to meet his mom's fiancé."

He laughed. "Yeah, you did have a little psycho in your Kool-Aid. I'm actually at the airport now. My flight's been delayed. Did you download the file I emailed to you onto your phone?"

"I most certainly did." She opened the door before Edward had a chance to ring the bell or knock. "Hey, Edward. What are you doing here?"

"I said I'd take you to the airport."

Brows furrowed, she remembered him offering a ride, but she didn't remember telling him their flight time. She didn't want to encourage him in any way. "I can take a taxi. And how do you know my flight time?"

He stepped inside. "I saw your itinerary on the coffee table last night."

"Homeboy is keeping tabs on you," she heard Sean say over the earpiece.

"Let me finish up this call," she said to Edward. "You're not funny, Sean."

"Yes I am. My plane is boarding now. Have a safe trip."

"I'll call you after we settle in our hotel."

"Sounds like a plan. Take your laptop. I have more goodies for you to download."

"Gotcha. Have a safe trip." She disconnected and gave Edward her full attention. "I can't believe you came."

"Who is Sean?"

If his question hadn't sounded so accusatory, she would have answered, but since it did, she replied, "Who are you, the phone monitor?"

"I'm sorry. Just after last night, I was worried about you. I've gotten a little overprotective."

"I appreciate your looking out for me, but it's not necessary. Just like it wasn't necessary for you to come here. We could have easily taken a taxi."

"Why would you take a taxi when you have a ride? Where's Miss Bertha?"

"I'm in the kitchen. Come on back here."

They entered the kitchen where Bertha was nibbling on a Saltine.

Edward bowed his head slightly. "Good morning, Miss Bertha. I'm Edward Knox. Are you ready for your trip?"

"More than ready. What are your intentions with the baby?"

"Stop it, Granny." Joy dampened a paper towel. "He's

giving us a ride to the airport."

"I've been to Los Angeles a few times." He pulled a folded sheet of paper out of his back pocket. "I've taken the liberty to print out a few places I think you'd enjoy." He set the printout on the table. "Let me load your bags in the car. I'll be right back."

Joy handed her grandmother a paper towel to wipe her hands and mouth. "Why don't you like Edward?" she asked once she was sure he was out of earshot.

"I didn't say I don't like him."

"Umm hmm. He went to the trouble of coming up with this list and printing it in large font just for you."

"He scares you. That's enough for me not to like him."

"Irrational fear. I don't want to push a friend away, a true friend, because I've suddenly become paranoid." Which she would have done had Edward not shown up to give them a ride to the airport. "I scare myself more than he scares me. Now don't get me wrong, I'm not interested in Edward romantically, and he knows that, but I shouldn't push him away."

* * *

"He's done nothing wrong. He's been a good friend, and I like him," Edward heard Joy say as he neared the kitchen. "So leave him alone."

"Okay, I'll give him a pass, for now. We'd better get out of here before that mother of yours shows up."

"My thoughts exactly, and she's not my mother, just your daughter."

Bertha giggled. "How about we call her your father's wife?"

"Deal."

Confident Joy would be his, Edward entered the kitchen. "I have you all loaded up. Time to hit the road."

"Thank you for this list of places to visit," Bertha said graciously. "You didn't have to go to so much trouble."

He wheeled Bertha from the table. "No trouble at all. On the back is the number of a friend of mine. If you need anything, don't hesitate to call him. He's also a gerontologist."

"So thoughtful," Joy said. "I'll call him first thing in the morning."

"I'm not sick," Bertha fussed. "I'm old."

"Granny, I'm just calling to let him know we made it into town and to thank him."

The ride to the airport was uneventful and quiet. Edward couldn't get over Joy defending him to her grandmother. No matter how much Joy denied her feelings for him, the way she allowed him to touch her body as no other man had and the way she took up for him showed differently. Patience. It would take love, patience and time before she was truly his. Somehow, he'd have to help heal her wounds of childhood before she could accept him as more than a friend.

Then there was this Sean. He had wanted to grill her about this person. Was Sean a male or female? The call sounded so cordial. It must have been a female, if not, Joy would have surely tried to hide the call or rush the person off the phone. *Definitely a female. Probably one of her co-workers.* He'd have to be more careful in the future to keep his jealousy at bay.

At the airport, he helped Joy and Bertha check in at the curbside booth, then hugged Joy. "Have a good time in California. Call me if you need me or to just say hi."

"I will. I take it you're picking us up?"

"You take it correctly." He knelt down to Bertha. "It was a pleasure meeting you, Miss Bertha. If Joy gives you a hard time, call me." He handed her his card and a baggy of low-sodium Saltines. "Here's a little snack for the flight. You have a two-hour layover in Denver, so don't worry about having to hold yourself until you arrive in Los Angeles. Eat and drink plenty of fluids."

"Thank you."

"Hey, where's my treat?" Joy teased.

He handed her a stick of gum. "Here you go."

* * *

Not even a half hour into the flight, Bertha had dosed off in her first class seat. The excitement of the trip had exhausted her. Truth be told, Joy was tired also. Besides going to bed late, she hadn't slept well. She slipped the ear buds into her ears, turned on the gift from Sean she'd downloaded onto her phone and leaned back in her seat. Sean had told her he had a treat for her. She'd been tempted to listen to whatever he'd sent when she downloaded it, but had promised to wait until she was on the flight.

"Hey, Sweet Thang," came his sexy voice. She already liked the treat.

"If you haven't already, sit back in your seat, close your

eyes and enjoy the ride."

Eyes closed, she fully relaxed in her seat.

"You and I are the only passengers on the plane. With hours to kill, how should we spend our time? I have an idea, but I wonder if you will agree."

If he had in mind what she had in mind, hell yeah she agreed.

"You can read my mind, can't you? We want the same thing."

Everything he said, she could see, hear, feel, from his undressing himself then her, to his kneeling before her and tasting her sweetness. As his hands roamed her inner thighs and he pulled her from the back of the seat onto his hardness, she almost squealed in delight.

How could this be happening? The how didn't really matter, the what did. And the what felt so good, too good. He cried out and she just as she was about to join him...

Bertha shook her arm. "Wake up, Joy. You're about to make your dreams public."

Thoroughly embarrassed, she looked around. "I'm sorry."

Bertha giggled. "What are you listening to?"

"Believe me, you don't want to know."

In her ear, Sean said, "Damn, girl, I hope I didn't make you call out on the plane." She heard him laugh. "I got a little carried away there. I need to shower. I'll have more treats for your trip, but these need to be listened to in private." She turned off her phone.

"This man is going to be the death of me."

"Was that your Angry White Man?"

"Sean, his name is Sean. And yes, that was him."

"Why do you like him so much?"

She removed the ear buds and gave her grandmother her undivided attention. "Because I don't have to defend myself with him. He accepts and likes me for who I am."

"What about Edward?"

"He took my vibrator," she said softly. "Need I say more?"

Bertha laughed. "You're right. He should be horse whipped."

Chapter Nine

The yard always needed grooming when Sean visited his mother's D.C. home, and as usual, he'd mentally prepared himself to be the lawn guy. He took in the perfectly groomed yard. His mother had either hired someone to care for the yard, or she'd taken up gardening since she'd retired last year. His cell phone rang. The name on the caller ID brought a smile to his face.

"So how did you like your treat?"

"Loved it until I embarrassed myself on the plane." Joy laughed. "You are out of your mind, but don't stop. I love it. Have you thought about selling your recordings?"

"Oh no, little lady, I'm saving my talents for your ears only. How is your grandmother doing?"

"The flight was a little much for her."

"No it wasn't," he heard Bertha say in the background.

"Yes, it was. We're on our way to the hotel now. We could both use a nap."

"I left another little surprise for you at the front desk."

"Oooooo, I'll have to keep you. But I told you my hotel so you'd come visit, personally."

He laughed. "No way." His mother stepped onto the porch. When she saw him, her entire face lit up. He missed her, and knew he should visit her more than four times a year, but he also harbored anger toward her for continually taking his father back.

"I hate to rush you off, but my mom's running for me."

"Oh no, no. Go be with your mom. I just wanted to let you know we made it safely. Take care."

"You, too. Don't open your gift until we're on the phone tonight."

"Oh no, that's not fair. You can't make me wait."

"I had a feeling this might happen, so I got you two gifts. You can open one of them. You'll know which one."

"Go spend time with your mother, you horny dog."

Laughing, he disconnected. *Wow, a virgin has me whipped.*

Arms open wide and a humongous smile on her face, Connie, his mother, quickly approached the car. "Sean. My baby is home!"

Still tickled by his sweet thang, he exited the car. "Why all the big production?" He hugged his mom. "You'd think you hadn't seen me in forever."

"Well, two more days, and it would have been forever. Don't ever stay away so long again."

It had only been six months. They'd met up in Chicago when he was at a conference. "You are always welcome to come out to Los Angeles."

"You know I hate the west coast, and don't get me started on that Nakia."

"You'll be glad to know Nakia and I are history."

"Excellent! Why didn't you tell me?"

"You don't have to sound so pleased."

"Sorry, darling."

"I didn't feel like talking about her. She was a huge mistake I'd rather forget."

She peeked into the backseat of the rental car. "You might as well grab your bags. You're not staying at a hotel."

"I thought you may want a little privacy with your man," he teased.

"Boy, get your butt on in the house before I take a switch to you." She headed for the house.

He couldn't remember seeing her so playful in... forever. It did his heart well to see her happy. He took his luggage into the house and set it in the entryway.

"We're Q'ing in the backyard," Connie called out from the kitchen. "Come on back and meet my fiancé."

Though happy for his mother, he wasn't quite sure if he were ready to meet the new man in her life. "Let me take these to my room. I'll be right down."

"Hurry up."

After he placed his luggage on the bed and took a few minutes to regroup, he promised himself to give this man the benefit of any doubt he might have. He loved his mother, but she had the uncanny ability to fall for men just like his father. Ones who would break her heart and leave her humiliated. He descended the stairwell with prayers that this time would be different. She was older now, and so were the men she dated. Hopefully, this man had grown past his days of running the streets.

He entered the kitchen and saw his dad sitting at the table

shucking corn.

He plastered a smile on his face. "Hey, Pops." He pulled a beer out the refrigerator. His mother was obviously trying to get Sean to speak with his dad. She'd been hounding him for months on the subject.

"Hey, Sean. I was beginning to think you'd never return home. How is the newspaper business treating you?"

"Not bad. Not bad at all." The few times he was home, he didn't visit his father, except when he'd had that heart attack. After that visit, he'd thought he'd forgiven his father, but he hadn't. He nodded toward the back door. "So what do you think about Mom's fiancé."

He chuckled. "Never met a nicer fellow."

"Yeah, right."

Connie entered the house. "So what do you think?"

"About what?" Sean took a sip of beer.

"Darren is my fiancé, Sean."

Beer shot out of his nose, and he choked out "Dad? You're marrying, Dad?"

"Damn," Darren said nervously, "why did you have to say it like that?"

Sean ran his hands over his face. "You're joking right?" He checked the room for hidden cameras. "I'm being *Punked*."

"Now that was just flat out disrespectful." Darren stood. "I know I gave your mother a hard time in my early days, but—"

"Hard time my ass." He turned to his mother. "You can't be serious. How many times does he have to kick you in the guts before you—?"

"Now stop right there," Darren interrupted. "You watch your tone of voice when you speak to your mother."

"Oh, so now you're suddenly her protector? Where the hell were you when one of your women put her into the hospital? What kind of bitch shoots into a fucking house? What the hell? You would put your shit in any hole. Or should I say ho!" He spun toward his mother. "How can you forgive him for all the shit he's done? How much more is it going to take for you to see he's no good?"

"Stop it, Sean," Connie begged.

"No, I won't. Where was he at night when you cried yourself to sleep only to be woken by some woman pounding on our fucking door looking for his sorry ass?"

"I was wrong." Darren stepped between Sean and Connie. "Duh."

"Listen, son."

"Don't fucking 'son' me. Where was your ass when we were hungry, when our utilities were cut off? You could afford to keep your bitches well-clothed and fed, but what about your fucking wife and child!"

"Stop it," Connie demanded.

"Oh, so now you're defending his ass against me? Who was here for you, Mom? Who will be here to pick up the pieces when this bastard breaks your heart again?" He thumped his chest. "Me. And I'm tired of it. You must love being tortured, but I want no parts of it."

* * *

"I cannot believe this."

"Wait a second, Sean." Worried out of her mind, Joy peeked into her grandmother's connecting room, then returned to her side and curled up in the armchair. "What happened?"

"She's getting married."

"You told me you were going to meet her fiancé, so what's the problem?"

"It's my dad. What the hell is wrong with her?"

"Oh, ummm." At a loss for words, she could only manage a soft, "Wow."

"Wow is right. How can such a smart woman be so damn stupid? The only reason he ever took her back was when his woman of the month tired of him or he tired of her. He'd come home all apologetic. She'd take him back, and we'd 'play' the happy family until he'd move onto the next flavor of the month and start the cycle all over again."

"That's so sad. I don't know what to say."

"Have you ever been hungry? I mean missed a few meals and not by choice."

"No."

"I have. Too many times to count. I hate rice, Raman noodles, peanut butter, and macaroni and cheese."

"You just named my first semester college diet. My tuition was paid, but not much more. When my dad found out how I was living, let's just say my bank account mysteriously grew. I knew it was my dad, but he didn't admit to the gift for years."

"You're lucky."

"I agree. Tell me what happened to you."

"When we lived in D.C., my mom had a good-paying government job, but my dad moved us out in the middle of bum-fuck Virginia, and she had to quit her job. He'd shown her the math and kept going on about how transferring to the Fredericksburg office would mean the promotion he'd been working so hard for. I know my mom was hoping this new city would help them start anew. He promised things would be different. He promised." He drew in a deep breath. "Well, he didn't break his promise. They were different, in that they got worse. He moved us out there to be closer to his main squeeze of the month."

"Main squeeze?" she teased to lighten the mood.

"Yeah. Soon, he was gone more than he was home. The next thing I knew, my mom is taking just about any job she could find, and she forgot how to cook just about everything except rice and fucking beans. I remember days she said she wasn't hungry and for me to eat."

"Why didn't she return to D.C.?"

"We left humiliated. Hell, my dad had even screwed women at her job. There was nothing for us in D.C. Things got so desperate, we actually went to food pantries. And don't think my mom didn't go to my dad's job. The only problem was, he'd transferred and told them not to tell her where because they were having marital difficulty, and she was basically stalking him."

"What?"

"Yep, the son of a bitch stranded her in Fredericksburg without a job and ran off with a piece of ass."

Hand over her mouth, the right thing to say just wouldn't come to Joy. "I wish I were there with you."

"I do, too," he said softly. Minutes ticked away in comfortable silence. "You may get your wish."

"What wish would that be?"

"To make love with me, of course," he said with a laughter weighed down by sadness. "I'm not staying here for this. I'm heading home in the morning."

"Nah, I won't be getting that wish any time soon. My Angry White Man needs a friend right now, not a virgin slut."

They both laughed.

"You're one crazy woman."

"And you're one crazy man. A crazy man who needs to sit down with his father and express how he really feels."

"Oh I gave him a piece tonight. I'm done."

"You spent months online bashing women, but won't spend a few days with your parents."

"But my mom…"

"You're just as angry with her for choosing to leave you in such a bad situation. Stay in D.C. and talk to them."

"Maybe you're right."

"Maybe?"

"Okay, okay, you're right. I'll stay here and have it out with them."

"I didn't say you have to fight. Just let them know how you felt growing up. Better yet, write it down. Tonight write both of them a letter expressing your feelings."

"I'm tired of talking about this. What's on your agenda? Did you get your gifts from the front desk?"

She glanced over at the packages on the dresser. He'd been correct. It was easy to see which one she was to open. "Most definitely. Thanks for the chocolates. I can hardly wait to see what the other package holds, but I think I'll wait a bit on it."

"Are you sure?"

"Umm hmm. And if Granny is up to it, we're headed to the beach to see the sunset. That's what this trip was for." She looked over the busy city. In another hour the sun would be going down. Bertha wanted to see the sunset, but Joy wasn't sure if her grandmother would be up to it today. The flight took a lot out of her. Much more than Bertha was willing to admit.

"Well, enjoy your evening."

"I'll try. Go write those letters." She disconnected and set her cell phone to the side. "That's so jacked up." Her family had serious issues, but they seemed minuscule compared to what Sean had gone through. If anything, her family loved her too much, while his parents seemed too selfish to think of anything besides what they wanted.

"That's not fair. I don't know the whole story."

This glimpse into his childhood answered any questions she held about how his opinions on relationships were formed. Sean would never cheat or tolerate cheating, but because he'd been so hurt, he may never truly enter a relationship.

"Joy, come on," Bertha called from her room. "It's getting

84

late. I don't want to miss the sun setting."

She rose from the chair. "It sets every evening."

* * *

"I can die now." Bertha looked away from the setting sun to her grandbaby. "Thank you so much for indulging this old woman."

"Indulging an old woman my foot." Sitting on the ground beside Bertha's wheelchair, Joy grabbed a handful of sand and allowed it to fall through her fingers. "Why didn't you come sooner?"

"It's like you said. The sun sets every evening. That's true, but because it does, I took it for granted. I had plenty of time to see the sunset on the ocean, but the right time never came."

"Well thank you for *extorting* me into coming."

Bertha giggled. "Extortion is such an ugly word."

"Especially when it's your grandmother who's the extorter." She leaned back on her hands. "Do you want to go to Catalina Island tomorrow? They have a glass bottom boat excursion I think you'd like."

"Now that I've seen the sunset, I've seen it all. But if you'd like to go, of course we can go."

Bertha sounded past tired to Joy. This went beyond waking early, the long flight and the coming down from the excitement of the trip. As of late, Bertha sounded perpetually weary, and she slept more than she was awake.

"Would you mind just hanging around the hotel tomorrow?" Joy asked. "I have an idea for a novel and would like to start the outline. Now if you want to go out, we can. This is your trip. We can do whatever you'd like."

Beaming, Bertha said, "You'll be a famous author some day. No, let's stay at the hotel so you can create. I'm so proud of you."

"Thank you very much, Miss Lady. I don't know about famous, but I will be published someday." A cool breeze kicked off the ocean. "Do you need a blanket? I brought one from the hotel."

"Oh no, darling, I'm fine."

Joy watched her grandmother watch over the ocean. Something was wrong, terribly wrong. A withdrawn Bertha? No, this wasn't right. "What's wrong, Granny?"

"I'm tired, Joy. I'm just tired."

"Tired of living?" she asked timidly.

"I've lived a good, full life. Do I want to die anytime soon? No. I'd like to stay with you forever." Arthritis prevented Bertha from opening her hand fully. Fingers folded in, she held her hand out to Joy who gently took it. "A year, even a month ago I was afraid to leave you, but now." She brushed her knuckles along Joy's jawbone. "We're both ready now. If I were to leave tomorrow, I know you'd endure and become a better woman than you already are."

Tears streamed down Joy's face. The thought of losing her grandmother was just too much.

"Now, now," Bertha whispered, "don't cry. I'll always be with you."

"It's not the same."

"You're right. It's not."

Eyes closed, Joy lowered her head. "Did the doctor say something to you I should know about? This trip came so suddenly." She prayed harder than she ever had for God to give her a miracle. Yes, she logically understood that anything living will die, but this was her granny, her heart. How could she survive without her heart?

"No, he hasn't. I just know, and I'm at peace with it. I'm telling you because I want you to fully understand that when that time comes, it's what I want. I want you to accept that I will not be with you forever. At least not in this form, but my love for you will remain. I'll always be with you."

"I understand," she said for Bertha's sake, but she didn't like it. Not one bit.

The two sat quietly for a few minutes and enjoyed the peacefulness of the ocean as people strolled along the shore. Joy didn't want to think about life without her granny, so she wouldn't. When the time came, she'd just... She didn't know what she'd do, but she wouldn't waste another precious moment worrying about what was to come when she had her grandmother with her now.

"You really like that Sean, don't you?"

"Oh yes. Too much."

"I'm just glad you've finally come out of your shell. You've excelled in all aspects of your life except..."

"What, sleeping around?" They both laughed.

"You know it isn't that simple. You've never really dated or allowed people close enough to get to know you. But look at you with Edward and Sean."

"Yeah, I have two men dangling," she joked. "Seriously though, I'm worried about Sean. That business with his parents has thrown him for a loop." She had told Bertha everything on their ride to the beach. "How could his father do such a horrible thing, and how could his mother keep taking him back? That makes absolutely no sense whatsoever. I'm trying to be supportive, but I don't even know what to say."

"You're listening to him is the support he needs."

"I pray it's enough."

Back at the hotel, Joy helped Bertha prepare for bed and kissed her good night, then returned to her room showered and lay across the bed. She wanted to call Sean to see how he was doing, but didn't want to pester him.

Just as she began to dial his number, the cell phone rang and her heart sang out. "Hey, stranger. Long time no talk to." She propped a pillow under her arms.

"Ha, ha, very funny," Sean said dryly. "Did you go to the beach?"

"Oh yes. I've never seen a more beautiful sunset, and the sand. Wow, I didn't expect it to be so fine. In a way, it's soft."

"And your granny?"

"She loved it so much I had to wait for her to doze off before I could wheel her away from the shore. And mind you, though her chair is electric, it is not made for sand travel, but she insisted I take her down to the *real* beach close to the water. I need to join a gym. Whew howdy I'm out of shape."

He chuckled. "I'm glad she enjoyed herself."

"Me, too." Neither spoke for an extended period, yet they were still together. Curled up on the plush comforter, Joy whispered, "She's dying. She brought me here to let me down softly, but there is no softly for this."

"I'm sorry. I know how close you two are."

"She's in so much pain, and I know she's physically miserable and just wants it all to end. Her body has been slowly shutting down. She's suffering, and I know I'm being selfish for wanting her to stay, but…"

"Stop torturing yourself. Of course you don't want her to die. Stop fretting over things out of your control. Enjoy the time you have and make her life as comfortable as you can."

"You're right. It's just hard."

"I know, baby. But you can do it."

Her cell *beeped*, indicating a second call. She quickly checked her caller ID. "That's my dad. I'm sorry, but I need to answer this."

"Oh no. Go ahead. I was just checking on you. We'll talk tomorrow."

"Thanks Sean. Good night." She switched the call over. "Hello, Daddy."

"How's my baby girl?" he whispered.

Giggling, she said, "Are you sneaking to call me?"

"I had to hide in the bathroom. Your mother has been hounding me all day for your new number. How are you feeling? I mean, Edward said you had a bad patch the other night."

Face flush with embarrassment, she couldn't believe her ears. "He told you? Awww man, why can't I just die?"

He chuckled. "You are so dramatic. If you want to talk about anything, you know I'm here for you."

"I know, Daddy." She paused. "I'm just not ready. I may never be."

"I fully understand. When and if you're ever ready, I'm here for you."

"Love you."

"Love you, too. Now let me get out of here before your mom comes looking for me."

Chapter Ten

Tears streamed down Joy's face, and the lump in her throat kept her from crying out. This wasn't happening, she told herself. Paramedics weren't trying to jumpstart Bertha's heart. Her grandmother wasn't dying. She wasn't! She slouched onto the armchair and lowered her face into the palms of her hands.

A few seconds later, the nightmare became worse as one of the paramedic said, "I'm sorry, ma'am. She's gone."

Sorrow, agony, reality pulverized the lump in Joy's throat as she cried out, "Granny!" She ran to her grandmother's lifeless body and clung to her.

* * *

Sean continued scrolling through the list of flights to Atlanta. Unless he wanted to chance flying standby, the earliest flight he could book would be leaving in the morning. Granted, Joy probably wouldn't make it back to Atlanta before morning, but he still felt rushed to make an appearance in Atlanta. She had sounded past distraught over the phone, all he wanted to do was comfort her. Now he cursed himself for being across the country when she needed him.

He booked the morning flight and lay across his bed. Knowing Joy, she was blaming herself for Bertha's death. They were so close. She'd even told him how Bertha had actually been the one to set up Joy's Internet presence.

At a loss for how to help Joy, he felt inept. He reached over to the nightstand and grabbed his cell phone. *Why didn't I stay my butt in Los Angeles?* He dialed her number.

"Sean," she wept into the phone. "What have I done? It's all my fault."

"Stop this."

"I can't. I knew there was something wrong. I should have taken her to the doctor instead of flying her across the country."

He leaned against the headboard. "I know this isn't what you want to hear, but there was nothing the doctors could have done for her. Bertha knew this. That's why she was in such a hurry to go to Los Angeles. You made her dying wish a reality. Please, baby, please stop. She had a good life and loved you with all her heart. She doesn't want you doing this to yourself."

"But I feel so... I should have done everything within my

power to save her."

"Save her from what? Death is part of life. Look, I'll be in Atlanta tomorrow."

"Oh no. Stay with your family. I know you have a lot to deal with there."

"You need me. I'll be there."

"Sean, please don't come. My family is on their way here, and they will swamp me. I won't have a moment's peace. Stay with your family. Now don't get me wrong. I'll be blowing up your phone."

Even with the chuckle behind her voice, she sounded so sad, so defeated. "If you need me, call," he said.

"You know I will. And I expect you to still have that talk with your parents. Stay in D.C. Wait a sec... Oh that's my dad on the line."

He said, "Good-bye, baby," but wanted to say, "I love you." He disconnected, but had no intention on staying in D.C. when Joy needed him.

A knock at his door startled him.

"Sean, Sean, are you still there?" came his mother's voice. He'd forgotten his parents were coming over. He contemplated pretending he wasn't in his room, but quickly decided that was the coward's way out.

"Yeah, I'm here." He crossed the room and opened the door.

Eyes red and swollen as if she'd been crying, Connie hugged her son. Tears. Sean always hated seeing her cry. Usually it was the man who was standing behind her who caused them.

"Come on in." He stepped to the side and allowed them in.

Darren and Connie sat on the bed and held hands. Sean took a seat in the armchair by the window and watched the busy streets below. He needed the emotional distance.

"Son," Darren said softly, slowly, but received no reply. "Son."

Sean continued looking out the window. He couldn't watch his mother cry. Wouldn't. "I hear you."

"The things I've done... unforgivable, but I'm asking for your forgiveness. I have true remorse for my actions and punish myself every second of the day."

"So because you are *supposedly* punishing yourself, I should just let bygones be bygones and act like you won't hurt Mom again?" Three cars had exited the parking garage across the street since he'd sat down. Boy how he wished he'd been in one of them.

"I love Connie—"

"You have a funny way of showing it," Sean cut in.

"I've forgiven your father."

"Sounds like the same old song to me." He faced his parents. "I'm tired of this broken record of a family we have. If you want to forgive him for leaving us humiliated and destitute time and time again, that's on you, but don't expect me to buy this bag of bull."

"I've changed, Sean. I took your mother and you for granted. Then there was the booze... drugs... women. I'm not making excuses. I made choices. Really bad choices. And though I didn't show it, I've always loved you. I should have let you two go, but I couldn't. I was selfish. I wanted it all and you paid the price."

"From where I sit, you're still being selfish. Mom, why are you doing this? You were done with him. Why?

Head lowered, she softly admitted, "I can't forgive your father. I'll never forgive that man for what he did to us, and I'll never forgive myself for allowing it to go on so long." She lifted her head and connected with Sean's eyes. "But this man." She drew Darren's hand to her heart. "I love him. He's a good, God-fearing man. He makes me laugh. He's a good provider. He makes me cry tears of joy. He doesn't do drugs or drink. He's not a womanizer. He puts me first. And most importantly, he loves my son. All I'm asking is that you get to know him."

"I don't know, Mom. There's so much. I can't act like it all didn't happen. Like the man sitting beside you isn't the same bastard who..." Too drained to go into all the pain his father had caused, he returned to looking out the window.

"I don't expect you to forget or pretend I wasn't the ass that I was," Darren said. "You could curse me out every second of the day, and I'd take it because I deserve that and more. You have no reason to believe I've changed. You're right, this sounds like the same old song, but it's not. I just pray that with time you'll see that every breath I take is for you and your mother. I'll never leave either of you again. Never."

Sean wanted to believe, but couldn't open his heart to the pain again. "So what do you want from me?"

91

"The chance to earn your respect, your trust, your love." Darren crossed over to Sean. "I know it won't be easy. I put you through years of hell, and I don't deserve another chance."

Still watching the traffic, pretending he didn't care and wasn't affected by his father's words, Sean said, "You got that right. You don't deserve another chance."

Darren rested his hand on his son's back. "I love you and your mother. I'm sorry it took my almost dying to realize what I had done, what I had thrown away."

Sean remembered his father's heart attack two years ago. That was the last time Sean had seen him. "I have too much on my mind right now. Joy needs me..." he trailed off. He hadn't meant to mention Joy.

"Joy?" Connie rose from the bed. "Who's Joy, the new woman in your life?"

"A good friend. Her grandmother passed this morning, and I'm headed to Atlanta to show my support."

"Oh sweet Jesus." Connie covered her mouth with her hand. "I'm so sorry. You go on and support your friend. We'll be here."

"Connie's right. Go be with your friend."

* * *

The flight from Los Angeles to Atlanta had been hell. Life went downhill from there for Joy. Benjamin, who had worked his magic and had Bertha's body released to Joy within hours of her death, couldn't make it to the airport to meet her when they landed because he was at the funeral parlor. Bertha had left very specific instructions for her burial. The main one being her burial must be within forty-eight hours of her death. Joy had thought the request strange at the time her grandmother had made it and pointed out that family and friends who didn't live in the area wouldn't have time to be notified and make it to the services, but Bertha had been insistent.

When Joy finally arrived home, her sisters were waiting for her. She hadn't even stepped out of the taxi good before the chastising began. An hour later, her mother arrived and started in also.

Too tired to argue and in partial agreement with them, Joy curled into Bertha's favorite armchair and took the abuse. All she wanted to do was disappear, but no such luck came her way. In the morning, she'd have to rise and attend her grandmother's funeral.

"What's going on here?" Benjamin entered with Edward close behind. The three older women stiffened. "I could hear you from the driveway." He held his arms out. Joy didn't hesitate to run to him.

"Daddy." He wrapped his arms around her and held her close. "I'm so sorry, Daddy. I shouldn't have taken her to California."

"No, baby, this isn't your fault."

"Stop coddling her, Benjamin," Emily broke in. "Irresponsible. Completely irresponsible."

"Don't you think I feel bad enough already?" Joy snapped.

"That's more than enough, Emily. Edward, would you mind taking Joy to her room? I need to have a discussion with my wife and daughters."

"Of course not." Edward took Joy by the hand and led her away. The further she was from her mother, the better she felt.

Inside the room, she sunk to the bed and cried. Edward held her in his embrace until she calmed.

"Don't blame yourself. Your mother is wrong. When you left, I knew Bertha didn't have much more time."

"Why didn't you say something?"

"Because you would have tried to save someone who didn't need saving instead of allowing her to have her last wish." He glanced at his watch. "It's after ten. Have you eaten today?"

"No. I'm not hungry."

"A piece of fruit is all I ask. Then you can sleep. You look exhausted." He rose from the bed and headed for the door.

"Edward…"

"Yes?"

"Thanks for being here for me."

Chapter Eleven

Sherri took extra care to look her best for her first day at work. A part of her still couldn't believe she had a legitimate job. Granted, she used a little more than her word processing skills to obtain the position, but she still felt good. The salary wasn't much, but it would be hers. A strange sense of pride overtook her as the assistant from the counselor's office introduced her to the staff. She had been told Tony would be in meetings all morning and would arrive after lunch. By the time he arrived, she planned to know the inner workings of the office better than she knew how to please a man. But first, she had to read the personnel file of one Joy Warren.

The file just about put Sherri to sleep. Edward was too much man for that goody-two-shoe of a little girl. Once he had the child he desired, he would quickly tire of her and be ready to move on to a real woman—Sherri.

She glanced at the clock—10:47. Little Miss Virgin's grandmother's funeral would be starting soon. Edward would be spending a lot of time helping to console the little twit, which Sherri would use to her advantage. She had quite a bit to learn. Over the years, she hadn't used her computer for much more than surfing the Internet and chat rooms. Two hours later, she was knee-deep in an electronic tutorial on Microsoft Office products. Amazed at exactly how much she didn't know, she became intrigued with the programs.

"I can do this," she said confidently under her breath.

"I'll bet you can."

Sherri clutched her chest and spun around. "Oh my goodness, Tony. You scared the sh… mess out of me."

"Sorry."

The devilish grin spread across his face didn't fit his apology. Oh how she missed Edward's mischievous grin. The way he treated her over the years told her he didn't think of her as a whore at all. What man is faithful to a whore? It didn't make sense. If she could only give him the baby he desired. Of course he'd want a child of his own blood. She'd been stupid to think anything different.

"Is something wrong? Is everyone treating you right?"

"Everyone has been extremely kind. I just have a lot on my

mind." She smoothed her hair behind her ear. "I'm a little out of practice, but I'm catching on quickly." She motioned toward the computer monitor. "I've already made it through a few lessons."

"Good for you. If you need help, don't hesitate to ask."

"Thank you for this opportunity."

"We all need a break sometime. I'm glad you came aboard." He tapped the back of her chair. "Now let me let you get back to your studies."

"I left your messages on your desk."

"Oh wow, you're already ahead of my previous office manager. She always let the calls go to voicemail. Don't get me wrong, I know sometimes you're busy, but I do prefer having the phone answered when possible."

"Got it," she said with a smile, surprised he hadn't hit on her. "Could I get you some coffee, tea?"

"Thanks, but no thanks. I don't do caffeine after ten."

She watched as he entered his office without closing the door. Thinking back to her streetwalking days, Tony had always been a strange bird. Initially, he'd pay for her time and take her to a nice hotel where they would shower together, then she'd sleep in his arms all night. Oftentimes she wondered what kind of weirdo would pass up the pussy, especially pussy he'd paid for? *Nut.*

She glanced at the clock. The funeral should be over, and Edward would be consoling his little virgin. Tonight he'd probably be by Sherri's place to release pent-up energy. Thinking about his release had her pussy juices flowing. She may not be able to give Edward the child he desired, but she was his fantasy come true in the bedroom, kitchen, car, elevator, wherever they decided to make love. And he was her fantasy come true. Damn how she wanted to pleasure herself right now in prelude for what Edward would have for her tonight.

"Sherri, could you come here a second please?"

Broken out of the beginnings of a climactic daydream, she grabbed her notepad and went to see what Tony needed. "Yes."

Tony looked up from a message she'd taken earlier and stared at her a few seconds. "Are you okay?"

Memories of him suckling her inner thighs stole her voice. Edward was an expert lover, but she had to give it to Tony, he sucked twat to perfection! "I'm fine." She quickly scanned the room. The mini-blinds were closed.

"I couldn't understand this number." He held the message out to her.

"I guess I should take a penmanship course." Smiling sweetly, she closed and locked the door, then rounded his desk, draped her arms around his neck and recited the digits.

Eyes closed, he leaned his head back. "I'm sorry about Saturday. This isn't why I hired you."

"I know." She slowly unbuttoned his shirt. "I wouldn't have taken the job had I thought otherwise." She slipped a hand into his undershirt and caressed as she nibbled along his neck. "I'll stop if you'd like."

"Don't stop."

Satisfied she had Tony right where she wanted him— wrapped around her fingers—Sherri eased around in front of him and lifted her dress over her head, showing Tony what a wonderful job her personal trainer had done. *Women half my age would beg for a body like this.* She dropped her panties and bra to the floor.

The awe in Tony's big brown eyes turned her on even more. So what if what they had was only physical, she had love at home.

As she finished unbuttoning his shirt, he held onto her waist and pulled her close enough to take her breast into his mouth. This man had to have the most talented mouth ever. Disappointment pinched her when he stopped suckling to take off his clothes. The whole process couldn't have taken but twenty seconds, but that twenty seconds felt like an eternity.

Seated in his chair, he pressed the arms into the back position, then again pulled her between his legs, this time settling his mouth at the base of her right breast, teasing and taunting.

A moan fought for release, but she couldn't make a sound. They couldn't afford for anyone to hear the pleasure they were sharing. He took one of her pebble-hard nipples into his mouth, and she about lost it.

The satisfaction in his eyes as he placed two fingers into her said he knew exactly what he was doing to her. He had her creamier than the contents of a well-shaken can of whipped cream. If he kept this up, after she and Edward worked their issues out, she would keep Tony around. The only issue she could possibly see was his dick was quite a bit smaller than Edward's. The length wasn't the issue, but the girth. She'd become accustomed to Edward's unusual thickness.

She repositioned herself to straddle him, then lowered onto his dick. Just as she had feared, he wasn't thick enough for her, but he still felt damn good. Simultaneously, he grasped her butt and took her mouth. The added pressure to her clit was just what the doctor ordered. As he worked her into such a frenzy that he had to swallow her cries as she came, Tony was proving to her that size really didn't matter.

Once the two calmed, they used the shower in Tony's office to clean themselves. Edward rarely allowed her to lead in bed, and it looked as if Tony was more than willing. This was such a nice treat. She'd definitely keep Tony around.

Both dressed and lying on the couch in Tony's office with his arms wrapped around her, he said, "I know this is a bad time to mention this, but I was serious, I honestly did not hire you to supply my sexual needs."

"And I was serious also. I wouldn't have accepted the position if I had thought otherwise. Those days are over for me. Have been since C'Money..." she trailed off. She'd never tell how Edward had saved her life by killing her pimp. Guilt washed over her. Edward was a good man. He loved her and she should be more understanding of his want of a child. Especially with all he'd done for her.

"I know you had nothing to do with C'Money's murder, but why did you leave?"

"I saw his death as my chance to break free. I didn't want that life, so when I got the chance, I ran as far away from it as I could. And let's face it, all of his girls had motive to kill his ass, but no money. It would have been too easy for the police to pin it on any of us to close the case quickly. My best bet was to leave town."

He caressed her waist. "I understand... I was worried about you. I looked for you."

She rested her hand atop his. "You are too kind. Always have been, but I had to make a clean break."

"Remember how we used to talk about just about everything? I miss those days."

She fondly remembered those times. Tony was always sweet, too sweet and sensitive for her liking, but she had enjoyed the talks they would have.

"We never discussed how you ended up under those

circumstances. Don't feel pressured to tell me. You know I'm not like that. But what happened after you left?"

"I didn't have it easy growing up. My father threw me out the house when I was fourteen because I got tired of sucking his dick and his fucking me whenever he could get me alone," she said honestly. "Within a few weeks, I'd met C'Money, and he was taking good care of me. I guess you can figure the rest out from there. After C'Money's death, I went up north and fell in love," she lied. "I've been with him ever since."

After Edward shot C'Money, she'd moved into Edward's house. Edward had very wisely advised her not to leave the house, answer the phone or the door for the first two years. No one was to know she was still in Atlanta. The third year he allowed her to run errands to the grocery store and such. By the time the fourth year came along, she could move freely. In the fifth year, he purchased her a condo. That he'd gone to such extent to protect her from the police showed, yet again, he truly loved her.

"And until Saturday," she said sadly, "I'd been faithful."

His lips gently pressed against her neck, having her ready for round two. "What happened?" he softly asked and glanced at his watch.

The thought of that little girl taking her man was unbearable. She sat up. "Midlife crisis. He started acting strange a few months before he turned fifty. Then the next thing I know, he decided to take a month-long cruise *without* me."

"Oh." He crossed the room to the door and unlocked it. "That doesn't sound good at all."

"You can say that again." She moved from the sofa to the chair in front of his desk. "It took next to no snooping for me to find out he was having an affair with someone who is literally young enough to be his daughter."

"I'm so sorry." He took his seat behind his desk.

"I love him so much, and I've been trying to be understanding, but it hurts. Then you came along." She shook her head and averted her eyes from Tony. "When he called me a whore… He knows I left that life behind when C'Money was murdered. He knows how hard I've had it. I'm in a confused place right now and just needed someone to want me."

"I feel like a real ass. I'm sorry."

"No, no, it's not you. You didn't know. We've always had

this odd connection between us. Thanks for being here for me."

"Thank you for allowing me to be."

The chime for the end of the school day sounded, and within a few minutes, someone knocked at the door.

"Come in," Tony said.

"I'm sorry to disturb you," Nurse Michaels entered, "but my operation is this Wednesday, not next Wednesday. I'm sorry for the miscommunication." She nodded at Sherri. "Hello again, how has your first day been?"

"Excellent, just excellent. Everyone has been so kind."

"I'll show Sherri how to change your time card now," Tony said from his computer. "Sherri, you'll also need to make the arrangements for the temporary nurse to come in tomorrow to get the lay of the land. The contact numbers are in your Outlook address book."

She'd read through the address book earlier in the day and knew exactly who to call. "Sure thing."

"Well, I've got to get on. Have a great evening," Nurse Michaels chirped and left the two alone.

Long after the children and teachers had gone home, Sherri was still at her computer working through tutorials.

"Plan to stay here all night?" Tony asked.

Amazed at how much she'd learned over the course of the day, she wasn't ready to call it quits yet. "Time just flew by. I don't have Excel on my home computer and am in the middle of learning how to make charts."

"You're really enjoying this, aren't you?"

"Most definitely, but I know you need to get on home to your wife, so let me pack up."

"If you wanted to know if I'm married, you could have asked." He chuckled. "I've been married twice, now is not one of those times."

"I wasn't..." she trailed off. "I mean I was a little curious." She saved her progress and shut down the program.

"I lost my second wife because of my midlife crisis. I didn't cheat, but I became a real ass. I really hope things work out for you."

"Thank you for believing in me."

* * *

"Mom, who is that man over there?" Joy asked of the older, stocky, man with a full head of silver hair who sat alone at a table in the church's basement. She'd seen him at the back of the sanctuary and at the gravesite looking uncomfortable, yet grief-stricken.

Emily glanced up from her plate of baked chicken and green beans toward the direction Joy had nodded. "What the hell is he doing here?" she snapped, drawing the attention of Heather and Helen.

The shocked look on her mother's and sisters' faces completely threw Joy.

"It's time to go." Heather and Helen took Joy by the hands and tried to pull her up from the table.

"No." She snatched her hands back. "What is wrong with you guys? I haven't eaten in days. I'm hungry." She looked for the man, but saw someone else in the crowd she thought she recognized. Her heart began to race. It was him. It was Sean!

"Marshall, take the baby out of here."

She faced her mother. "Who are you calling a baby? What baby?"

Marshall held his hand out. "Don't make this hard, Joy."

Exasperated, Joy ignored her brother's outstretched hand and walked toward Sean. Before she knew it, Marshall showed just how big of a jerk he was and carried her out. She didn't bother kicking and screaming, but when they arrived at his SUV, she hauled off and punched him with all of her might.

"Don't make me turn you over my knee, little girl."

Joy narrowed her eyes on her oldest brother. She'd never liked him and didn't see her opinion of him changing any time in the near future. "This is the last damn time you're going to disrespect me."

"Watch your mouth."

"Since you obviously didn't get the *fucking* memo, allow me to inform you that I'm grown and will not tolerate your disrespect any longer."

Shock clear on his face, he stepped back as if sucker-punched. Joy rarely cursed, and had never cursed at him before, but she had to do something drastic to make him listen to her for a change.

"Joy!" Emily barked.

She spun around to see her mother.

"How dare you send this ox to carry me out of my grandmother's repast. What the hell is wrong with you?" So livid she could barely breathe, Joy turned away from her mother just in time to see Edward rush out the church with her father close behind.

"Joy, what happened?" Benjamin took her into his arms.

"Ask your crazy wife. I can't take this anymore, Daddy. I can't. Not now." She sank into the comforting embrace of her father.

"What has gotten into you?" Benjamin snapped.

"It's… It's… Uncle George is here. That bastard had the nerve to be here."

"What…? Where…?" Benjamin looked around.

"It's true, Daddy," Heather said.

"Who is he?" Joy asked.

"Your grandmother's brother," Benjamin said, voice filled with disgust and sadness. "We can't keep him from attending the funeral. I know he's the reason she wanted the services conducted so soon after her death."

Joy listened carefully to every word spoken about this mysterious Uncle George. They had a huge, close-knit family, so why hadn't she heard of this uncle previously, and why did everyone dislike him? *Be careful what you ask for.*

"I know, I know," Emily stammered. "I saw him and had to protect the baby." She wrapped her arms around Joy and her husband. "I'm so sorry, baby, forgive your mommy. You know I can be a bit over the top at times. I didn't mean to scare you."

"What's going on? Why are you all acting so crazy? So what if he wanted to come to Granny's funeral. It only makes sense." Truth be told, Joy didn't want to know why her family had such disdain for her uncle. Somehow she felt it was tied to the dark presence she wanted to stay in the dark. "I'm going home."

"You have to wait for the reading of the will," Marshall said.

"I don't want to deal with this right now! I don't want to listen to the reading of the will. All I want is my granny back!" She turned and bumped into Edward's solid body. First one tear, then another, and another fell from her eyes. "I want my granny."

"It's okay." He held her close and rocked her. "It's okay."

"I'm sorry, Joy." Marshall placed his hand on his baby sister's back. "I know you're hurting, but Granny left very specific instructions. She did things this way to make it easier on you, on us, in the long run." He pulled her from Edward. "And you're right. I shouldn't have carried you out here. I was completely wrong. Do you forgive me?"

"I still don't like you." She hugged him. "But I love you."

Chuckling, he admitted, "I love you, too, you little brat."

* * *

Joy, Benjamin, Nancy and Bertha's attorney were the only people left in the room for the reading of Bertha's last will and testimony. Bertha, being Bertha, had made a special video for the entire family. As she finished speaking to each person and telling them what she was leaving them, they were dismissed from the office. Thus far she'd given each member a personal message of love and a few thousand dollars, which shocked the whole lot of them. They'd all assumed Bertha was living off the retirement from her husband, social security and what her very generous children gave her.

Seated between Nancy and her father, Joy continued watching the video.

"Nancy, you've been such a faithful employee and a true friend."

"I miss you already," Nancy said to the image of Bertha on the screen.

"I know you'll keep an eye on my baby girl, but don't miss out on the life you still have ahead of you. I'm leaving you the house."

"Bertha no."

"And don't you dare say no. You love that house more than Joy and me put together. These are my last wishes, you have to follow them." Bertha smiled.

Tears streaming down her face, Nancy turned to Joy. "You can still live in the house, nothing has changed."

"And before you think you can outsmart me," Bertha continued, "Joy isn't to live there. It's time for the baby girl to grow up. She won't do that as long as we keep overprotecting her, so it's time to kick her out of the nest. She has until the end of the school year that I die in, then she must move out."

"That's not acceptable," Nancy said to the lawyer, Mr. Franklin.

"No, no." Joy took Nancy's hand into hers. "I'll be fine. I can't see myself staying there now that Granny is gone. I can't."

"Are you two done yet? If not, pause the DVD so you don't miss anything." Bertha laughed. "Boy howdy do I tickle myself." She waved them off. "It's okay to laugh, you know."

With that, Joy couldn't help but giggle. Her grandmother had always been a mess in the best way. "You are too much, Granny."

After Bertha calmed, she continued. "I've also left a nice nest egg for you, Nancy. Use it to travel to all the places we dreamed of going, but never went. I love you."

"I love you, too." She dabbed at her eyes with a tissue. "I love you, too."

"Now hug my two favorite babies for me before you leave."

Nancy hugged Joy and Benjamin, then left them alone with the attorney.

"Place this thing on pause until Nancy leaves. You know the routine."

The attorney paused the video until Nancy left.

"Okay, I guess you've resumed the video. Benjamin, you are a great man and I know Joy will say I'm not supposed to have favorites, but you are my favorite son. I want to thank you for loving my daughter. I know she has a strong will and can be a bit bossy at times."

"Humph, that's an understatement," Joy mumbled.

"Be good, Joy." Bertha wagged her arthritic fingers.

Joy laughed. "She knows me too well."

"Over the years, I've seen you act as a buffer between Joy and Emily, and I know you grow tired, but please don't give up. With me gone, Emily will become even more…"

"Controlling, overprotective, overbearing…" Joy supplied.

"Whatever Joy said." Bertha laughed.

"You two are horrible." Benjamin chuckled.

"Joy will need you, especially now that I'm leaving her the remainder of my assets."

Attorney Franklin rounded his desk with a box and set it on the floor before Joy.

"Go ahead, look inside while I speak."

Benjamin removed the lid and revealed books. Joy began sorting through the old novels as Bertha spoke.

"I've always been a tad bit before my time and a tad bit melodramatic."

Joy looked up from one of the books at the screen. "A tad bit?"

"Quite melodramatic," Bertha corrected. "Back when I was young, the only real choices for women were housewife, secretary, teacher. Like Joy, I loved to write. Since I knew the chance of a publisher purchasing rights to my novels were slim to none, I wrote under a pseudonym and didn't let them know I was a female. That box contains first edition copies of each of my novels."

"I think I've read just about all of these. Granny is famous!"

"Now you understand why I was so excited when I saw you'd caught the writing bug. Your grandfather, being a proud man, wouldn't accept the money my writing brought in, but instead invested the money I'd made from the novels. Over the years the portfolio has grown quite nicely."

The lawyer handed a copy of Bertha's holdings to Benjamin.

"Then about seven, maybe eight years ago, the publisher got in touch with me and wanted to rerelease my series. My original contract said that once the novel was out of print, the rights reverted to me. By the time they contacted me, women authors were finally finding their books in the national chains, but I still didn't want to remove the mystery behind my books. You know the story from there. The series was released and picked up by a movie studio, and at the end of the day, you are thirty-six million dollars richer."

"What?" Joy choked.

"Someone get Joy a glass of water." Bertha laughed. "Whew howdy this is fun. Yes, I said thirty-six million. And you'll continue receiving royalties from my work. You now own all the rights."

"Daddy, Granny is rich! Did you know?"

"I had no idea." He shook his head. "I really had no idea."

"Now, Joy, I love you, but you are too kind-hearted. You'd give every dime you have to the children. Don't get me wrong. I'm all for helping them out, but to help keep you from giving your money away, you'll receive a hundred grand a year for the next ten years, then you'll receive a million a year. Neither of you are to tell anyone of my secret life or the amount of wealth I accumulated. Well, let me amend that last statement. Joy, when you marry you must have a prenuptial agreement and you can't tell your husband about the wealth until after you're married."

"Well thanks for letting me tell my husband."

"Joy, you love teaching and writing. Now you can do both."

"I'm in shock," she mumbled.

"That makes two of us, baby girl."

Chapter Twelve

"Where did Mother get a hundred grand?"

"If she had wanted you to know, she would have told you," Benjamin replied. "I'm fed up with how you've been treating Joy." Over the years, he and his wife rarely fought, but when they did, Joy was usually the subject matter. He dropped his robe on the foot of the bed, then slipped under the covers with Emily.

"You are always coddling that child."

"She's not a child but a grown woman. And your performance at the repast was completely unacceptable. Actually, your behavior since you decided to put your virgin daughter on the auction block for the first eligible bachelor has been completely unacceptable."

"I didn't mean to tell Edward. It just slipped out. He is so perfect for Joy, and I knew Mother would like him also. He can give her guidance."

"I love you with all of my heart, but if you make me choose between you and my child, my child will win every time. Stop it and stop it now."

"Benjamin, I'm…"

"You're what? Treating our daughter like she can't think for herself, making her feel inadequate, humiliating her at every turn? That's not love but you covering for your own failures." He fluffed his pillow and turned away from his wife.

A few seconds later, he felt Emily's hand on his shoulder and her body ease close to him. "I failed my baby. That's why she's…"

"She's what?" He pushed her hand away and rolled toward her. "She's a successful young woman with a kind heart, but because she won't follow your dreams for her instead of her own dreams, you demean her at every turn."

"That's not true. I'm encouraging her to set her sights high."

"And what's wrong with being a grade school teacher?"

"You don't understand." She wiped the tears from her eyes.

"I know you wanted to be a teacher. I told you to be whatever you wanted. You're the one who chose to follow a different path."

"But I couldn't. You know my parents. They crushed my dreams because they wouldn't allow me to go into a dead-end job, and they were correct."

"You made your choice and Joy has made hers. What if teaching were a dead-end job? Hell, I wouldn't give a damn if Joy decided she didn't want to work at all. I'd support her, but that's not Joy. She loves to work. And working with the children is what she lives for. You act as if she's taken off on an immoral career path."

"I know. It's just sometimes I worry about her. We're not getting any younger. She needs someone to love and be loved by."

"You'll be lucky if she ever forgives the way you've been treating her. How could you blame her for Bertha's death?"

"I was grieving."

"So the hell is your child!" He pushed himself out of bed.

"Where are you going?"

"A hotel."

"Please don't leave, not tonight, I just buried my mother. I love, loved her so much. I'm so sorry I took my grief out on Joy." She wiped the tears from her eyes. "I'm so sorry. I love her so much."

"You're jealous of your own child. Between your jealousy and your guilt for her being molested, you're driving a wedge between us. Like I said, I love you with all of my heart, but I won't allow you to continue taking your pain and guilt out on *my* baby." Because he did love Emily and knew she needed him, he crawled back into the bed and cupped her into his body. "I do love you, but you have to stop this. Please. I don't want to lose you."

"I love you, too." She turned in his arms. "And you're right. I didn't even realize I was jealous of her until now. She has the life I've always wanted. With all of my success, I'm the only failure because I didn't fight for what I wanted. Then I let that bastard hurt her."

"It wasn't your fault, and you're not a failure."

"I failed my baby. I'll never forgive myself. Mother never forgave me. She took my baby from me, and she was right."

"Stop this self-pity. You made a mistake. We all did."

"I can't believe he showed up at the funeral. What if Joy

starts having the dreams again?"

"Edward was right. We shouldn't rush her into something she's not ready for." He held Emily close. "You need to go back to therapy." She tried to pull away, but he continued holding her. "I'll go with you, but you're returning. First the loss of Bertha, then seeing George after all these years... Hell, we all need therapy."

* * *

"I thought I told you to stay in D.C with your parents." Joy couldn't sleep, so she called Sean.

"Who says I'm not in D.C.?"

"I saw you at the repast. You stuck out like a sore thumb, being one of the only young angry white guys there in a sea of black."

He chuckled. "Okay, you got me. But I did come back to D.C. I have unfinished business here. How did you know what I look like?"

The dark, edgy image of him she'd downloaded had her panties wet. Seeing him in real life... The image hadn't done him justice. She fanned herself. "It's called the Internet. I looked up every Sean who is a feature writer for the L. A. Times. It took all of ten seconds for a picture. And I must say, you are one incredibly handsome Angry White Man."

"And you are one incredibly sexy virgin."

Laughing, she said, "You are too much."

"I'm serious. Dark hair, pearly white teeth, doe-brown eyes, slender yet still curvy enough for a man to hold on to, and don't get me started on those full red lips of yours. Damn, woman. You know that sexy-ass teacher all the boys dream of losing their virginity to, that's you. You had me wanting to go back to school."

"Awww, that's the nicest thing anyone has ever said to me," she joked, then calmed. Sean had become her true friend in such a short time, and she truly appreciated him, loved him. She hugged her pillow close, wishing he were there to wrap her in his strong arms. "Thanks for coming. You were the only bright spot I've seen since Granny passed."

"It was a beautiful ceremony. You have an enormous family."

"It's the longevity." The older, stocky man who sat alone at a table in the church's basement came to mind. "I found out

Granny has a brother, but…"

"But what?"

"Have you ever been afraid to speak something because the spoken word gives whatever it is life? Even if in your heart, you may know whatever is true whether it's spoken aloud or not?"

His sigh filled the line. "I was afraid to say how my father felt about me for years, and now that I've finally accepted it, can speak about it, have moved on with my life, he's trying to change the script."

"If you don't mind my asking, how did he feel?"

"As long as I kept telling myself that my dad loved us, I was making excuses for his behavior. Once I admitted he didn't give a damn, the excuses stopped and I was able to move on with my life. I thought my mom had also, but hell. She's planning on remarrying that bastard."

Glad to have a break from her own issues, but saddened Sean was in pain, she asked, "Do you think people can change? Maybe your mom has fallen in love with the man your father is instead of holding onto the resentment for the man he was."

"The shit he did to us…" he trailed off. "If you only knew."

"You haven't moved on with your life."

"What?"

"You said you moved on with your life after you accepted your father didn't give a damn, but that's not true. If you had, you would have forgiven him by now. " The line went silent, but Joy knew he was still there.

"Maybe you're right. It's just hard to let go. When I see him all I see is the man who put us through so much pain and I'm… I'm afraid he'll hurt her again. Why would she trust him?"

"I don't know. I do know that you have a legitimate reason to be angry. Your anger may never run its course, but don't lie to yourself and say you've moved on." She chuckled nervously. "I think we both need therapy."

"Maybe you're right."

"Two times in one night. Here, here now. Let me try for three. Granny used to say that forgiveness isn't for the offender but the offended. You'll never be free from the pain until you truly forgive him." The doorbell rang. "Who could that be?"

"What?"

She rose from the bed and grabbed her robe. "Someone's at the door. Probably Mom here to apologize for acting crazy today. I swear to God I want to run away from home at times."

"Well, I don't want to keep you. Good night, Joy."

"Good night, Sean." She set her cell phone on the nightstand and rushed to answer the door. "Edward?"

He'd been walking toward his car and turned to her. "I'm sorry. I shouldn't have come so late."

"Oh no." She opened the door wider. "Come in. I can't sleep and could use the company." Once near her, he drew her into his arms and hugged her. This was what she needed, to be held, loved. "I miss her."

"I know, baby. I know." He kissed her forehead, then took her by the hand and led her fully into the house.

"I think I may stay with Jonathan until I figure out where I'm going to live."

"What?"

"Oh, you haven't heard." They lowered themselves onto the couch, and she snuggled close to him. "Granny gave the house to her assistant, which is fine with me, but I have to be out by the end of the school year. It's Granny's way of making me grow up. I'd stay with my parents until I find a place, but Mom has been tripping more than usual. Jonathan is my only sibling who has any sense."

"You should stay with me. I have extra rooms at my place."

"Oh no, I'd never impose on you like that. Plus, I'd hate to give you the wrong idea. We're friends."

"Exactly, friends." He took her by the hand. "And I'm worried about you. You need time to be alone without being alone. I understand that. I also think you have the wrong idea. Yes I'm attracted to you and would like more than friendship, but I'm not delusional or desperate. You've let me know your feelings, and I've let you know mine. I can live with friendship. And as your friend, I'm asking you to let me be a friend. If the shoe were on the other foot, wouldn't you open your home to me?"

"Yes," she admitted softly.

"You need a break from your family. Allow this friend to be a friend. No strings attached. That is except the string of friendship."

Now she felt like a real jerk—an arrogant one at that. "You're right. I'm sorry. But only a few weeks."

"However long or short you need." He scanned the room. "Do you have plans for your grandmother's things?"

"She left instructions for what she wanted to go where. Mostly everything stays. I get her novels and anything else I want from the house. I've been storing our family photos electronically for years." Reminded of the pictures they'd just taken the other day, she teared up. "I miss her."

* * *

Sherri couldn't believe Edward had moved that frigid, little cunt into their home. She'd driven to his place for a late-night snack—his dick—when she'd rounded the corner and seen him and what had to be his little virgin carrying suitcases into his home. She'd parked and watched them unload their cars. The twit had her dark hair in one of those awful pageboy haircuts that framed her lifeless face. *She looks like a child ghost*, Sherri quipped and drove away. If Edward thought she'd cut and dye her hair to look like that, he had another thing coming. She did not imitate little girls. All she knew was he'd better hurry up and impregnate the ghost so they could get back to their life—with their child. Sherri looked forward to raising a baby. Unlike Edward, she didn't care that the child wouldn't be of her blood. A baby was just what they needed to be a complete family.

Horny as hell and angry Edward wasn't available, she drove over to Tony's house. She needed to vent and fuck, and Tony was good for both. She stopped her Lexus in front of his two-story, Georgian Colonial styled home. The large white house with matching picket fence was a lot of room for one man. She wondered if he were as single as he'd claimed.

A light was on in what appeared to be the living area, so someone was probably awake. She turned off the ignition and grabbed her clutch purse. If a wife or girlfriend answered the door, she'd act like she had the wrong house.

Decision made, she exited the car. Delicate daisy-like flowers lined the cobblestone path to the front door. Everything about Tony's home was too beautiful, too pristine, too perfect to be real—just like Tony.

Her finger hovered over the doorbell. Maybe she should just walk away and find her pleasure elsewhere. This was her boss and she loved her job. Anxious laughter tickled her. One day on a legitimate nine-to-five had Sherri considering passing up good dick, or in Tony's case, exceptional tongue.

She turned and headed back down the cobblestone path. Men ready to go down on her were a dime a dozen, but the feeling of pride she'd felt while working was rare.

"Sherri?" she heard Tony say. "Is that you?"

She turned and smiled. "None other but. I'm sorry, I didn't realize the time." She motioned back to her car. "I was just leaving."

"What's wrong?" Dressed in shorts and a black T-shirt, but no socks or shoes, Tony approached her. He was quite a bit taller than Edward and had a cowboy swagger to his step that had her wanting to ride him all night long.

"It's nothing, really. I didn't mean to disturb you so late. I wasn't thinking." She backed away, but he continued to approach.

"You wouldn't be here so late if something weren't wrong." He gently took her by the arm and led her into the house. "Talk to me."

The exterior perfection of Tony's home had nothing on its interior perfection. His home could easily be featured in *House Beautiful*. "Are you bisexual?" she asked, but regretted it instantly. "I'm sorry. I don't know what's wrong with me today. I don't usually stereotype people like that and even if you were, who cares?"

He chuckled. "I'm not gay or even metro-sexual. This," he motioned around the palatial home, "is my sister's doing." He led her into the kitchen. "The house is on the historical home tour. She had the audacity to marry and move to Seattle but didn't want the house empty, so she asked me to live here. She has maid and lawn services maintain the place." He opened the refrigerator. "Water, beer, orange juice or Pepsi?"

She pulled one of the ladder-backed chairs from the table. "That explains a lot. Juice please." She'd wondered how a principal of an elementary school could afford to live in a multi-million dollar neighborhood.

He grabbed a small bottle of orange juice and handed it to her. "All I do is pay utilities. I couldn't pass up this deal. Do you want a glass?"

"No thanks. This is fine."

He took the seat diagonally across from her. "So what has

you out so late?"

"Why can't all men be like you?" She twisted the top off the orange juice.

"What, living in their sister's home rent-free?" He winked.

She laughed. Tony was caring, kind, sweet—too weak for her. She needed a real man, but Edward's little virgin would be perfect for Tony.

"Seriously, though, what happened?"

"I went to my boyfriend's house and..." Real tears fell from her eyes. She'd given Edward ten years of her life, and he wanted to toss her aside because she couldn't give him a child. "He wants children I can't give him. He won't even consider adoption. I know that's why he's with this other woman." She placed her hand on her chest. "I know it."

He reached across the table and thumbed the tears from her cheek. "I'm sorry. You don't deserve to be treated like this. No one does." He pushed away from the table and knelt before her. "You're not happy. What are you going to do to change your situation?"

"I don't know. I honestly don't know." And she didn't. After the baby was born, the twit would want to be a part of the child's life, but Sherri wasn't having it. Given time, she was sure she could convince Edward to sue for full custody. With his money and connections, he'd win, but how long would it take?

"What do you want out of life, Sherri? Don't you want to be loved and respected?"

"Of course." She knew Edward loved and respected her, but she couldn't give him what he needed, a child of his own blood. Unlike Tony, Edward was a real man who wouldn't allow anything or anyone to keep him from what he wanted. "He loves me. It's just he wants a baby so badly."

He looked as if he wanted to say more, but backed away to his seat. "Why are you here?" he asked softly.

"I don't know. I was so hurt. I don't know. I shouldn't have come. I was trying to leave when you saw me. I'm sorry." She pushed away from the table. "I should leave."

He took her by the hand and pulled her close. "Don't leave."

She gazed up into his warm brown eyes and was lost in desire. He lowered his lips to hers, and she opened freely for him. This was what her wounded ego needed, to be loved tenderly, sweetly—the opposite of Edward.

He lifted and carried her into the bedroom just off the kitchen. Once he set her down, she began to unbutton her blouse, but he stopped her.

"Allow me." He unbuttoned her blouse and tossed it to the side. Large, his hands were large, yet gentle. She didn't usually like the gentle touch, but tonight it was perfect, he was perfect. He undressed her and laid her in the bed, then undressed himself and lay halfway on top of her with his heavy cock rested on her thigh.

The soft glow of the moonlight illuminated the room enough for her to see every ripple of his abdomen. She ran her hand over his well-defined chest. "You've taken very good care of yourself."

"I was thinking the same thing about you."

He caressed and kissed every inch of her body. When she'd beg him to enter her, he would say, "Not yet," and continue on his mission of exquisite torture. Orgasms overtook her twice—without penetration or him using his expert tongue skills on her clit! Just when she knew she could take it no longer, he flipped her onto her stomach and entered her from behind. He thrust into her with such force the neighbors would think Georgia was experiencing an earthquake.

The feel of his hard cock reaching into her depths and tapping her G-spot and his balls slapping her ass, the grip of his strong hands on her waist holding her steady, the guttural groans and smell of sex that filled the room shot an orgasm through her the likes she'd never experienced before.

"Oh God!" She clung to the comforter and tears fell from her eyes. This wasn't possible. How could anything feel so good?

Chapter Thirteen

Six weeks later...

Joy waited in the executive chair of Jonathan's office and looked out over Atlanta's afternoon traffic. Jonathan had always been her favorite sibling. Unlike her other siblings, Jonathan had disappointed their mother with one of his life choices. When Joy was a teen, he'd been an alcoholic and lost his wife, children and job because of it. After the divorce, he'd moved in with Bertha until he could get himself together. Jonathan had a few relapses those first few years, but hadn't had an alcoholic beverage since Joy was seventeen, and now he owned one of the top investment firms in the southeast region of the country.

Thoughts of Bertha brought tears to her eyes. There was something special about "granny time." Whenever family members hit a rough patch in their lives, Bertha had a way of smoothing that patch enough for them to make it over.

"Hey, little bit." Jonathan entered his office and dropped a file on his desk. "Get out of my chair."

"I was here first." She ran her hands over her cheeks.

He pulled her out of the chair and took his seat. "So what do I owe the pleasure of this visit?"

She moved a stack of papers to the side and planted her butt on his desk. "Money, I need the hundred grand Granny gave me."

"What the hell do you need that kind of money for? And get your ass off my desk. I have chairs. Use one of them."

When she moved to California she'd miss irritating Jonathan. "I'm homeless and would like to purchase a place of my own." She rolled a chair around from the conference table to his desk.

"A hundred grand sounds like a lot to you, but it's not much at all. Investing in a house is good, but you're not buying a million dollar home."

"You got that right."

"You have excellent credit. Twenty percent down on a modest home will keep your payment well within your budget."

She couldn't tell him the amount of her trust fund and didn't want him to know her plan to move away. She'd need extra cash until she could find a new job and thought saying she wanted to buy a house was the easiest way to get at her cash. "I have lots of somethings to fall back on. Make that someones: Mom, Daddy, Heather, Helen, that jerk of a brother Marshall and of course you. I want a low monthly payment."

"A low monthly payment is good thinking, but I can't allow you to spend your entire inheritance."

"You've been investing fifty percent of my check. I can afford to take out a hundred grand." Thanks to Jonathan, she had a very nice portfolio. She paid all the bills at Bertha's, but the house had been paid for, so she'd been able to invest nicely over the years.

"What part of you are not using your inheritance don't you understand. Find a few places you like, and after I look at them for you I'll put the money down myself."

"I don't want you paying for *my* house. I'm grown and have my own money." She could kick herself for allowing him to invest the inheritance for her. He'd caught her when she wasn't thinking clear. Now she'd have to go through hell to get her own money.

Brow raised, he asked, "Are you done pounding your chest? I don't like you staying with Edward, but I don't want you spending the little you have." He picked up his phone and punched a few buttons. "Lori, isn't your brother a realtor?" he asked his office assistant. "Good. Little bit is ready to get her own place. Clear my schedule for tomorrow. We're going house hunting." After a few seconds, he hunched his shoulders. "I don't know. Little bit, house or condo and how many rooms?"

"Don't bother, just give me my money."

"Three bedrooms and two baths minimum," he said into the receiver. "Condo or house doesn't matter. Just ensure it's low maintenance and has twenty-four/seven security."

"That's not what I said."

"Thanks." He hung up. "It's all arranged."

"Jonathan, listen to me. I truly appreciate your volunteering to swing the down payment for me. I truly appreciate your wanting to ensure I don't get ripped off and that I find a proper home. You take excellent care of me, and that's one of the reasons I love you so much."

"I love you, too, little bit."

"But I want—no need—to do this on my own."

He stared at her a long while. "You sure about this?"

"Yes."

"Fine, but not until you tell me what you need the money for."

How the hell does he do that? For as long as she could remember, he had been able to tell when she was planning to do something she shouldn't. "I'm up to buying a house or condo. I don't know which one. I'm leaning toward condo because I hate yard work. I don't know. I may need to rent somewhere a few months first and only have a few thousand in my savings account."

"Tell me what you're up to and don't make me repeat myself."

"Why are you my favorite sibling again?"

He chuckled. "Because I'm always on your side. Maybe not in a way you want, but I'm always here for you."

"You swear not to tell anyone?"

"Only if I see fit. Do you want the money or not?"

She reached into her back jeans pocket and pulled out the acceptance letter for the writing summer retreat she planned to attend. "You know how much I want to write." He was her only sibling who acknowledged her love of writing as more than a hobby and encouraged her to follow her dreams.

"And?"

She handed over the letter. As he read, a smile lit up his face. He hopped up from the chair and pulled her into his arms. "Congratulations, little bit." He swung her around. "I'm so proud of you." He set her down. "I wish Granny were here for this."

"I showed her the letter a few days before she passed." She took the letter from him. "I'd planned on taking her to Los Angeles with me for the summer, but now... Well, I think I'll stay in Los Angeles after the retreat is over. I need a change of scenery."

"Good for you."

"Good for me? You mean you aren't going to try to talk me out of moving across the country?"

"Nope." He returned to his executive chair. "You'll only be a flight away. I'm still not giving you a hundred grand. What do you need the money for?"

"Somewhere to live and to support myself until I can find a job."

He picked up his phone and hit a few buttons. "Lori, little bit is moving to Los Angeles for a few weeks, maybe longer. It's a secret, so if anyone asks, you don't know anything." He reached his hand out to Joy. "Hand me the letter." She handed over the letter, and he proceeded to tell Lori to find a nice apartment near the location of the retreat and charge it to his personal account.

He hung up. "It's done. When do you want to leave?"

She couldn't think of the words to express herself, so she remained silent.

"Earth to little bit. When will you be ready to leave? I don't want you staying with that pervert a minute longer. We can get your things tonight and move you to my place until your flight."

"You are unbelievable, but I'm not fighting it."

"What?"

"You are just as controlling as everyone else in my life."

"You're the baby of the family. Hell, I have children older than you."

"Whatever, and Edward isn't a pervert."

"The hell he isn't. I still can't believe Mom set you two up. What was she thinking?"

"That I need a fourth father." She flashed a quick smile. "After I finish the retreat, I'll tell Mom where I am, but this is an intense program. I can't have her breaking my concentration. I've finished three manuscripts and want at least one of them ready to submit to agents before summer's end."

"Fully understandable."

"My ticket is for day after tomorrow. The retreat starts next week."

"Give your ticket information to Lori on your way out. I might need to change your flight."

"You are entirely too controlling. There is nothing wrong with my flight."

"I'm going with you to make sure you get settled in and we can look at a few condos. Give Lori your ticket information on your way out. Good-bye, little bit. I'll be by to get you tonight after work."

"Unbelievable." On her way out, she left her flight information with Lori. If she didn't do things Jonathan's way, she knew he wouldn't help her make the great escape from her mother and sisters.

* * *

Bare feet drawn into the cushy armchair and curled beneath her body, Joy tried to relax. The armchair was the only piece of furniture she'd taken from Bertha's house. She'd sit in it whenever she needed to feel closer to her grandmother.

When she'd first agreed to the temporary stay with Edward, she'd been apprehensive, but agreed. Bertha used to say, "Always follow your first mind," and this was a case where she wished she had followed. Edward lived up to Emily's expectations and tried to "guide" Joy into doing his will. His "guiding" equaled manipulative control as opposed to her mother's blatant control. In the end she wanted neither, but felt the manipulative control was worse. She could hardly wait to move to Los Angeles and be free of all of the control freaks.

"If your coursework doesn't start until next week, why are you moving out now?" Edward asked in an accusatory tone Joy didn't appreciate one bit. If he didn't change his tone of voice soon, the conversation would be over. "And I'm still not happy about your springing this retreat on me without any notice."

"First off, I told you I'd only be staying a few weeks, so how am I springing anything on you? Secondly, if I want to visit my brother, then I'll visit my brother. Thirdly, why do you care where I go?"

"Are you serious? Why do I care?" He neared. The hardwood floor sounded as if it would crack beneath his heavy steps. "Don't you know how much I love you? Ever since Bertha died, you've become distant. Now you want to run off across the country. I'm worried about you." He placed his hand on his heart. "This isn't about what I want. You're running from your family, but you need them more now than ever."

"I said I'm going to visit my brother, you should be happy." Since her granny died? He'd only known her a few days before her granny died so who was he to judge how she was before as opposed to after. She was onto his game. Many times in the past six weeks he'd used her "family" as an excuse for her to follow his will. He was worse than her students who thought they were getting away with something.

The doorbell rang. "That must be Jonathan." She slipped her feet into her sandals.

"Jonathan? That explains everything." He held his hand up to her. "Stay seated. I'll get it." Edward let Jonathan into the house. The two exchanged pleasantries that didn't sound pleasant to Joy.

"You have everything ready?" Jonathan asked Joy.

"Everything except the chair." She tapped the old armchair. "Can you have someone pick it up for me?"

"Sure. I'll have it shipped to you."

"That won't be necessary," Edward said. "It's in my possession. I can go ahead and have it shipped. But since you'll only be gone for this retreat, you might want to just leave it here for your return. I'll even move it to your room."

"Her room? You seem to be confused. Joy doesn't live here. She was a guest and is moving on. Thank you for the offer to ship her chair, but I'll take care of it."

"What the hell is wrong with you?" Edward stepped up to Jonathan. "She's your sister, not your lover."

"Yes, my sister who I'm protecting from your ass."

"Hold up, both of you." Joy wedged herself between the two. Jonathan had taken a disliking to Edward before he'd even met the man. "You're both acting insane. Let's just go, Jonathan."

"Stay away from her." Jonathan grabbed the two largest suitcases and headed for the door. "Little bit, let's go."

Joy wrapped her arms around Edward. "I'm sorry. You know how protective my family can be. You've been a true friend and I appreciate it."

"I said let's go," Jonathan barked from the doorway.

"Stop being a prick and take my bags out."

He stalked out.

"I don't know why he's acting like such a jerk. I truly appreciate you giving me a break from the crazies." She put Edward in the category of controlling crazy, but kept that tidbit of information to herself. "Thank you for all you've done. I'll call you from California." She tried to back out of Edward's embrace, but he held on.

"You don't have to leave with him if you don't want to."

"I haven't seen much of Jonathan or my dad lately. I want to spend time with them before the retreat."

"You know I'm here for you, right?"

"Of course."

Jonathan entered the house and grabbed two more of her bags. "Let's go!"

"I guess it's time for me to go." She kissed Edward on the cheek. "Thanks again, for everything." She picked up her last bag and carried it out to Jonathan's Escalade. "There is no excuse for you being so disrespectful." She tossed the bag into the backseat. "Like it or not, Edward is my friend. What in the hell is wrong with you?"

"There's something about him I don't like. I can't pinpoint what it is."

"Oh give me a break. You didn't like him on general principle. Don't get me wrong. Because Mom made the introductions, I was anti-Edward at first, too. But I wasn't being fair. It's not his fault Mom drives me crazy."

He smacked the steering wheel. "Shit, you're right."

She stared at her brother. "I'm right?"

"Yes, little bit, you're right." He opened his door. "I'll go apologize."

"Well look who wants to play adult. Good for you. While you're in there, grab my computer. I left it in the guest room." She pulled out her phone to call Sean.

* * *

"Son of a bitch!"

Edward watched Joy and Jonathan through the window. Why the hell did Joy's favorite sibling, the only one she listened to, have to be the one who hated him. He snatched the curtain closed and stomped about the living room.

The man's dislike of him didn't make sense to Edward, and poor Joy was stuck in the middle. The way she'd stood up to Jonathan impressed Edward and showed him she was falling in love with him. She'd be his if not for Jonathan's interference.

The doorbell rang. He calmed himself so Joy wouldn't see him out of sorts, then opened the door, but it wasn't Joy.

"Little bit forgot her computer, and…" Jonathan ran his fingers over his salt-and- pepper hair. "I'm sorry about earlier. I was out of line." He stepped fully into the house and closed the door.

"Since day one you've had it out for me. What the hell have I ever done to you? I love Joy. I'd never hurt her."

"It's not you. Hell, my family is full of a bunch of controlling asses. She doesn't need another in her life. I've been taking my frustration out on you. I'm truly sorry, but this is for the best. Granny was right. We're smothering Joy."

"What?"

"Before Granny left for Los Angeles, she made me promise to protect Joy from the family, including myself. I have nothing against you. I'm sure you're a fine man, but you're just as controlling as the rest of us. That's why Mom picked you, but I'm not having it."

"What are you saying?"

"Joy isn't coming back to Atlanta to live if I have anything to say about it, and I do. I'm sorry. I know you have feelings for her. You may even be in love with her, but you aren't what's best for her."

"And who the hell are you to decide who is best for Joy."

"I'm the brother who helped Granny raise her. In my heart she's my child, not my sister. Where's the guest room? She forgot her computer."

Edward couldn't believe this was happening. Jonathan was literally taking Joy from him. He retrieved her computer and returned to Jonathan. "Don't do this. She needs her family. She needs me."

"No, she doesn't. We're crippling her. I'm sorry, but I have to put Joy first." He held his hands out for the laptop.

"You're making a mistake." Edward handed over the computer.

Chapter Fourteen

Sherri didn't know which to kill, the morning sunlight for blazing through the hotel window or her cell phone for ringing at this God awful hour. She glanced at the clock—10:32. Okay, so it wasn't a God awful hour, but it sure felt like one. She grabbed the phone without checking the caller ID. "Hello."

"Where the hell are you?"

"Edward? Wha… what's wrong?"

"I'm at your fucking condo and you're not here. That's the fucking problem. Where are you?"

"Wait a second. I'm putting you on speaker." Edward started cussing about something, but she was too tired to care. She'd spent all night talking to Tony about her life since C'Money's death. She was ready to make a change and appreciated having someone behind her to support that change. Real support. She pressed the speaker button and set the phone on the nightstand. Tony was nowhere in sight, so she guessed he'd gone to find something to eat.

"Edward." She clapped her hands to get his attention.

"… the son of a bitch. And your ass…"

"Edward! Stop, take a breath, and tell me what's wrong."

"Who the fuck do you think you're speaking to?"

In no mood for Edward's shit, she pinched the bridge of her nose and blew out a long breath. "I'm sorry. What did you need?"

"Where are you?"

"In New York, why? Is Joy giving you trouble?" She covered her mouth with her hands. She'd just revealed she knew who he was seeing.

"No. She's headed out of town for a few weeks, so I thought I'd give you some time."

Grateful he didn't catch her slip, nervous laughter bubbled up in her. Six weeks away from Edward had been a crash course twelve-step program. After she admitted her life had become unmanageable, she took inventory of where her life was and the life she dreamed for herself and wasn't happy with what she saw. *No more.* It was time for her to take steps down the path of life she wanted to travel.

"What's so funny?" he snapped.

"Me. You were right." She hugged a pillow close and spoke toward the phone. "I love you, but I'm not what you want. And to be honest, I don't blame you. I chose to be a whore. Your personal whore." More nervous laughter escaped her. "No wonder you don't respect me. I wasn't even respecting myself. I was lying to myself."

"What are you saying?"

"I'm saying I'm not a whore anymore. I want to be someone I can be proud of. I love you and am sorry I let you down, let us both down." Tears filled her eyes. This was hard. Edward had saved her life and been her lover for ten years. She cared for him deeply, loved him, but now realized she wasn't in love with him. Six weeks of sobriety had been enough time to cleanse her system and step out of denial. She'd never be more than a whore to him or with him.

The line went silent.

Tony entered the suite. She placed a finger to her lips and pointed to the phone. She'd told him everything about Edward and her relationship except that Edward's new squeeze was one of his teachers and she'd taken the job to spy on her. Turned out she liked Joy. The girl had spunk. She also knew about the writer's retreat and that there was no way Edward could have known about it or he would have tried to stop her. The woman was smart. She'd probably figured out Edward's game a long time ago. Sherri only wished she'd been half as smart.

"Look, I'm sorry I haven't called," Edward finally said, "but I've been busy. How much do you want me to put into your account?"

"I'm serious. I'm not a whore anymore. I wish you the best in life." She watched Tony undress. He'd become more handsome with each passing day. At first she'd thought him weak, but now realized Edward was the true weakling.

"I'm not taking your ass back, fucking whore!"

"Good-bye Edward. I love you and wish you the best in life." She picked up the phone, disconnected, then blocked Edward's number.

Tony slid under the covers with her. "Come here." He cupped her into his body. "You're not a whore."

"I honestly thought I'd had it all. I was such an idiot." The feel of his warm body against her back and his arm wrapped around her comforted her. "Thank you," she whispered.

"For what?"

"For seeing me for who I am, even when I didn't see myself." She rested her hand on top of his. "This reminds me of when you first started picking me up. At first I thought you were some psycho. Who hires a whore then just holds her all night? Then I looked forward to the days you'd come. What was all of that about?"

"I was married. It was my way of staying faithful. Stupid. I know. The marriage didn't last. We were having issues before I found you and shouldn't have married. Then after the divorce I was free to make love with you."

"I remember our first time. It was the first time I felt wanted. I felt loved, but couldn't admit it. It didn't make sense. You knew nothing about me except that I was a whore. It didn't compute. In all honesty, it still doesn't. Why Tony?"

"I've known you since we were in second grade."

"Wha...?"

"You knew me as little Anthony."

Completely surprised, she flipped over and faced him. "No way!" Little Anthony was the class runt and her next-door neighbor. They'd always gotten along and were best of friends, but she never told him of her home life of abuse.

"Yes way," he teased and stroked her hair behind her ear. "I knew what your father was doing to you. I even called the police, but because I was a child, they completely blew me off. Thinking back, I should have told the teachers, but I didn't know. And my parents wouldn't have wanted to be involved. I'm sorry." He pressed his lips against her forehead.

Tears fell from her eyes. Little Anthony had always been protective of her. They'd protected each other. She should have known he knew her life was a nightmare.

"Since the day of the interview, I'd wondered how you knew my real name. For a few moments, I thought you were some sort of stalker, but there was something about you." She wiped the moisture from her face. "I should have known." She gazed deeply into his eyes to find her old friend. Little Anthony looked back at her, but the rest of his body was completely different.

"You've grown."

"You can say that, Charlene Duerr."

"Oh how I hated my name. I think I'll go back to being

called Charlene." She reached forward and stroked his chest. "I can't believe you're Anthony." She shook her head. "Besides your eyes and your kind heart, I wouldn't know you."

"When you left I wasn't even five feet tall. My junior year I began to shoot up. By the time I graduated, I was over six feet, my hair had darkened, I switched from glasses to contacts and my voice had lowered. I went from looking like my mom to looking like my dad."

"Oh my God, you do!" She pointed at him. "You look like Mr. Shapiro. It's all coming back to me. I didn't even think of your dad as handsome, but damn. You have one handsome father."

His cheeks reddened. "Why thank you."

"Little Anthony Shapiro." She inched closer. "I can't believe it's you." Even as children, Tony had been there for her. All this time she'd had what she never believed she deserved, someone who loved her. She brushed her lips over his, kissed.

She rolled onto her back and gazed up into his eyes. *I love you, Anthony Shapiro.* Truly in love for the first time in her life, she was scared. Not of Tony, but of her past ruining his career if others found out about their affair.

"Is something wrong?" he whispered.

"Besides your not being in me, no."

He nudged her legs apart with his knee and settled between her legs. "I aim to please."

Pleasure-filled bursts shot through her as he rubbed the head of his penis on her clit. The heat, pressure and the pre-cum combined with her love for him made her climax.

"That's it, Charlene." He eased into her. "You were made for me."

Still on a climactic high, she wrapped her legs around his thighs and reached for the heavens. Tony made love with his entire body to her entire body. With Tony she gave and received more than body. With Tony it was mind, body and soul. Her body tightened around him. She grasped onto his buttocks, then forced her hands to the bed to keep from ripping off his skin.

His eyes rolled back and he drew in a sharp intake of air.

"That's it, Tony." She contracted her vaginal walls to increase his pleasure, but ended up increasing her own.

This orgasm was too powerful. It was going to give her a heart attack, but she didn't care. Her legs unwound from Tony's thighs, and her hips arched up from the bed. The orgasm possessed her entire being.

* * *

The soft rumble of Tony's snore comforted Charlene in ways she'd never imagined—at least never imagined for herself.

I'm in love.

Charlene had never been so scared in her life. How had this happened to her? How had she gone from Sherri to Charlene? And what was she going to do about it. This wasn't about being saved. Over the weeks, he'd pointed out that only she could save herself, and she agreed. This wasn't about the sex, which she found to be unbelievable with Tony. This wasn't about needing a provider. Thanks to Edward's generosity over the years, she owned her car, condo and had nearly two hundred grand in the bank. She'd done ten years with Edward, that last check of a hundred grand made for one hell of a severance check.

The morning slipped into afternoon, but she didn't want to move from within Tony's arms. Reality would eventually set in, and he'd realize they couldn't be a couple. She loved him too much to jeopardize his career if people found out about her past. With as vindictive as Edward could be, if he woke up on the wrong side of the bed, he'd make sure to ruin her and Tony's lives.

* * *

"So do you plan to run away from me again?" Joy adjusted her earpiece.

"I wasn't running. I was protecting your virtue," Sean said. "This should be interesting with you in the same city."

"Very."

"How is family day coming along?"

"We're in Best Buy. Daddy and Jonathan were debating which oversized television is the best. Truly exciting, but I'm in the computer section. My laptop has been acting odd lately. I think it's time for a new one."

"Were you able to download the goodies I sent for your flight?"

The last batch of goodies almost had her call out on the plane, so she didn't want to wait to see what he had in store for her this time, but she would. "Jonathan will be on the flight with me, so no goodies on the plane. I can't believe he's escorting me across the country like an unaccompanied minor. I love my family, but they are smothering me." Edward was a nice person but as controlling as her family. Sean was the only person in her life who didn't try to control her, and she loved it in him.

She read through the system features of one of the laptops and only understood the screen size. "I need a *Consumer Reports* magazine on laptops. What kind of computer do you have?"

"I have a Mac."

"Oh, you're one of *those* people." A few of her co-workers owned Macs and looked down on any other computer.

"Yes, I'm one of *those* people. When you get here, I'll let you see mine."

"A little game of show me yours and I'll show you mine? Sounds like fun." She moved over to the Mac section.

"I love the way you think. Are you sure you're a virgin?"

"Last time I checked."

"Well my sexy, little virgin, be sure to purchase a laptop with a good webcam."

"What on earth would I do with a webcam?" She ran her fingers over a thin Mac. The concept was interesting, but its slight size worried her.

"You really are a virgin," he joked. "I want to see you come."

This conversation was making her panties wet. "And end up on YouTube. No thanks. Before I forget, thanks for sending me the list of condo complexes."

"Don't think I didn't notice the subject change. It's okay, my sweet thang."

She'd love nothing more than to be his sweet thang. When they first started talking, she'd been horny as hell and he was a way to help alleviate some of the frustration, but their relationship had grown to much more.

They continued their conversation, which led to a debate over renewable energy. Instead of telling Sean of her temporary move to Edward's home, she'd allowed him to assume she'd remained at Bertha's house. While she stayed with Edward, she hadn't experimented sexually with him—not that he hadn't wanted to try. She hadn't wanted to give him the wrong idea and she wanted to save herself for Sean. But was she giving herself the wrong idea with Sean? Was she holding out for love he'd never give?

"You ready to go, little bit?"

She looked over her shoulder and saw her brother and father. "I've been summoned. I'll call you tonight."

"Tonight it is. If you act right, I'll tell you a bedtime story."

"I promise to behave." She disconnected and followed her brother and father out of the store.

"Who was that?" Jonathan asked.

"Sean," she said without thinking. "He's one of those Mac people." She looped her arm around her father's arm. "I'm hungry."

"He?" Jonathan and her father said in unison.

"Yes he."

Her father and brother snuck a glance toward each other that she caught. If she could snatch Sean's name back into her mouth she would, but it was too late now.

The ride to *Pappadeaux Seafood Kitchen* had been quiet, too quiet. She'd rather have their silence than their grilling, so she was grateful. The oyster trio and fried alligator appetizers had been delicious, and her brother and father had remained quiet for the most part, so all was grand in the world of Joy.

Just as she was about to fork a bit of almond-crusted trout, her all-time favorite food, into her mouth, Jonathon ruined the moment with, "So who the hell is Sean?"

"Watch your mouth," Benjamin warned. "Who is Sean?"

"Why are you my favorite brother again?" She tasted the trout, which was cooked to perfection. "Oh this is delicious. They'd better have *Pappadeaux* in Los Angeles or I'm moving." She ate some of the spaghetti squash. "Simply delicious. Can I have yours, Daddy?"

Benjamin spooned his squash onto his baby girl's plate. "I take it this means you aren't telling us who Sean is?"

"Thank you, and I haven't decided yet." She ate another bit of melt-in-your-mouth trout. "We're only friends, but someday I'd like for it to be more, and you all would scare him off."

"Maybe he needs to be scared off." Jonathan cracked open a lobster claw and fished out the meat.

Joy loved lobster, but hated all the work you had to go through to get to the good part. She flashed the most angelic smile she could conjure in her brother's direction. He set the sweet meat of the lobster claw on her plate. "Now I remember why you're my favorite."

"So, little bit, what does this Sean do to support himself?"

She proceeded to tell them everything about Sean except how they met, where he lived and the sexually charged portions of their conversations. Maybe she'd tell him the bedtime story tonight. "He's the greatest. He even came to Granny's funeral."

"Oh really," her father said. "Why didn't you introduce us?"

"By the time I saw him, your son was carrying me off like he was some sort of psycho caveman. Did you know he bought me a new car? I had to speak to him long enough to thank him for it."

Jonathan cracked the other lobster claw. "You're spoiled." He dipped the meat into the melted butter.

"Extravagant apologies is one of the few benefits of being the baby of the family. Don't hate."

"So this Sean fella. How long have you known him?" her father asked.

"A few months, and I don't want to talk about him anymore."

"Fine, have it your way. Jonathan, I'll be traveling to Los Angeles with you two. Can you book my flight?"

"Daddy, no."

"Jonathan."

"I'm on it." He broke out his cell phone. "I'll have it booked in a few minutes." He chuckled. "I can't believe you thought you could mention a man's name without Dad meeting him. You do know the family you come from, right?"

"I didn't even say where he lives."

"Which means he's in Los Angeles. You might as well call him and set up a meeting. You're lucky it's Dad instead of Mom."

Jonathan had a point, but she still wasn't happy.

Chapter Fifteen

"You owe me for this."

Sean's low, sexy voice caressed Joy's body. "How ever will I repay you?" she purred with thoughts of ways she'd like to repay him.

"The webcam is a good start. Damn you're hot. Slide your hand between your breasts to your pussy."

Lying naked in the bed with her new computer with webcam, she moved her hand between her breasts.

"Slow down. I want to savor every millimeter your hand travels. I want to feel you. Close your eyes and listen to my voice. Feel my hands on your body. "

Eyes closed, she followed his soft-spoken instructions. Sean was with her. With just enough pressure his hands were touching her body in all the right places. His fingers, not hers, slipped into her heat, fondled her clit and brought her to completion.

"That's it, baby," he said. "That's it. God how I love to hear you come."

She opened her eyes in just enough time to see cum shoot onto his chest. Oh how she longed to be there to hold him in her hand, take him into her mouth, taste him. She could hardly wait to arrive in Los Angeles and... And what? Fear of what was to come drenched her. She was in love with him and wanted his love in return, but knew he wasn't ready for a relationship and may never be ready. Just as she hadn't wanted to lead Edward on, maybe she was leading herself on with Sean. Maybe it was time to back away from sharing such intimacy.

She rolled away from the webcam, away from her feelings. "I'm all sticky. I'll be right back."

"I need to clean myself also. I'll call you in a few."

Fifteen minutes later, she nudged the curtain to the side and looked out the window of her brother's guest bedroom. She wanted to run away from everything, including how she felt about Sean. "Thanks again for agreeing to pick us up from the airport." That he'd volunteered to pick them up at the airport had put silly notions in her head. Silly notions she wouldn't allow to convince her he wanted anything more than their erotic games and someone to debate.

"You sound like you're a million miles away. I can barely hear you."

"Sorry, my earpiece is stuck on stupid, so I have you on speaker." She switched from speaker and held the cell phone to her ear. "Can you hear me now?" she joked.

"Wow, I didn't see that one coming. You should take your show on the road."

"Very funny." She sank onto the bed and hugged a pillow close. "I was thanking you for picking us up tomorrow."

"It's nothing."

"But it is. You know full well my father and brother think we're an item. I know what I want out of our relationship, but what do you want? What's going to happen when I move there?"

"Nothing has to change when you move here."

A tiny part of her wanted him to say, "I want happily ever after with you. Why else would I want to meet your father and brother?" She forced herself out of denial—a large part of her wanted him to want happily ever after with her. That same part could easily slip back into denial if they continued sharing such intimate moments.

"You've gotten quiet on me," he said.

"I've always been honest with myself."

"That's a good way to be. I try, but miss the mark from time to time."

"I can't believe I'm about to say this, but I'm falling for you." Falling her foot. She was in love and knew it. Honesty with herself was so much easier than being honest with him about her true feelings. "This." She motioned around the bed as if he could see her. "We have to stop. I don't want sex, I want to make love, and what we're doing will lead to sex."

Awkward silence filled the line.

"Just my luck. My virgin slut turns back into a nun on the eve of her moving to my city."

They both burst into laughter. "You are so wrong for that."

Once they calmed, he said, "So we're friends."

"Yes, friends without benefits." That he so easily accepted the end of their intimacy told her she'd made a painful, yet correct, decision.

* * *

"What the hell just happened?" Sean dropped his cell

phone on the cushion and leaned back on the couch. One second Joy had been her usual sexy, fun-loving self, the next she'd become a construction worker who was an expert at building blockades.

Who was he kidding? Not himself, for sure. He knew exactly what had happened. Joy was protecting her heart from him, and he couldn't blame her. How many times had he said he didn't want a relationship while everything about Joy screamed, "Relationship material!"

It wasn't that he didn't want a relationship. He wanted nothing more than to have a committed, respectful, monogamous relationship with Joy, but he'd been shown time and time again that the type of relationship he wanted was a myth.

"Nothing has to change? What the hell? Nothing has to change! Stupid, stupid, stupid." Of course things would change. They couldn't help but change with her being in the same city. Fear of a failed relationship with Joy had cornered him. He'd pushed her away emotionally to protect himself.

"What am I doing?" he mumbled. "What do I want?" He knew what he wanted—Joy. *A freaking virgin has more courage than I do.*

The cell phone rang and broke him out of his musings. "Hello," he answered without checking the caller ID.

"Hello, darling. It's not too late, is it?" his mother asked.

He glanced at his watch. It was after midnight on the East Coast. Apprehension in his mother's voice coupled with the late hour worried him. "I should be asking you that. Are you okay?"

"I'm fine. Maybe not fine, but I'll do."

Grateful for the reprieve from his non-relationship with Joy, he asked, "What's going on?"

The line remained silent.

"Mom?"

"I..." She inhaled deeply. "I want you to give me away at my wedding."

"Hell no!" *Shit.* Two times in one night he'd spoken without thinking and regretted it instantly. "I'm sorry. I shouldn't have spoken so harshly." *First Joy, now this.* "It's just you know how I feel. This is a mistake. How can you ask me to do this?"

"Because you're the most important man in my life, and I

want your blessing."

"I can't—"

"Please hear me out," she interrupted.

The pain in his mother's voice silenced him.

"I've changed," she said softly. "All those years ago I literally thought I'd die without Darren and accepted his behavior, but no more. I'm sorry I didn't grow into the woman I am while you were young. The first time he cheated on me, I should have been strong, should have cared about myself more than I feared losing him. I should have put you before my fears of being without your father. I can't go back, baby. I'm ashamed of who I was. How my inaction hurt you. I was just as emotionally abusive to you as your father."

"No, Mom—"

"I'm not done. I'm your mother. I should have protected you. Please forgive me."

Overwhelmed with emotion, he found himself on the verge of tearing up. The anger and disappointment he'd felt toward his mother had always laid right beneath the surface and would pop up from time to time, but her admission had uncovered it fully. "I needed you."

"I know, darling. I failed you. Your father and I both failed you, but no more. If you don't bless this marriage, then it won't happen. I'll never put anyone before you again."

"No! Don't put this on me. If you want to marry, then marry."

"Darren and I have already discussed this. We've caused you more than enough pain. It's time we put you first."

Enraged, he pushed up from the couch. "This is some bull. You're manipulating me. You're no better than any other woman. Hell, you are every woman." Joy came to his mind. Her timely switch from virgin slut to a prudish nun was her way of manipulating him into giving into a relationship with her. A relationship where she'd take his heart and tear it to pieces some day.

"No, darling, I'm not. Maybe I came about this wrong."

"You're damn skippy you did."

"I'm not trying to manipulate you."

"Oh really? You know full well I'm against this fucking marriage. If you wanted to put me first, if you weren't trying to manipulate me, you two would have just broken off the engagement and told me you had changed your minds. Instead, you hand me this crock of bull."

"Darling, please."

"Don't 'darling please' me. Look, you want my blessing? I give it. Get married. I don't give a damn." He disconnected.

* * *

"What do you mean you're going to California for a few days?" Emily asked Benjamin. "Is this about Joy?" Earlier, Benjamin had called and left a message that he'd be flying to California with Jonathan in the morning to escort her to some writer's camp, and she might stay on the West Coast.

He grabbed a few T-shirts and boxers out of the dresser and put them in a carryon bag. "I explained everything."

"I'm coming."

He lifted his gaze from the suitcase to her. "No you're not. You're one of the main reasons my baby is moving across the country."

The anger in his voice couldn't be mistaken. She hadn't heard this kind of rage from him since they discovered Joy had been molested. She turned from his cold gaze. Many years ago he'd shut her out. Unlike this time, he hadn't said he blamed her, but she knew he had. How couldn't he? She blamed herself.

"Be reasonable. She can't stay in California alone." She wiped tears from her eyes. "Who'll watch over her?"

"She's thirty-three, not three. I think she'll manage."

"Please don't take her from me." She faced her husband. "Please, she listens to you. Tell her how sorry I am. I just lost my mother. I need Joy home."

Hard, angry lines on Benjamin's face softened. He reached out for her and drew her into his arms. "Joy's growing up. We have to give her the freedom to be."

"You sound like Mother." She soaked in the love of her husband. "I miss her so much. Joy is so like her."

"And so like you, just less controlling." He chuckled. "I don't want to, but we have to let her go."

Chapter Sixteen

"Stop dragging your tail, little bit."

"I'm coming." Joy increased her pace. "I'm coming." One of Jonathan's long strides equaled two of Joy's strides, but that wasn't the reason she lagged behind her brother and father. In a few too-short seconds, she'd be face-to-face with her Angry White Man.

She'd barely had time to see him, yet he'd had more than enough time to burn quite an impression on her, she thought. Strong chiseled features without looking like Stonehenge, short dark hair with a slight wave that begged for her fingers to explore, the bluest of blue eyes deeper than the deepest portion of the ocean, lips—oh God she didn't want to think about his lips and how she wanted them to roam her body. *Why couldn't he just be eye candy? At least then I'd have half a chance.* It would be hard enough to navigate their "relationship," no sense in complicating things with sex, she reminded herself.

In the baggage claim area, she felt Sean's presence but didn't see him. Since Jonathan and her father were preoccupied at the conveyor belt waiting for their luggage, she slipped away to find Sean. It seemed as if everyone in the Los Angeles area decided to hang out at the airport baggage claim just to block her view.

"Looking for anyone in particular."

The sound of Sean's low, sexy voice sheathed her in warmth as his arms slipped around her waist. Back rested against his chest, she relaxed completely. "You'd better be my Angry White Man or there will be trouble."

"Well, I'm angry, white and a male, so you must mean me."

She turned in his arms and gazed up into his stormy blue eyes. Behind the passion that matched her own, she saw pain. She cupped his jaw with her hand. "What's wrong?"

Eyes closed, he placed his hand over hers, then embraced her. "How do you know me so well?"

"You're my best friend."

"Best friends forever, huh?" he said with humor in his voice.

"Something like that." Cheek rested against his chest, she listened to his steady heartbeat and enjoyed sharing an embrace.

The rushing travelers and airport noise seemed to vanish. "Are you going to tell me what's wrong?"

After a slight hesitation, he admitted, "I said some horrible things to my mother. Things I shouldn't have said. I'm out of control. That wasn't me. I don't like what I've become."

"You decide who you are." Of all the ways she'd imagined their first embrace, an embrace of consoling wasn't one of them, but it was still nice. Too nice. That he felt comfortable enough to allow her to console him truly touched her and gave her hope that they could be more than phone sex buddies.

"Excuse you."

Joy glanced over her shoulder at Jonathan. She expected Sean to release her, but instead he turned her in his arms. With one arm he held her possessively with her back to his chest, with the other he held out his hand.

"Hello, I'm Sean, and you must be Jonathan, the sibling Joy actually likes."

That crack brought a short-lived smile to her brother's face. The two men shook hands.

"And you must be Judge Warren." Out of the corner of her eye she saw Sean bow his head. "It's an honor to finally meet you." He shook hands with her father.

"It's a pleasure to meet you. Please call me Ben."

As usual, Joy couldn't read her father, but knew she'd be hearing from him.

"Thank you, sir. Joy has told me so much about everyone, I feel as if I already know you."

"Wish I could say the same," Jonathan grumbled. Joy narrowed her eyes on him in warning.

"My car is this way." Sean took the two large daisy-print bags that were beside Ben and led the way. Jonathan took the final two large bags and followed the rest of the group.

Joy found herself almost trotting to keep up with the long-legged men. Not that she minded trailing behind Sean. The man wore the hell out of his jeans and had a swagger that would make any cowboy jealous. "We haven't had any real food all day. After we check in, how about we go out to dinner? My treat. That way you two can get the grilling of Sean over with."

"Sounds like fun," Sean tossed over his shoulder. "What do you want to eat, and it's my treat? Think of it as my 'welcome to California' gift."

"Do you have Pappadeaux? It's my favorite restaurant."

Sean stopped midstride and turned toward her. Jonathan tripped to keep from bumping into Sean.

"This is the *West Coast* and you want Pappadeaux? Don't insult me. I'll pick somewhere to eat."

Jonathan laughed. "I like him."

* * *

Freshly showered, Tony slipped under the sheets with Charlene. After their long day of sightseeing and shopping, he'd gone on a walk to give her time to herself. When he returned, she was already in bed, seemingly asleep. He'd bet she thought she was less desirable to him wearing his T-shirt. He eased over to her side of the bed and spooned her into his body.

"Relax," he whispered in her ear in response to her tense body. "I just want to hold you." The erection in his briefs wanted him to do a lot more than hold her. Hell, he wanted to do a lot more, but sex wasn't what she needed right now. She'd come such a long way since she'd left Edward. She wasn't a new person, but the person she'd been afraid to show all of these years.

The call from Edward had disturbed her more than she would admit. Since the call, she'd been building a protective wall around herself with him on the opposite side of it. Maybe she was afraid she'd never be free of Edward and didn't want to involve him. Maybe she thought he couldn't protect her from Edward. Maybe she thought he would leave her because he didn't want to deal with her Edward issues. Maybe she was afraid Edward would come after him. Whatever the maybe, he'd be there to give her the support she needed. He couldn't protect her from her father but times had changed. They weren't teens anymore. No way in hell would he stand by and allow anyone to hurt the woman he loved. Never again.

"Tony," she said softly and rolled toward him. "I've been thinking." New York's nightlife provided enough light in the room for him to see her big, sorrow-filled, blue eyes look away.

"It's okay." He twirled one of her golden locks between his fingers. "I know that call from Edward upset you. You're not alone."

"I just don't think this is the right time for us to…"

"We've waited our entire lives. The time is perfect for us." Hand rested on her waist, he could feel her tremble under his touch. "What's your greatest fear?" He nudged her chin up with his knuckle so she'd look into his eyes.

No words came from her, only tears.

He kissed the tears away. "I'm sorry I didn't know how to protect you when we were teens. I'm sorry for the life you've led. We're not children anymore. No more running away from problems. You can count on me. Let me do my part."

Eyes closed, she said, "I love you too much."

Heart singing, he held her close. "Now that's my kind of problem."

She wedged her hands between them to his chest and pushed away. "I love you so much I'm willing to let you go. It's for the best."

"The best for whom? Not us. You didn't answer my question. What's your greatest fear?" If she didn't stop biting her bottom lip, he was sure it would fall off. Oh God he knew this wasn't the time, but he wanted to take her lip into his mouth.

"You're too good for me, Tony. What happens when Edward comes after you because of me? You're a principal. You love what you do and are good at it. What happens when people find out you're dating a whore? You talk protection." She rolled away from him. "I have to protect you from your feelings. You could lose everything because of a worthless whore. I won't let that happen."

The way she so easily degraded herself pissed him off. Her father, C'Money and Edward had beat her down emotionally and made her think she wasn't good enough for better. He saw it as his duty to show her otherwise. "You're not a worthless whore. You're the woman I love." He cupped her into his body. "What do you think will happen? Edward will take out an ad saying you used to walk the streets, he murdered your pimp and now you're married to me?"

She flipped toward him. "Married?"

"Will you be my wife?"

Brows knitted together, she stammered, "You'd marry me?"

Forehead pressed against hers, he said, "That's what people who are in love do. I refuse to allow fear to keep us apart."

Shock evident in her voice, she repeated, "You'd marry me?"

"In a heartbeat. I'm not letting you run away." He leaned

forward, took her bottom lip into his mouth and suckled gently.

Shock apparently worn off, her fingers laced behind his neck and she opened to a full-fledged kiss. With the betrayal and cruelty she'd suffered at the hands of the men in her life, he'd understand if she never opened her heart to anyone, but she trusted and loved him enough to give him a chance, and he wouldn't blow it.

* * *

Like magic, Tony's touch made Charlene's insecurities and fears disappear. No man ever made her feel so desired, so beautiful, so loved.

He suckled from behind her ear, along her neck and caressed the tender flesh between her thighs. To give him better access to her overheated body, she pulled his T-shirt over her head and tossed it to the side. When she reached to unfasten her red silk bra, he stopped her with two simple words, "Allow me."

And allow him she did. The care he took to undress her left her feeling delicate and loved—two things she never thought would be associated with her. Innocence stolen many years ago, she refused to allow Edward or anyone else to take this from her. What she shared with Tony was worth fighting for.

Breasts cupped in his hands, he suckled one pebble-hard nipple then the next. Her clit twitched in response and eager anticipation.

"Tony," she managed to rasp out.

"I know, precious." He captured her lower lip between his teeth and nibbled, all the while massaging her clit with the tip of his dick. The heat of his pre-cum set her senses on fire in all the right ways. She lifted her hips to take him in, but he moved.

"Not yet."

She gazed into his eyes and wanted to cry. Being under him, accepting his love and loving him in return felt more right than anything had ever felt in her life.

"This is forever. Do you understand what I'm saying?" he asked. "I want forever with you."

Not in the mood to debate a given—of course this was forever—she moaned more than said, "Yes, forever, with you."

With that, he gave her what she wanted and plunged into her inch after glorious inch until he was buried so deep he claimed her soul as his. Hips tilted up to meet his forceful thrust, she watched their glistening bodies. His long length slipped in and out of her. The slap-slurp sound played the most lovely tune. The aroma of sex filled the air. Heaven. She knew she'd died and gone to heaven because nothing on earth could be this good.

"Oh God!" Her pussy walls clamped around his dick and held tight. She felt him in, out and around her all at once. She balled her fists and banged them onto the bed to keep from tearing his skin off his back. Orgasms didn't feel like this. Over the years she'd had many of them and knew they weren't this powerful.

He shoved her left leg upward and changed his angle just a touch to the right and repeatedly hit a G-spot that shattered everything she thought she knew about being pleasured by a man. Tears fell from her eyes, and her entire body quivered. She'd been fucked good many times, but this was something completely different, mind-altering. The term "making love" had always been too flowery for her. She'd looked down on people who used it. No she wanted to use real terms, but what she and Tony were doing she couldn't classify as fucking. This was better. She finally understood, making love required mind, body, soul and love.

So she'd be on top, he flipped them both over.

"Ride me," he rasped out.

Thick, creamy cum coated his dick and balls. So much so that she had a better idea. She pulled him up behind her and offered her ass to him. Worried he'd be put off by her offer, she ground her ass into his crotch and gave him the choice of, "Both are ready and waiting for you."

Brow raised, he grinned. "I absolutely love you." He slipped his fingers into her pussy and brought her to completion again. She came so hard the juices literally dripped down her legs. Weak in the legs from so much good loving, she wasn't sure how much more she could take.

He massaged her inner thighs, took much of the moisture, then used his left index finger to slowly finger-fuck her ass. She naturally pushed back into him with soft moans of, "More."

"Relax, precious."

She couldn't help but wonder how he expected her to relax when he had her every nerve ending tingling. She saw him reach for the lubricant, which was on the nightstand next to the bed. Body relaxed the best she could, she was rewarded with his smooth entry.

In and out he stroked, his pelvis repeatedly hit her ass with a slap of his balls right behind. All the while his right arm wrapped around her, he massaged her clit.

She hit yet another climax. *Impossible.* "Oh God…"

He grasped her hips and delved in harder, deeper.

"That's it, baby." She tightened her butt cheeks and forced herself back into his strokes. She glanced over her shoulder and watched him. Face contorted, he looked to be fighting off his impending orgasm. "Come for me, baby."

He pulled out then slammed back into her. His whole body quaked. "Aw shit."

"Yes, baby, yes." She reached back and caressed his hand. "That's it." She worked her hips. "That's it."

* * *

Charlene stepped out of the shower and wrapped herself in one of the plush, white hotel towels. Tony was more than she had dared to dream of. He stepped out of the shower. She opened her towel. "Care to join me?"

A sly smile tipped his lips. "I'd love nothing more." He joined her in the towel, kissed her into oblivion, then carried her back to the bed. "I want to make love again, but if we don't take a break, we'll both be in pain. I hate getting old."

"Not old, more mature and you brought me to completion so many times in that last session, I lost count. No young man could do that." She chuckled. "I'll bet no ordinary man could do that."

"You are good for my ego." He kissed her forehead. "When are you going to marry me and make me an honorable man?"

Fear of Edward's reaction lingered. She didn't know what she'd do if her love of Tony hurt him.

"Charlene, speak to me."

"I'm just afraid. If anything ever happened to you…"

"It won't. Believe in the strength of our love."

"That won't stop a bullet. He murdered C'Money and was abusive. For years I blamed myself for his abuse, but it wasn't me. It was Edward."

"Then you need to decide where you want to live. We will move."

Brows furrowed, she pushed away from him. "You can't

give up your career. This is what I was afraid of. That Edward would ruin everything. I love you too much to let you give up everything for me."

Tony chuckled. "I love you, but you can be quite conceited at times."

Of all the replies he could have given, that wasn't one she'd expected.

"I'm not giving up anything for you. I love doing what I do. I've also always wanted to start a private school. I have the business plan and funding. It just didn't feel like the right time, not until now. We can live just about anywhere in the country."

"And what about when Edward finds me." It was time to come clean. Completely clean. This was the man she loved and who loved her. "It's just…" She went on to tell him why she'd applied for the position at his school. After she finished, he remained silent and just stared.

"So you were stalking Joy?"

Now she wished he'd remained silent. Ashamed of her actions, she couldn't look into his eyes. "Initially, I wanted to see my competition, but I fell in love with you and became friends with Joy. Having true friends and love have changed me."

He lifted her chin. She didn't see anger or disgust in his eyes.

"We didn't change you. We allowed you to be Charlene." He pulled her close. "Thank you for sharing everything with me. Now we can protect ourselves. What do you think Edward will do?"

"Once he realizes Joy isn't coming back, he'll try to hunt me down. He won't be able to accept I don't want him. To him I'm his property." A chill ran down her spine. "He'll hunt me down and kill me."

"No, baby, no. I won't let that happen. We're in this together. Promise me you won't run."

"I love you so much."

"Love isn't enough. I need you to stand and fight with me, not run from the confrontation."

Tears fell from her eyes. "If anything happened to you because of me…"

"If anything happens to me it will be because of Edward, not you. And I don't plan on standing by and allowing him to do anything to us. Are you with me in this?"

"Yes, I'm with you."

Chapter Seventeen

Even the slightest glance from Sean had Joy ready to rip her virgin card to shreds. How could she stay away from him when staying away was the furthest thing from what she wanted? For the umpteenth time, she reminded herself that he said he wasn't ready for a relationship and that she should listen to him. If she indulged in a full-fledged sexual relationship with him, her emotions for him would run out of control and she'd be hurt when she wanted to move their relationship forward and he still thought they weren't in a relationship. Just as she'd stopped all sexual contact with Edward to keep him from getting the wrong idea, she reaffirmed she must stop herself from doing the same in regards to Sean.

Easier said than done.

A cool breeze kicked off the ocean. *I love it out here.* She leaned her head on Sean's shoulder. After they'd checked into the hotel, he took them out for dinner to the best seafood restaurant she'd ever been to. The crab cakes were unbelievable, and there was no way that succulent, melt-in-your mouth crustacean on her brother's plate had been your everyday lobster. Someone had packed twice the flavor in every bite. Fat and full from dinner, she'd suggested they hang out at the beach, which was only a few blocks from the restaurant, while their food digested some.

Seated on a beach towel with Sean's arm draped around her waist loosely, she glanced over her shoulder at her brother and father who looked quite comfortable in lawn chairs. Thankful Sean kept beach supplies in his trunk, she returned to convincing herself not to allow her relationship with Sean to become more complicated.

Sean removed his arm from around her. "Would you like to go for a walk with me?"

"I'd love to."

He helped her stand, then pulled his car keys out of his pocket and held them out to Jonathan. "You guys don't have to wait on us. The hotel address is plugged into the GPS for you."

Jonathan didn't make a move to take the keys. "How very thoughtful of you, but we can wait."

Joy fixed her mouth to tell Jonathan to stop acting like a

jerk.

"Thank you for the offer," Benjamin said. "My body is still on East Coast time. I'm ready to turn in. Jonathan and I will be leaving shortly. We'll leave your keys in Joy's room."

Jonathan snarled, but otherwise remained silent.

"Thank you, Daddy." Joy hugged her father, then her brother. "Stop being so grumpy."

Hand in hand, Joy and Sean strolled along the shore. Though she wanted to discuss their "relationship," she couldn't find the right words to start the conversation. "We've become the cliché couple walking along the beach at sunset. An editor would probably suggest rewriting this section of a book."

"To fit the cliché, we'd be on the beach alone," he said, humor clear in his voice. "In all the times I've been to the beach, I've never been the only one here to enjoy the sunset." They continued their walk in silence.

He drew her hand to his heart. "I don't know how to proceed with us."

Relieved he was ready to discuss their situation, she looked up into his sea-blue eyes and about drowned in the restrained passion she saw there. Nerves atwitter, she agreed, "That makes two of us. I know we have to be completely honest about what we want and our fears."

"Let's start with wants first. What do you want?"

"Oh no, you first."

"Chicken," he teased.

They came upon an area with boulders and large rocks that reached all the way into the water. He led her over to the rocky area. "Let's grab a seat." They climbed up a few rocks onto a bolder and watched the sun's pink, purple and orange extravaganza of a goodnight salute with several other couples. Show over, the majority of the spectators left.

"It's so beautiful out here. I'm glad Granny got to see it before she passed."

"Did I ever tell you she called me?"

Mouth wide open with surprise, Joy wondered why she was surprised. "Granny was a mess. What did she say?"

"That you deserve someone as full of life as you, not some bitter asshole."

Joy laughed. "Yep, that sounds like Granny. I'm sorry about that."

"Don't be. She's right. I don't want to be some bitter asshole who makes his mother cry. That's not me. I can't believe I hurt her like that." He cupped Joy's hand to his chest and gazed into her eyes. "I've fallen in love with you and want a complete relationship with you, but I'm damaged goods. My greatest fear is that I'll hurt you. This is crazy. I truly believe what I've always wanted is right here, but my track record with women isn't the best. Hell, it's atrocious and I don't want to take my past out on you."

Her hearing paused after he said he loved her. She replayed the "I've fallen in love with you" portion a few times, then had to take a few seconds to listen to and absorb the rest of what he'd said. "I love you, too." Nervous laughter tickled Joy. "My greatest fear is that you'll project your experiences with the women from your past onto me. I'm not them. I'm me."

"Then we're in agreement. That we shouldn't pursue a relationship. Not right now anyway."

"No, we're not in agreement."

"But you just said—"

"I said I have fears. We both do. Now that we've admitted what they are, we can work on them. If you're waiting on a hundred-percent guarantee that we'll make it, that'll never happen."

Sean looked around, leaned close to Joy's ear and whispered, "You're a virgin. You're not getting my ass sent to hell for deflowering you and breaking your heart. No thanks."

She burst out in laughter. "You are crazy."

He joined in the laughter. "I'm afraid so." They both calmed. "I'm joking, but I'm also serious. I have never felt the way I feel about you. We've gotten to know each other on a level I can't explain. I don't want to let that go. I want it all with you, but I know I'm not ready. I have too many issues I need to work through."

"I hate it when you're right. I shouldn't pressure you into something you're not ready for. That's just asking for trouble. So where do we go from here?"

"I can't believe I'm saying this." He shook his head. "I really am crazy for this." He whispered into her ear, "I want to make love with you, but I won't." He sat up. "At least I'll try not to. Not until I'm ready to put a ring on your finger."

Laughter bubbled out from Joy. "Did you just say you're

saving yourself for marriage?" One of the few couples who remained looked their way, but she couldn't help it. This was too funny to contain. "I'm sorry. I shouldn't laugh." She hugged Sean. "I am truly in love with you."

Her cell phone vibrated in her back pocket. "Jonathan and Daddy must be back at the hotel." She pulled out her phone and answered without checking the caller ID. "Hello."

"Why the hell didn't you call when your flight landed?" Edward snapped.

Joy's smile dropped. "You must have the wrong phone number. Please hang up and try again." She disconnected.

"What happened?"

"I don't know what Edward's problem is, but—" Her phone vibrated. She looked at the caller ID and saw it was Edward. "Hold on a second, Sean." She connected the call. "Hello."

"I'm sorry, Joy. I was just worried."

"Why? Did you hear about a plane crash or something?"

"No, no, it's just."

"This is not a good time to talk. I'm too angry and may say something we'll both regret. Good-bye, Edward, and don't call me back. I'll call you when I'm ready." She disconnected.

Sean stared at her a long while. "So, what was that about?"

"I could really shake my mom. What on earth possessed her to think Edward would be right for me? I have told him a million times I'm not interested in him like that. I even told him we could be friends, but he keeps..." She shook her head. "I don't want to ruin our perfect evening talking about Edward and my mom."

"Let me get this straight. You told him you could be friends?"

"Of course I did. I'm not interested in him romantically, but a friendship I can do."

He smiled.

"What?" she asked.

"It's just I must be getting better because I don't think you're cheating on me with the old coot."

"You are wrong for that."

"I'm serious. This is a big step forward for me. My trust has been betrayed so many times."

She hit at him. "Be quiet."

"Seriously though. The virgin in you is really showing. Men don't think like women. When you told him you could be friends, that's like saying he has a chance with you."

"No it doesn't."

"Not to you, but to him, it does."

"But I told him in plain English that I do not want him in the romantic capacity. That the most I could offer is friendship and if our friendship would mislead him into thinking we could have more, then we need to end our friendship. There is no room for misinterpretation in what I said."

"In your mind you two are just friends. But according to the phone call you just received, he doesn't think of you as just his friend." He led her toward the main street.

"I'm calling him back now and telling him we can't be friends."

"You don't have to prove anything to me, Joy. I'm trying to turn over a new leaf. To trust again."

"This isn't for you. I don't want him thinking we have something that we don't." She took out her phone and dialed Edward.

"Joy, baby, I'm truly sorry. I shouldn't have spoken to you like that. I was completely wrong. Let me make it up to you. I can book a flight and be there by morning. I'll show you the time of your life."

"Edward, I'm sorry, but I think it's best if we just cut all ties. You've been a great friend, but…"

"Joy, no."

"This is for the best. I'm sorry. Please delete my phone number and email address. Good-bye." She disconnected. "I feel like a complete jerk. I wasn't trying to mislead him. I thought we could be friends."

"I know." Sean took her into his arms. "I know, baby."

* * *

"What a bitch!" Edward threw his cell phone against the wall. Bits of plastic, glass and electronics scattered.

"No, it's her fucking brother. I knew his ass was trying to take her from me." He stomped across the room to the bed Joy had used. "Their whole family is full of a bunch of perverts." He snatched up the photo album he'd just filled and flipped through page after page of Joy. One day when she was at work, he'd had cameras hidden throughout the house.

He lowered himself to the bed, picked up the pillow and pressed it to his nose. Her scent still lingered, but wouldn't linger long. He needed Joy back home with him. He set the pillow down, then turned to his favorite section of the album—Joy in the shower, in the tub, dressing, undressing. "She's mine. They can't have her."

Many a night he would enter her room and watch her sleep, so peaceful. If he could just get rid of her meddling brother and father, she'd be where she belonged—in his bed. The thought of her hot, tight, wet pussy had his dick diamond-hard.

He unzipped his jeans and wrapped his hand around his throbbing member. "One day," he said to Joy's picture. "I'll teach you how to," he stroked himself, "pleasure me as I want to pleasure you. Soon all obstacles will be out of our way."

* * *

"So what's your plan, to pout all night?" Sean took the television remote control off the hotel nightstand and plopped his butt onto the bed.

"It's either pout or seduce you. The choice is yours."

"Pout on, my dear virgin."

Joy kicked off her shoes and went into the bathroom. Though she'd told Edward on numerous occasions she wasn't interested in anything more than friendship, she should have known better than to move in with him—even temporarily. Of course he got the wrong idea. "I'm an idiot." Disgusted, she turned on the water and yanked a washcloth from the towel rack on the wall.

"You all right in there?"

"I'm fine. I've just never broken up with anyone before." She moistened the washcloth and wiped her face. The cool water felt good on her skin. "Especially someone I wasn't going with," she mumbled. "How did I get myself into this?" She stared at the curly-haired, brown-eyed woman in the mirror. "What's wrong with you?"

"Are you talking to yourself? I can barely hear you."

"I'm talking to the idiot in the mirror." She washed her face, neck and hands, then crawled onto the bed next to Sean and took off her jeans.

"What do you think you're doing?" he asked.

"Stop being a scary cat." She tossed her jeans to the chair.

It had been a long day and she wanted to relax. If he couldn't handle it, too bad for him. "Hand me your cell phone."

"What are you up to?" Eyes transfixed on her bare legs, he pulled his cell phone out of his back jeans pocket and handed it over to her. "And I'm not a scary cat."

She scrolled through his numbers. "Say that in about thirty seconds." She found the number she wanted and dialed.

"What are you doing?"

"Hold that thought for another twenty seconds."

"Hello," came a groggy, yet lovely female voice over the line.

"Hello, ma'am, I'm sorry for calling you so late. My name is Joy Warren."

"Oh, Sean's friend!" She cleared her throat. "It's no trouble. I was just falling asleep to a book. Is something wrong with Sean?"

"No ma'am, not at all. Wait a second. Let me put us on speaker." She looked at the LED screen. "How do you put this thing on speaker?"

"Who is that?" he asked.

"Oh never mind. I see the button." She pressed the speaker button. "Wow, I did it without hanging up on you."

"Joy, I'm not asking again. Who is it?"

A shiver went down Joy's spine. Someone had stolen her mother's spirit and possessed Sean with it.

"This is your mother, darling."

"Joy, what's wrong with you?" he bit out.

"You sound like my mother. Stop it." She held the phone, face up, between them. "As I was about to say before I was so rudely interrupted." She winked at Sean. He snarled, but she saw smoldering desire underlying his anger. "Your son has been bending my ear all evening about how horrible he feels for speaking to you so harshly yesterday. He was completely out of line and let his shock and anger say things he didn't truly mean. I told him he needs to tell you instead of me, but as you see, I didn't get too far with that approach, so I took it upon myself to let you know." So he hadn't been bending her ear about his disagreement with his mother all evening. This little lie was for his own good.

Sean shot what Joy interpreted as his disapproving stare. She almost smiled. If he wanted to shake her with a disapproving look, he'd have to do a lot better. His look couldn't even almost compete with the disapproving looks of the children in her family.

"It's hard for Sean to trust," Joy continued, "but he wants to try. He's trusting that you know his father better than he does and would be honored to walk you down the aisle."

"Sean said that?"

"Nah, I'm reading his body language." Currently, his body language said he wanted to kill and kiss a certain virgin. She hoped he'd opt for the latter. A sweet smile curved Joy's lips at the thought of their first kiss. Would it lead to more? She could hardly wait to find out.

He inhaled and exhaled a deep breath. "She's right. And I'm sorry for acting like a complete jerk. I'd be honored to walk you down the aisle."

Squeals shot through the phone and startled Joy. She drew a hand to her chest. "You okay, ma'am."

"Yes, yes, yes. I couldn't be better. And stop with this ma'am stuff. Call me Mom."

Sean's brows spiked up.

"Sure thing, Mom." *She likes me*, Joy mouthed and winked. "I am sorry about calling so late. I was raised better, but I had a feeling you'd be up and just as upset as Sean has been. I don't like seeing him distraught."

"I'm the one who should apologize. Sean, baby, the way I sprung everything on you was a shock I could and should have prevented. I made things worse with my approach. Please forgive me."

"There's nothing to forgive." He held onto Joy's free hand, and she knew she'd been forgiven of her little transgression of calling his "mommy" on him and telling a tiny fib.

"Yes there is. It wasn't easy for me to trust the man your father is today. Even though I forgave him years ago, I didn't forget and held it against him. I didn't want to make the same mistakes again. It took years to build a trust we'd never had before. Years for me to see him as the man he is today, not as that asshole I allowed to hurt us time and time again. I wasn't thinking clearly and expected you to just accept him because I'd done all the legwork. I knew he'd changed. But in reality, you have reason to doubt my judgment with men. I'm sorry, baby. I wasn't fair to you."

"Thanks, Mom. You don't know how much your words mean to me. And I'll try to see and judge Dad for the man he is now."

"That's all I ask."

Sean held Joy's hand to his heart. "I guess we'll be seeing you in a few weeks for the wedding."

"Don't you two even think about checking into a hotel. You'll stay here."

"I'm looking forward to meeting you in person, Mom."

"I feel the same way about you. Unfortunately, my son took after me when it comes to the opposite sex. Fortunately, he has taken after me and improved vastly in that area. I think we'll both make it. Call me anytime, Joy."

"I most certainly will."

"On a sadder note. I was truly sorry to hear about your grandmother's passing. When Sean received the news, all he cared about was getting to you."

Sean's cheeks reddened. "Mom, really. You two are speaking about me like I'm not here."

"I'm sorry, darling. I worry about the damage my poor decisions have done to you. But Joy is... Well, what can I say? I love you, baby. I want you to be happy."

"Okay, Mom. I'll call in a few days with our flight arrangements."

"Good night, baby. Good night, Joy."

"Good night." Joy disconnected and handed over the phone.

Conflict clouded his eyes. "Don't ever do anything like that again." He set the phone on the nightstand and drew her close.

"When Granny passed, my mom had unresolved issues with her. God forbid if something had happened to your mother before you had a chance to let her know how you feel. Time is too precious to let pride and anger keep us from those we love." She would have mentioned his relationship with his father, but chose not to push the issue, yet. "I'm sorry, but I'm in love with you. I couldn't just stand by."

He weaved his fingers through her curls to the nape of her neck and rested his forehead on hers. "I like the sound of that."

"Of what?"

"You're in love with me." He brushed his lips over hers. "I want to make love with you so badly."

153

"I was just feeling the same thing about you."

"You're not going to make this easy on me, are you?"

More interested in showing than telling, she suckled his bottom lip.

He groaned, then breathed life into the words he'd typed to her in the chat room. He took the sensitive flesh of her lower lip into his mouth, nibbled, teased until her lip tingled. The slip of his tongue into her mouth made her virgin body quake with need.

This was it. She knew she'd finally lose her virginity tonight. And that her first time would be with the man she loved was special in a way she hadn't foreseen. Enough of the analyzer in her. Time to enjoy the moment. Time to bring out the naughty, sex-starved girl who resided within her.

He nuzzled her neck with his nose, pressed her against the bed and covered her with his body. The thought of a man overpowering Joy had always lurked in the recesses of her mind and terrified her, yet no inkling of fear crept in when Sean was near.

"Am I too heavy for you?"

"No, I'm fine. Better than fine."

He descended on her lips, and she tasted him fully. The bulge that ground against her leg discombobulated her mind with anticipation.

He broke the kiss, and tugged at the bottom of her shirt. "This needs to come off. Sit up a little." After he helped her out of her shirt and bra, he cupped one of her breasts in his hand. "I knew they were real. Thank you." He lowered his mouth to her nipple and suckled. The heat and pressure were glorious.

Not to be outdone, she lifted his shirt over his head and tossed it to the side. She wouldn't lie. Edward was in nice shape and very handsome, but Sean. She fanned herself. Tapered waist, six pack, broad shoulders, the stuff romance heroes were made of but in real life and right before her happy little fingers. Nervous to look below his waist, she gazed into his eyes. He had the most beautiful eyes she'd ever seen. She'd always hated her mud-brown eyes but loved his ocean-deep baby blues.

"Are you scared?"

"No, not really."

"Then why won't you look below my waist?"

"So you noticed that, huh?" Face heated with

embarrassment, all she could do was close her eyes and lower her head.

"Are you sure you're ready?"

"More than ready. I was trying not to be rude or objectify you."

He laughed. "I'm a man. I live to be objectified." He placed her hands on his chest. "I have dreamed of the day your hands would roam my body." He guided her right hand down to his hardened dick. "All of my body."

She rubbed the bulging denim.

"I'm about to bust my zipper. May I finish stripping or should I pour ice down my pants?" He toyed with his belt buckle.

"Strip."

He backed out of the bed. "Cover yourself and don't watch. I'll be there in a second."

"I don't get to watch?" She finished undressing and covered herself.

"Only if you're comfortable watching all of my manliness," he teased.

Such a good man. This time she allowed her gaze to caress his entire body—*simply magnificent.* She could hardly wait for the day he was as confident in their relationship as he was with his body.

He rejoined her in bed. "I love you, Joy. And I'll do my best to never hurt you." He drew her close.

"And I'll do my best to objectify you every chance I get."

"That's my virgin." He nipped her lower lip. "Straddle me."

Lying on his back, he held his dick down, covering the head with his hand.

This made absolutely no sense. How would he penetrate her like this?

With his free hand, he guided her to settle on the length of him. The mouth of her vagina wrapped around him. Holding her thighs, he rocked her back and forth. Within seconds, she moved of her own volition. How could she not, when it felt so divine?

He pulled her into a kiss where he didn't swallow her face. The man should give kissing lessons in his spare time. Nix that. She wanted him all to herself. Eyes closed, she stopped analyzing every move and enjoyed the moment.

"That's it, baby." He pressed her lower back deeper into the grind.

A rush flowed through her. "Oh…"

"Just let go." He took one of her breasts into his mouth and she had no choice but to let whatever was holding her back go because it refused to stay. Moaning, she released all inhibitions and rode him like a prized stallion. Coming hard, she cried out.

He held onto her hips and continued to work her over his dick. Lowering from the high he catapulted her to, she gazed into his face and saw strain. Amazed anyone could have so much control, she quickly lowered herself and took his engorged dick into her mouth. Hours of frank conversation with Sean taught her everything she ever wanted to know about giving decent head, but she knew that she needed more practice. Not that any of that mattered at this moment. He was already on the verge of hitting his climax.

"Oh God" he said breathlessly. "Come up here…" He pulled her up then held his dick with one hand and onto her with the other as cum shot out of him onto her waist.

She wrapped her hand around him and milked him until he was dry.

"Whoa…" He lay on his back. "Damn." He propped himself on his elbow. "I'm sorry about that." He pulled off one of the pillowcases and cleaned her waist off with it.

"Don't be." Heart still pounding, Joy tossed the pillowcase, then rested her head on Sean's chest. "There's no way intercourse can be better than that. If it is, we do need to wait because I'm not ready to die."

He kissed the top of her head. "You're incredible."

"I was just thinking the same thing about you." She moved back to bring his face into view. "Seriously though, why can't we make love?"

"It's hard to explain."

"Try."

He laid his arm across her waist. "I envy you. You have no inhibitions emotionally or sexually. You're my dream come true. While I," he hunched his shoulders, "am your worst nightmare waiting to happen."

"That's not true."

"Let's be honest. If we don't make it, the chances are high

it will be my fault. I've been screwed over too many times to count. Besides being an emotional cripple, I'm a tad bit jaded."

"A tad bit?"

"I have serious trust issues and don't want to take them out on you. I'm so in love with you that I can't make love to you until I'm sure I can trust myself enough to trust you completely."

Hurt, she drew her hands to her chest. "You don't trust me?"

"I do, for now, but that could be the euphoria of first love. Try to see this from my point of view. I've had nothing but shitty relationships with women from the time I was born. I'm not blaming it all on the women. Hell, a lot of the fault is mine. I don't want my disastrous streak to continue with you. I love you too much. I need to do things differently with you. I need time to sort out my issues and truly believe that the love I've envisioned exists." He caressed her face. "I'm sorry I can't give you what you want, but I can't keep going into relationships the same way and expecting different results. With you I want forever."

The love she felt from him overwhelmed her in a good way. She'd be there to help him see there was no boogie man to steal what they shared and someday they'd have their happily ever after. "I understand. I truly understand."

Chapter Eighteen

Joy led Sean to the door. "I wish we could stay in bed all day."

He pulled her bare butt into his jean-clad crotch, and she felt how much he wanted to stay in bed all day also. "I have an article due. I'll pick you up for dinner and dessert at my place tonight." He slipped his hands around her waist and fondled her clit. "This will have to hold us both over."

Back pressed against his chest, she rocked her hips to encourage him to finger-fuck her. "This is so not fair," she groaned.

"You're going to be the death of me." He lifted and carried her across the room, then dropped her onto the bed. "Spread your legs."

She gladly spread her legs and fingered the juices that had gathered.

He kicked off his shoes, shoved his pants and briefs off, then straddled her so his rock hard dick dangled above her mouth. One lap of his hot tongue over her clit just about did her in, but she was not one to be outdone.

As his tongue, lips and mouth set her pussy on purr, she licked, sucked and caressed his dick and balls. Fucking. This was pure "D" fucking out of carnal need, and she loved it. She pumped his tongue.

He slipped his long fingers into her, and she cried out, "Oh God!" This was unbelievable. Still stroking him with her hand and sucking him, she hit her climax and had to keep from biting down.

He jerked in a little deeper than she'd liked, but not so deep that she gagged.

"Oh shit." He exploded in her mouth, but continued his oral assault.

The salty taste of his cum wasn't bad, but she didn't like the consistency.

"Spit, baby." He returned to overstimulating her clit. "I'm going to make you come again."

She didn't see a good spot to spit. He quickly reached over the side of the bed, handed her the wastebasket. The man had to be a mind reader. She spit into the can, then lay back. "I just had an orgasm that just about made me lose my mind. It's too soon to try again."

"Oh ye of little faith." He rotated his body, put her legs over his shoulders and his mouth squarely at the juncture between her legs. "Help guide my head."

One to follow instructions, she guided his head from her clit to her pussy as needed. Nearing the second climax she had thought wouldn't come, she pumped his tongue. He rose slightly and suckled her clit.

Tears came to her eyes as the second climax ripped through her. Her body arched off the bed, and her vision blurred.

"That's it, baby. You taste so good." He kissed along her waist, to her breasts. She was so sensitive, she couldn't take it and jerked away. He chuckled. "Want to try for a third orgasm before I leave." He kissed her lips and she tasted herself on him.

"I thought you loved me. Why are you trying to sex me to death?"

"You started it. Why weren't you wearing panties?"

She rolled her eyes. "As if my wearing panties would have stopped you."

They showered quickly and dressed. This time she put on panties and a T-shirt before she led him to the door. "Tonight." She opened the door and saw a woman leaving from Jonathan's room across the hall.

"I'll be by around six." Sean nodded a good morning to her brother, then drew Joy into his arms and kissed her. "Instead, call me when you're done, and I'll be by."

"Sure thing."

"It's time for you to leave," Jonathan barked. "Get in the room, Joy."

"Your parents raised you to be a gentleman," she shot back. "Walk the young lady down to her car and leave me alone."

"You have two seconds to get your butt in the room."

Embarrassed Jonathan treated her like a baby in front of Sean, she readied to put him on blast, but Sean stepped between them.

"If you think I'll allow you to disrespect Joy, you are sadly mistaken. Joy is a grown woman, and what we do is our business. I know you will always be her brother, and I'd like for us to get along, but your behavior is unacceptable. I will not tolerate it."

"Who the hell do you think you're speaking to?"

"I didn't stutter. You."

The woman who had spent time with her brother said a quick "good-bye" and rushed down the hallway.

Joy stood between the feuding men. "Both of you please step back and regroup. Thank you, Sean. You are my hero. I'll see you later."

"The hell he will."

"And you." She faced her brother. "If you don't stop acting like a Class A Prick, I'll make your life miserable, and you know I can do it. I'm hungry, did you order room service?"

The two men continued starring at each other. "Please, Sean, I need you to be the adult in the room." She looked around. "Adult in the hallway."

He kissed her forehead. "Call me when you're ready."

"Thank you." She hugged him. "I owe you one."

"You owe him nothing. And you're naked. Go put some clothes on."

"I'm not naked." But she had forgotten she wasn't appropriately dressed to be in the hallway. "I love you."

"Love you, too, baby." Sean kissed her, then headed down the hallway.

Jonathan followed her into her hotel room. "What the hell was that about?"

"Did I grill you about the woman who left your room?"

"This is different." He closed the door, stalked over to the desk and pulled out the room service menu.

"No it's not. You're just being your usual jerk self, and it's gotten way past old." She sat on the end of the disheveled bed.

"Yes, it is." He handed over the menu. "I want scrambled eggs, bacon, sausage, hash browns and orange juice."

"You can't eat all of that junk. You'll have a heart attack. I'm ordering boiled eggs, one order of bacon we can share, fruit and if you act right, a cheese Danish we can split."

"I'm a man who was with a woman all night. I need real food."

"You should have thought of that before you handed me the menu to order."

"You're just angry because I scared off Sean."

"That, too." She called in their order. "It will be here in fifteen minutes."

"We need to have a discussion about… Sean. Sex isn't something you enter into lightly."

"This coming from a man I'm assuming met a woman last night and took to bed."

"Like I said, that's different." He sat beside her. "She's not a virgin, and we're both grown."

"I'm grown, and being a virgin is highly overrated. By the way, I'm still a virgin and it's not from lack of my trying. Sean's the one who wants to wait until we're engaged," she said in hopes of Jonathan seeing Sean wasn't some sex-crazed maniac but someone who wanted a real relationship with her.

"Did you just say he slept here last night and you're still a virgin?"

"Not in those words, but that's what it amounts to."

He laughed. Not a little chuckle, but a full-fledged belly laugh. "I can't believe this."

"Let me in on the joke."

"I hate to tell you this, little bit, but Sean is gay."

Somehow her hearing didn't work properly. She could swear he'd said Sean was gay. "What?" A knock at the door drew her attention.

"I said your boy is gay."

After the night she and Sean had shared, there was no way he could be gay. "Does the thought of me being a sexual being bother you so much that you have to come up with this craziness?" She went to answer the door.

"Thinking of you as a sexual being is disgusting, but that's not why I say he's gay."

She opened the door. "Good morning, Daddy." She stepped to the side. "Come in. Your knuckleheaded son was just about to explain to me why he thinks Sean is gay."

"This should be interesting." Benjamin entered and took a seat in one of the armchairs by the window. "Anyone order breakfast?"

"I ordered it," Joy closed the door and sat on the bed. "Well, Jonathan?"

"He stayed the night and you're still a virgin. That would not happen with a straight man."

"Just because you're a pig doesn't mean all men are."

Benjamin chuckled. "You two are entirely too funny." He resituated himself in the chair. "Normally, I'd agree with Jonathan on this, but Sean seems like one of the good ones. I think he'll put you before his needs."

"Bull. Be careful, little bit. He's on the down low."

"She'll be just fine," Benjamin continued. "As a matter of fact, after breakfast, I think it's time for us to be heading back to Atlanta," he said to Jonathan. "Now that I've met her fella and looked into this retreat, I think Joy can handle the rest without us."

"She doesn't even have anywhere to live."

"Lori emailed me a very nice list of units to explore. I want to do this on my own."

Shaking his head, Jonathan paced about the room. "I don't like this, but... I guess you're right. We need to let her do this on her own." He stopped. "I'll pay your first year's rent or mortgage and down payment."

"Is it my place?"

"Yes, it will be your place. I just don't want you struggling to survive. A hundred grand is nothing nowadays. Especially in Los Angeles."

Benjamin crossed over and hugged his baby. "You're all grown up. It's time we start treating you like it."

Overwhelmed, she didn't know what to say. "Thank you. Thank you both for believing in me."

* * *

"Looking good, Edward. You must be living right." Alonzo Montoya walked across the mosaic-tiled floor into the parlor. "When you said you were dropping by, I had the cook prepare lunch for us."

"You shouldn't have gone to the trouble." Forty-three years ago, when Alonzo was thirty, he was the most sought-after hit man in the game, but a double life sentence stopped him in his tracks. Since his release, he'd been living well in an Atlanta gated community for the more-aged population.

"It's not a big deal." Alonzo lowered himself into his Lay-Z-Boy. "Don't ever get old, son. Don't ever get old."

"If I'm not aging, I'm dead, so I think I'll keep aging." Edward settled on the couch. "Have you been testing your sugar?"

"Every day. I'm down to one hundred three. Now we both

know you didn't come all the way out here to talk about my diabetes. I haven't heard from you since your little girl, umm," he snapped his fingers, "Joy moved in with you. You ready to pop the question? You aren't getting any younger you know."

Edward and Alonzo's relationship moved from doctor and patient to friends upon their first meeting. Over the past three years, they'd gone golfing, fishing or just shot the shit on most Saturdays. "I'm sorry about—"

"If you apologize for choosing the company of a beautiful young woman over that of an old man, I swear to God I'll slap the shit out of you," Alonzo cut in. "When do I meet her?"

Edward laughed. "Sorry about that." He calmed. "I'd hoped to bring her by today but…"

"But what?"

"I don't even know where to start."

"How about the beginning?" He resituated himself in his chair. Even at seventy-three, he was a physical force to be reckoned with.

"As I mentioned over the phone, she comes from a very protective family and when she moved in with me, I knew there'd be trouble."

"You should've married her like I said and you wouldn't have to worry about that protective family anymore. What's wrong with young folks today? Why are you so afraid of marriage? Fucking wimps. Back in my day, she'd be fat with my baby by now."

"We barely knew each other when her grandmother passed. Then the right time never came."

"Listen up, son. My generation is the last with any sense. If you find a good woman, you'd better snatch her up before someone else does. What happened to Sherri?"

"She was never a possibility for marriage. She can't give me the children I've always wanted. She'll remain my lover."

Alonzo nodded in approval. "Be careful to keep your women separate. Never disrespect your marriage by letting Joy know about Sherri or any other woman."

"I won't. My problem will be Joy's family." He shook his head. "Her brother came over the other day and moved her out to California. He's made her break all ties with me."

Alonzo leaned his old body forward. "Wait a second. Did you just say this man came into your house and took his sister?

163

And I thought she had a job? Teaching or something, right?"

"There are things I haven't told you. Her family is full of a bunch of perverts. The fuckers let her uncle molest her when she was young, but she doesn't remember. And now her brother has been priming her to finish what that fucking bastard started."

"What the hell?"

"It's true, and I have to save her. I don't know how, but I will." He ran his large hands over his face. "I hate to ask this, but... but do you have any connections left."

Alonzo looked around, then at Edward. "Define connections."

"I don't want to do this, but I can't stand by and let him hurt her." He glanced over his shoulder to ensure no one was around. "Her brother must die. It's the only way."

Big grin spread across his face, Alonzo said, "I've always liked you."

"I'm sorry for putting you in this situation, but I don't know where else to go."

"Leave everything to me. I can't stand fucking perverts. I'll need his name, home and work addresses, pictures."

"I knew I could count on you. Thank you. I'll gather the information for your man. Just let me know how much he wants."

"You're not paying anything. I'll cover it."

"I can't let you pay for this."

"If anything goes wrong, I don't want you connected in any way. My ass is old and knows jail better than the outside world. They can't do anything to me."

"I can't let you pay."

"Of course you can. As they say, you can't take it with you." He paused. "Are you sure you want to do this. Once I get the ball rolling, it's almost impossible to stop it."

"I'm sure."

Chapter Nineteen

Charlene opened the door to her condo unit, then stepped to the side to let Tony in. After dropping their bags off at Tony's they'd picked up a few large boxes and made it to her place to pack a few things.

"I can't believe we're moving in together. Are you sure your sister won't mind?"

"You're my fiancée who has a psycho ex. Of course she won't mind my getting you out of the line of fire." He set the collapsed boxes beside the couch, then looked around. "Nice place."

"I thought Edward spent so much on me because he loved me." Disgusted with her own stupidity, she closed the door. "This condo is an expensive mousetrap and everything in it," she motioned around, "the bait. All I want are some clothes and my birth certificate and stuff. I guess I'll sell the rest and donate the proceeds to a women's shelter. Maybe my epiphany will be able to help someone else."

He hugged her. "You've come a long way, baby. I'm proud of you."

"I couldn't have done it without you."

"That's not true." He released her. "Edward wants you back, but you've decided you don't want the life he has to offer you. I know you wanted the office manager position at the school to spy on Joy."

Embarrassed, Charlene rolled her eyes. "I am so sorry about that."

"But look how you turned it around. Within a few weeks, you had everything running smoothly and you know the systems better than I ever did. You're smart. You're beautiful. You're full of life. You're your own woman. You don't need me. You want me, and that makes me feel like the luckiest man on Earth."

Compliments. Edward rarely complimented her, and when he did, it was related to sex. "I love you so much."

"I love you, too. I'd love you even more if you got me some packing tape."

Elated such a great man loved her, Charlene practically floated to the pantry in search of packing tape. When she moved into the condo a few years ago, she'd bought tape. Now she hoped she could find it or she'd be taking a trip to the drugstore.

Finding none on the lower shelves, she pulled a stool into the pantry and searched the top shelves.

"Who the hell are you?"

The shocking boom of Edward's voice knocked her off the stool to the floor and fear held her there.

"Charlene!"

A few seconds later, Tony rushed into the room with Edward close behind. Tony pulled her off the floor into his arms. "What happened?"

"What the fuck is going on?" Edward demanded. "Who the hell is Charlene? Did this whore tell you her name was Charlene? Sherri, really? You think you can change your name and wipe out what you are?"

Worry in his eyes, Tony seemed oblivious to Edward. Instead, he felt along Charlene's body as if he could tell if she were injured. With Tony, she felt precious.

"I'm fine. Just a little embarrassed. Thank you." She began to pick up the stool, but Tony grabbed it first. She didn't know how she'd calm Edward down, but she needed to think of something fast.

"What were you doing?" Tony asked.

At times she could be slow on the uptake, but this was ridiculous. Why was he completely ignoring Edward? Just in case he knew what he was doing, she followed his lead. "I was looking for the tape on the top shelf."

"What the fuck are you doing in my house with my woman?" Edward interrupted.

Edward could be violent and she didn't want Tony hurt so she tried to step between the men, but Tony gently pushed her behind him.

"Who do you think you are, this bitch's protector?" Edward barked.

Looking down on Edward, Tony calmly said, "It's time for you to leave."

"What the... Who... This is my damn house. I pay the bills in this bitch."

"Show me your legal claim to this property and your receipts for the bills?"

Utter confusion overtook the anger on Edward's face. Talk about a Kodak moment! Charlene wished she had a picture of this. Now that she'd had time away from Edward, she could clearly see him for the manipulative-bully that he was. He was no different than the bigger kids on the schoolyard who pushed around the smaller ones. Glad he'd finally met his match, she stood taller. Tony may not be as loud as Edward, but he didn't need to be.

"Are you fucking serious? Who the hell are you?"

"I'm Charlene's fiancé and—"

"Fiancé?" As if sucker-punched, Edward stumbled back. "Fiancé? Is this a joke? Did you know she's nothing but a whore?"

"Then what does that make you, a John or pimp? And why are you here?" Tony turned to Charlene. "Do you want him here?"

"No. Please Edward, just go."

"The lady has spoken." Tony took out his cell phone. "Do I need to dial nine-one-one? I wonder what your patients will think when they see their doctor being hauled off by the cops for threatening his ex."

Pointing at Charlene, Edward bit out, "When his stupid ass gets tired of you, don't come running back to me." He turned his rage to Tony. "She's playing you for a fool. She'll bleed you dry in no time." Edward stormed out.

Charlene locked the front door. "I'm so sorry."

"Don't be." Tony hugged her. "I didn't know what to think when I saw you on the floor. I was afraid you'd broken something." He caressed her, calming her racing heart.

"Hearing Edward startled me and I fell. I was so confused, and the way he left is so not Edward. I've never seen him back down. Never."

"I've worked in elementary education for twenty years. I know a bully when I see one and know even better how to handle them. Bullies feed off fear and use intimidation to control others. I'm not afraid of him and he can't intimidate me." He sat on the couch and pulled her along. "He just walked in like he owns the place. What's the process to have the locks changed?"

"I'll call the super." She cuddled with him. "For a little bit there, I thought you'd lost your mind."

He chuckled. "I could tell, but you fell right in and let me handle it. Thank you for having faith in me. I'd never let him hurt you. You know that, don't you?"

"Yes." She leaned her head on his shoulder. "I wish that was the end of him, but he'll be back."

"And we'll be ready for him." He wrapped an arm around her. "Do you think we should warn Joy?"

Charlene thought for a bit. "She should be fine. I'll bet the only reason he showed up here is he figured out he can't control her so he decided to come back to a sure thing. But you showed him."

"No. You did. I could tell you were scared at first, but you didn't cower or back down."

"You are so good for my ego." Joy came to her mind. "I really admire that young lady."

"Who, Joy?"

"My motives for getting to know here weren't pure, but…" She hunched her shoulders. "I don't deserve to have such a great friend and fiancé. I'm not the same person anymore."

"Edward's a predator and a bully. He took advantage of you when you were vulnerable and tried to do the same to Joy."

"But she had his number. I'm so glad she had more sense than I did. Did you know after her grandmother passed she went to stay with him?"

"No. I didn't. I'm shocked."

"She was looking for somewhere to get away from her family. He thought he'd take advantage of the situation, but she wasn't having it. Within two weeks, she'd won me over, and I wanted to invite her to stay with me, but under the circumstances, I couldn't. When she told me about the writer's retreat I knew she planned on moving to California. Good for her. She'll be fine."

* * *

Unable to believe he'd been relegated to picking up a common whore off the street, Edward asked the young woman, "Do you know how to deep throat?"

"I can for you."

He rolled up his window and continued his search. Seven girls. He'd tried seven different girls and not one knew how to deep throat properly. And if one more bitch bit his dick, he'd ring her neck. Until Sherri came to her senses, he'd have to make do. Ignoring her had been a mistake. The illusion of a relationship was what had kept her in line all those years. He'd gotten sloppy, and now some asshole was giving her the illusion.

Now he may need to train a new bitch. Damn he missed Sherri. It took years to teach her how to fuck.

A short while later, he found someone with a similar build to Joy who may be suitable. Wearing the most hideous blonde wig he'd ever seen, her eyebrows were black, so at least she had the correct hair color.

"You think you can take my whole dick into your mouth? I want to feel it go down your throat. No biting."

Leaning into the car, she purred, "I'd love to."

"You take drugs, smoke?"

"What is this, an interview?"

"You could say that. If you suit my needs, this will be very lucrative for you. Get in the car."

"A high roller, huh?" She jumped into the passenger seat but left the door open. "I need to see some money."

"I need to see your arms and gums." She complied. Seeing no signs of drug use, he pulled out a few hundred bucks and tossed them at her. "You want to continue to the next stage of the interview or not?"

Picking up the money, she beamed. "Yes. Whatever you want." She closed the door.

Instead of taking her to his home, he checked into a midrange hotel and set his bag on the small desk by the window. To negotiate a good price, he'd have to show her he had money without revealing just how much. Grooming a new bitch was a lot of work. Maybe he should just propose to Sherri to get her back.

"You look a million miles away," said his new prospect. "What about my interview?" she asked coyly.

This girl had potential. Maybe he should keep her and Sherri. That way when he needed to let Sherri think she had some control, he wouldn't have to do without. Yes. That was the ticket. "Joy. Sometimes I'll call you Joy and don't want to hear any shit about it."

"Call me whatever you'd like." She eased her hand down to his crotch and squeezed gently. "Nice package."

Yes, she would do, and her resemblance to Joy was a bonus. Missing Joy, he took the wig off the young lady, and sure enough, her hair was thick and blacker than coal. "Don't ever wear that thing around me." He finger-combed her hair. "You're beautiful."

A genuine smile tipped her lips. Stroking a woman's ego was a key to dominating her. Get her dependent on you for praise and her well-being. Once you have her trust, take the praise away, and she'd do whatever you want to regain it. Where he'd fucked up with Sherri was getting too comfortable. Every now and again, you had to give the praise and let her think she had the upper hand. Telling her about Joy had been another mistake of comfort. At the end of the day, a whore was still a female, and you had to make them feel special.

He slipped his hands under her mini skirt and caressed her butt. On second thought, why bother with Sherri? She was old, worn out and her new mark may cause trouble. Eventually, he'd tire of her and throw her ass out on the street. No fool, Edward would be ready when she crawled back, but things would never be the same. She'd have to work hard for the money. No more easy life for her.

She eased his pants zipper down. "Is there anything you want?" Hand wrapped around his dick, she stroked.

Gazing into her dark eyes, he longed to be with the real Joy, to feel her hands exploring every inch of him. Moans from when he'd made her come still resonated within him. All he needed was one night with her. "For you to undress and lay on the bed."

Smiling, she undressed him, then herself and lay on the bed with her legs wide open. There was no way she'd been working the streets for long. Her pussy was too pink and juicy to have been used very often. What a boon for him, he mused. The way she'd gotten into the car before he'd shown her a dime should have told him she was green. She was still trusting. Yes. Sherri was definitely more trouble than she was worth.

She slipped her fingers into her pussy and fondled her clit. "Like what you see."

Now if he could only get her to be quiet. "Dangle your legs over the edge of the bed." He joined her in the bed and straddled her. Looking forward to trying out each hole on her body, he replaced her fingers with his. *Moist and hot.* Just like he liked it. She clamped her legs around his hand and pumped. Glad she enjoyed sex, she looked to be the perfect replacement for Sherri.

He crawled along the bed over her, then looked down into her face. Until the testing came back, he'd have to make due with her mouth. He turned in the position for sixty-nine, leaned forward and sniffed her pussy. His Joy came to mind. The first time they made love would be special for both of them. She'd waited her entire life for him, and he wouldn't disappoint.

He could see his Joy beneath him, eagerly awaiting first penetration. Slowly he entered her and was rewarded by her liquid heat. Knowing she was a virgin, he kept his pumps shallow, as not to hurt her, but it was hard. Her body clamped onto him and tried to pull him in deeper. With each stroke, he thought he'd lose it.

Her hands gripped onto his butt. She wanted more, and he'd gladly oblige. Deeper and deeper he drove until he came so hard he was sure his dick would fall off. Crying out, he gripped onto the bed. He looked down at Joy, but it wasn't her. Snapped back to reality, he held himself in the gagging girl's mouth. "Don't you dare let go. Take a breath and swallow." He returned to shallow strokes until his body couldn't take it anymore.

Laughing, he rolled off the girl. "Damn, that was wild." He wanted a repeat performance, so he knew he'd have to give a little something and make her feel special.

* * *

Terrified and confused, Angie couldn't catch her breath. He'd practically suffocated her. Warned about biting, she feared what he'd do if she bit down to get him off of her.

"I hope I didn't hurt you." He pulled her close and kissed her forehead. "I'm sorry. I'll teach you how to do it so you don't gag. I got carried away." He took her breast into his mouth, then worked his way down.

Do it correctly? Hell, deep throating was one of the first things she learned to do. It was to be her specialty. But she'd always been in control of the depth and pace. If anyone needed teaching, it was him. Unsure whether to run or stay, she remained still. What had just happened?

Head planted between her legs, he lapped the juices that had collected there. Laying back, her body began to tingle. After the wad of money she'd seen, he could keep her quite well. And he'd said he wanted to deep throat. Deciding she was overreacting, she calmed. He'd apologized and was now trying to make up for getting carried away. Next time she'd be ready.

A buzz ignited between her legs. Holding onto his head, she guided his mouth as she pumped. No normal John would go so far to satisfy a prostitute. She needed to do whatever she had to do to make him a regular.

On the edge of an orgasm, the buzz intensified and spread throughout her body. "Yes... yes..." The orgasm sent her body into spasms. He continued to suckle until she begged him to stop.

Heat of the moment over, Angie got under the blankets. "Am I hired?" she joked.

"It depends." He lay his head on the pillow and watched her.

"On what?" she asked, playing along. He was at least twenty years older than her, but he was handsome and had money. She wondered if he were married or what.

"If you pass the drug test."

She laughed. "Funny."

"I'm serious."

Laughter ended, she stared. "You *are* serious."

"Dead, so if you do any type of drugs, I suggest you tell me now." He went over to the small table by the window and grabbed his bag. "I want to hire you, but I have to ensure you're clean and free of disease."

Stunned, all she could do was stare as he drew her blood and swabbed her vagina. He said something about being a doctor, but it was all lost on her.

"Did you hear me?"

"I'm sorry. What did you say?"

"I think you'd be a good fit." He put the tubes of blood in his case. "You didn't answer about drugs."

Still tripping that this man had actually drawn her blood and given her a pap, she stammered, "I only smoke pot from time to time. Exactly what is it you want from me? What's the job?"

"I'll explain in a minute." Naked, he put away the samples in a small case, then sat on the edge of the bed. "I have strong sexual urges, ones my fiancée wouldn't understand."

Now everything was falling into place. He wanted a prim wife for show and a whore for the bedroom. As long as he paid well, she didn't care.

"I'll buy you a car, set you up in an apartment and pay you a grand a week to be at my beck and call, sexually. I love my fiancée, so don't get any Julia Roberts, *Pretty Woman* ideas. I'll treat you nice, but can't give you a relationship outside of the bedroom."

Jackpot! "Are you serious? You're going to put me up in my own place and pay me a grand a week to have sex?"

"There are some parts of myself I can't share with her. You understand and will enjoy our special time."

She didn't enjoy being gagged, but for a grand a week and free room and board, she'd learn to love it. And he was getting her a car. Hell yeah she'd suck his dick or whatever else he wanted sucked for that kind of money. After giving Carlos, her pimp, his cut, she didn't make that kind of money in a month.

"I expect you to be exclusive to me. No pimps, and I don't care what you do with your free time. I work long hours, so will probably only call on you once or twice a week, but when I call, I expect you to drop everything for me. And what I say goes. If I want to fuck your pussy, ass, mouth, whatever I want, I get."

His talk got her a little hot. Ready for round two, she said, "Damn, I want to fuck you right now to seal the deal."

"That makes two of us, but not until after the tests come back negative for STDs." He caressed her inner thigh. "Truth be told, I shouldn't have gone down on you, but I couldn't resist."

All this talk of him sharing this part of his life with her and not being able to resist her had her feeling some kind of way. How had she gotten so lucky, she wondered. She scooted over so his hand would brush against her clit. "I don't have anything. I always use condoms." Seeing he'd firmed up again, she held him with her hand and squeezed. His length was average, but he was thicker than most men she'd seen. His girth probably lent to her gag reflex being activated. His size wasn't his fault. She was sure they could work something out. Especially for the money he'd be dolling out. Ready to ride him, she eased closer. Having that thick dick in her would be a treat.

He tangled his fingers into her hair, then pushed her head down to his crotch. She sucked him off, thinking this was what she got for getting him excited again when he'd said he didn't want to have intercourse before the tests came back.

Chapter Twenty

Two weeks later…

Bluetooth secured snuggly in her ear, Joy held out her phone to take a selfie. "I'm about to send a picture now, Mom." Smiling, she clicked the photo. "I'm getting good at this." She sent the picture as a text to her mother, father, and siblings. "The church is beautiful. I think they purchased every lavender and pink flower on the East Coast. When I get married, I want deep purples and golds. Then my gown can be electric green," she said to annoy her mother. "That way it will stand out."

"You're wearing white. I have a few gowns in mind for you. Are you and Sean talking marriage yet? When do I get to meet him? Since you're on this side of the country, why don't you come for a visit? I promise not to give him the third degree. Oh the picture came in. You're so beautiful."

"Thank you." She watched guests pour into the church. "We just came over for the wedding. I have to get back to camp and he's headed to Washington for an interview. How about you and Daddy come visit me? My place isn't all decorated yet, but there's no rush. I have a spare bedroom that actually has a bed in it."

"I'd love to! I miss my baby girl."

"I miss you, too," Joy said honestly. "I do not live in a building with armed guards. Don't tell Jonathan's paranoid butt."

"He's just looking out for your best interest."

"It's a nice neighborhood and close to the camp. I have a month-to-month lease until I can find a job. I want to live close to work. When I choose my final place, I'll let him pay for it."

"That sounds like an excellent plan. The money Mother gave you won't last long. I know you can take care of yourself, but let us know what you need. How is the job hunt going?"

"Good. I want to work in a public school, but I have an offer from a private one. If need be, I'll take the job with the private school until I find what I want."

"Have you heard from Edward?"

"No. Not really." After she told him to lose her number and email address, he emailed her once apologizing for pushing too hard. He wished her the best in life and hoped they could be friends again someday, which made her feel like a complete jerk for the way she'd spoken to him. "I'm so embarrassed. You should have heard me. Actually, I'm glad you didn't."

"Heard what? Did something happen?"

"Let's just say I pulled from my inner Marshall and was a complete butt hole." A few of the attendees looked around at her. Voice lowered, she relayed their entire conversation to her mother. "Sean was right. My being friends with him would have led him on, but he didn't deserve to be disrespected."

"You should apologize."

"I want to, but I don't want to lead him on."

"Darling, you don't keep from doing the right thing because others might misinterpret it. He's a big boy. He can either deal with your moving on with your life or not. You live in Los Angeles now. You don't have to worry about leading him on anymore. Send an apology email and be done with it."

"I guess you're right."

"Of course I am. Oh, your father's coming in. Benjamin, book a flight for Los Angeles. The baby's *invited us* for a visit. Have someone take your picture with Sean. I need to go. Love you."

"I love you, too. See you in a few days." She disconnected, then went into her email account. *No sense in putting it off any longer.*

Hello Edward,

I pray these lines find you well.

Allow me to apologize for our last discussion. There is no excuse for my being so rude. You were a great friend to me and deserved better. I hope you find it in your heart to forgive me.

I want the best for you and pray you find your Mrs. Right.

Joy

She read what she'd typed to ensure there was nothing misleading. Straight and to the point, it was perfect. Seeing the ceremony would begin soon, she sent the email and felt better instantly.

Placing her cell phone into her purse, it vibrated. She glanced at the caller ID. "Hey, sexy," she answered quietly.

"Hey, beautiful, I need your assistance in the female robe room, please."

The urgency in Sean's voice set off alarms in her head. "What's wrong?" She eased out of the pew and rushed along the hardwood floor toward the room they were using for his mother's dressing room.

"I just need your assistance with Mom."

Standing outside the dressing room's door, Joy took a few seconds to catch her breath, then knocked.

Sean opened the door and pulled her into the room where she saw his mother sitting there with tears streaming down her face, ruining her makeup job.

"What happened?" She knelt before Connie.

"I can't go through with the wedding. I just can't."

She narrowed her eyes over her shoulder at Sean.

Shoulders hunched, he said, "Don't look at me. I didn't do it. I came in, and she was in here crying. I tried to get her to tell me what was wrong, and she cried louder."

"May we have a moment alone? I think a little girl talk is in order here."

"You women are crazy." Sean kissed his mother on the cheek. "Whatever you decide works for me. I'll be outside the door standing guard." He left the two alone.

"Where is your maid of honor?" Joy liked Connie, but didn't know her well and thought she may need backup.

A fresh batch of tears streamed down Connie's face. "I... I... overheard her saying I was a complete idiot for taking Darren back. That I'm about to get what I deserve." She wiped her face. "I'm just so tired of everyone saying I'm a fool that I told her to get out. Maybe I am the fool. Can everyone be wrong?"

Joy placed her hand on Connie's lap. "So these people saying you're a fool, do they know Darren as he is now, or the man he used to be? Do they know him better than you? What evidence do they have? Or are they just stating their opinion."

"You're so sweet. I pray Sean doesn't screw things up with you." She lowered her gaze to her lap. "I'm scared. I took him back so many times... Each time I thought this was it. That he'd changed. I don't want to be played a fool again."

"Then I'll tell Sean to call off the wedding." Joy began to stand.

"No… don't… I just need time to think."

"Be honest with yourself. Back when you continually took him back, did you really believe he'd changed, or had you hoped he'd changed? Were you in denial? Are you in denial now?"

Connie thought a few moments. "I had been lying to myself back then. Deep in my heart, I knew he hadn't changed."

"And now?"

"I'm in love with him. I want to believe, but I'm afraid."

"Your son takes after you. Because of his previous relationships, he's afraid of giving himself fully to me. How can you guys live in fear like that?"

Connie held Joy's hand. "I'm sorry, darling. I'm afraid I've ruined my son. His opinion of women isn't the highest, and a lot of that mistrust is because of me. I need to be a role model for him. I was afraid of being alone. That's why I kept taking his father back. Now I'm in love with Darren, but afraid to marry him because of history. You're right." She nodded. "I need to stop making choices based on fear."

"So are you going to marry the man you love or continue to live in fear? Is the wedding on or off?"

"My makeup is a mess." Nervous laughter escaped her.

"One of the great things about having two much-older sisters is they taught me how to do makeup properly. Much too conservative for any normal person, but perfect for a wedding." She pulled Connie over to the mirror. "I'll have you looking Cover Girl fantastic in no time flat. Sean!"

He opened the door. "Yeah?"

"The wedding is on. Give us ten minutes."

"Gotcha. I'm glad you're going through with this, Mom."

"Really?"

"Yeah. I want you happy. And if Dad makes you happy, so be it. I'll let everyone know you're running a little late." He closed the door.

Joy applied Connie's makeup the best she could, and was quite satisfied with the results.

"I know this is late notice, but… I no longer have a maid-of-honor. Would you do me the honors?"

"Oh my God! Are you kidding? I'd be honored!" She looked down at her peach dress. "I don't match your lavender and pink theme."

"I don't care and the maid-of-honor should wear a

different color than the bridesmaids. You look perfect." She held Joy's hand to her heart. "Sean had better not mess things up with you, or I'm getting rid of him. I'm serious."

As if on cue, Sean entered. "It's time to get married. Throw your faces on and let's do this."

* * *

Weddings had been a major part of Joy's life for as long as she could remember. From her siblings marrying and remarrying to her cousins, nieces and nephews, weddings were a big deal in her family. Of the many weddings she'd attended, none had been as lovely or drama-filled as Connie's. So many doubters attended, wanting front row seats to what they thought would be a train wreck, and it saddened Joy. No wonder Connie had second thoughts. Had it been Joy, she would have eloped. Your wedding day should be special in the best ways, but Connie's had been ruined in many ways.

Done eating chocolate-covered strawberries—for now—she watched Sean on the dance floor with Connie. Ever since his mother said "I do," he'd been laughing, joking and having a good time. No matter how much he protested, she knew he wanted his parents to have their happily ever after.

"Had I known you were going to eat all of the chocolate-covered strawberries, I would have ordered double." Darren chuckled as he moved her empty plate to the side and set a plate of the dark-chocolate-covered delights before her.

Face heated with embarrassment, she stifled a giggle. "They're really good."

"I'm just playing with you. Eat. Eat. Sean told us you love them, so we made sure there were plenty."

"Really, Sean told you that?"

"He wanted certain items on the menu. How many weddings do you know that serve almond-crusted trout and spaghetti squash? I'd say my son is quite taken with you."

Heart warmed, she looked from Darren over to Sean who had moved on to talking with some men she didn't know. "He's such a sweetie."

"No, he's not. You just bring out the best in him. Thank you."

"For what?"

"Ever since you came into his life, he's been more…" Shoulders hunched, he shook his head. Growing up, Sean may

178

not have been around his father much, but they sure had the same mannerisms. "I don't even know how to describe it. He's been angry, for good reason, but lately he's been trying to work through the anger. He even calls me from time to time without cursing me out. It's a refreshing change."

"I'd love to take the credit, but it wasn't me. I think he's been ready to move on for a while and your wedding gave him a reason." She bit into one of the strawberries. Sweetness of the berry mixed with the bitter of the dark chocolate to perfection.

"I was a horrible father and husband. I'm glad you don't know that other guy. He died."

Gazing into his eyes, she saw sincerity and an older version of Sean. "Don't worry about the naysayers. Just focus your love on Connie. My brother Jonathan was a mean alcoholic and womanizer. He lost his family to his drinking. I'm sure people who knew him back then wouldn't believe who he's become today. One of the things he had to do was cut people off who brought negativity into his life. Even my parents for a while."

Darren nodded. "Excellent suggestion."

"I come up with a good one every now and again." She bit into another delight. "I know I've said this a million times, but these are delicious."

"You trying to bribe my lady with sweets?"

Recognizing Sean's voice, she turned and faced him. "Someday I want a strawberry patch."

"Today, I want to dance with the most beautiful woman in the world. You mind if I steal her, Dad?"

"Have fun."

Sean pulled her up from her seat and escorted her to the dance floor. Sean calling Darren Dad hadn't been lost on Joy. Secure in Sean's embrace, she rested her head on his chest and rocked to the ballad playing.

"It feels good to see Mom happy. I know I acted a fool at first, but I'm glad they didn't listen to me."

"I'm glad they didn't either. She survived before and if for some reason Darren slips back into his old ways, she'll survive again."

"You're right. She's a big girl now."

Gazing up into his eyes, they were still as blue as ever, but the storm that raged in them had finally passed. The transformation hadn't happened overnight, but it did happen.

Just as she knew it would. New storms would rage from time to time, but she wasn't worried. He'd be better equipped to navigate storms now.

Head rested against his shoulder and arms wrapped around him, she continued to sway. "Why can't life always be this calm?"

"We'd die from boredom."

"I guess you have a point. I sent Edward an apology email. I've been feeling like a complete jerk. I was too hard on him."

Sean chuckled lightly. "I'm shocked it took you so long. You're a softy."

"I guess I am."

"Why are you telling me?"

"Because I don't want to keep anything from you. I knew you would have never found out, but if I'm emailing a man who was interested in me romantically, I think I should tell you."

"I'm not that psycho you met a few months ago. I trust you. You don't need to report your activities to me. I don't want to live like that."

"I know I don't. I just wanted to." She watched Darren pull Connie from a conversation to the dance floor. "I'm so happy for them." She nodded toward the happy couple.

"That makes two of us. I had a breakthrough the other day. I don't want to live worrying about what might happen. It expends too much energy. Make informed choices and move on. Sometimes things will work out. Sometimes they won't."

"Wow. I am rubbing off on you," she teased.

He glanced at his watch. "You ready to leave?"

"We're supposed to wait until your parents leave for their honeymoon."

Hand in hand, Sean led her to his parents on the other side of the dance floor. "Will you be leaving soon? Joy says we can't leave until you do."

Darren laughed. "I was just asking Connie the same thing."

Shaking her head, Connie said, "These two are so much alike. Yes, darlings. We are leaving soon." She hugged Joy. "You're such a sweet thing. If Sean gives you any trouble, call me."

"Don't encourage her, Mom."

* * *

Disappointed in himself, Edward continued with the flow

180

of traffic toward Angie's place. Not only had he forgotten to charge his phone, but his stupid car charger didn't work. Normally he wouldn't care, but Alonzo would be contacting him soon with an update on the hit.

Damn he missed Joy. He hadn't heard from her since Jonathan spirited her off to California. Knowing her spiteful brother, he'd probably gotten her into the writing camp to separate them. Grooming his own sister for himself... *What a fucking pervert.* Not to worry. His days were numbered.

The three-bedroom bungalow he'd bought for Angie came into view. After the super had the audacity not to allow him into "Sherri's" condo, Edward decided no more middle men. Instead of renting Angie an apartment, he purchased the house. Impressed with her new home, she'd sucked his dick like her life depended on it. By now she'd be done unpacking the crap he'd bought for her.

Pulling into the driveway, he decided the day hadn't been a total bust. Angie's drug and disease test results had come back negative for the important stuff. She'd said she smoked pot and that came up positive. To allow her some fun, he told her he didn't care about her pot smoking as long as she didn't have the entire house smelling like it. She promised to keep the smoking confined to one well-ventilated room.

Inside, he slipped the spare set of keys into his pocket. An oversized sectional took up much of the living room and a flat screen television took up much of the wall. Why anyone needed such a large television was beyond him, but these small expenses went further in reeling her in.

"Angie, I need to use your charger." He'd purchased her the same phone as his, so at least his dead cell wouldn't be an issue much longer.

"I didn't hear you come in." Charger in hand, she rushed from the back of the house. "I love this place. Love it, love it, love it!" She handed over the charger. "I can't thank you enough."

He hated to admit it, but her excitement turned him on. "As long as you treat me right, I'll treat you right. We have a mutually beneficial arrangement. You're looking as sexy as ever today." The T-shirt and jeans she wore were nothing special. He'd just needed to stroke her ego a little each day until she couldn't live without the strokes.

A broad smile lit up her face. "Thank you."

Charger and phone plugged in, he looked around. "When you picked out all this mess, I didn't see how it would all fit together, but this place looks nice. Good job."

Like a proud peacock, she pranced about the room. "I think I may look into interior design."

At least she wanted to do something constructive with her free time. This new generation of whores could teach Sherri's a thing or two. Buzzing to life, his phone alerted him of a text message from Alonzo's burner phone and Joy. He knew his patience would pay out and she'd contact him. Excited, he read her message.

Hello Edward,

I pray these lines find you well.

Allow me to apologize for our last discussion. There is no excuse for my being so rude. You were a great friend to me and deserved better. I hope you find it in your heart to forgive me.

I want the best for you and pray you find your Mrs. Right.

Joy

"Yes," he breathed more than said. He went through the text again. This time reading between the lines. He'd known if he gave her some space, she'd realize how much she loved him and come back.

"That must be some message." Angie eased over and stroked his dick through his pants. "You're getting hard."

"It's my fiancée. She misses me as much as I miss her."

"How sweet. You know what I miss?" She unzipped his pants.

* * *

Upon returning to Sean's mom's house Joy's first order of business was to strip out of the dress and shoes. Spending seven hours in a pair of shoes meant for four hours tops had not been one of her better ideas. The shoes looked so good with the dress, she couldn't help herself. Comfortable in her underclothes, she packed for their early morning flight. Tomorrow promised to be a long day. When you added in the time zone change, she had nine hours of the friendly skies to endure.

Sean entered the room wearing his briefs and a T-shirt and carrying his shaving kit. "Had I left this behind, I'd be upset." He packed the kit away in the suitcase.

"That was such a lovely ceremony."

"Yes it was." He drew her into his arms. "I'll be happy if ours is even half as nice."

"Yeah," she said wistfully. "Hold up. What did you just say?"

He knelt before her. "Joy Warren, would you do me the honor of becoming my wife?"

Too excited to speak, all she could do was kneel down and hug him.

"Does that mean yes?"

Overwhelmed with joy, she nodded. "Yes... Yes."

He nibbled on her bottom lip until she opened up for him. Sean had changed her mind about kissing. For them kissing wasn't a slob fest where she fought for her life. Instead, their kissing was an all-encompassing pleasure-filled experience that left her lips tingling and her body aching for more. Now that they were engaged, she'd get the "more" she wanted.

He lifted her camisole over her head and tossed it to the side, then unfastened her bra and let it drop to the floor.

The bulge in his briefs called to her, but she'd play it cool. Instead of going for what she wanted, she caressed his chest as he lifted and threw his T-shirt. Fingers gliding over the ripples on his chest, she leaned into him. "Mine."

"All yours." He tipped her chin up and gazed into her eyes. "All mine." He pulled her up as he stood, then led her to the bed. "All mine." He lowered her panties, planting light kisses on her legs as he made his descent.

Now what? The moment she'd been waiting for a large part of her life, and she didn't know what to do.

He dropped his briefs, then cupped her face and kissed her lightly. "You seem conflicted. Do you want to wait until our wedding night?"

"No... I'm just..." She lay on the bed with him. "I know we've been enjoying each other, but this is different. I can't explain. I want you, but I don't want to ravish or make this just about my losing my virginity."

Pressing her back, he caressed her inner thigh. "It's not."

He slipped a finger into her, then another. "I want to make love for the first time in my life with the only woman I've ever been truly in love with." Working his fingers in her, he took one of her breasts into his mouth.

Gyrating slowly on his hand, she weaved her fingers through his hair. Making love didn't take thought and planning. It took following your heart.

He lay on his back. "You on top."

She straddled him.

One hand on her hip and the other holding his dick, he guided her down. "As you lower, splay your legs behind you."

Taking her time to lower onto his hardness, she savored first penetration. Hands on either side of him, she rotated her hips on the head of his dick.

"Umm, that's it." He wound his hands around to her back and repositioned her as she continued taking him in.

Inch by inch he filled her until he lit a flame at her core. With each stroke, the flame grew hotter and hotter. Numerous good sensations flowed through her at once, leaving her breathless.

Stroking from beneath her, he took her breast into his mouth and suckled.

Shocked her clit throbbed, she gasped.

"That's it." Hands at the small of her back, he gently pressed.

"Oh my..." The added pressure somehow caused a cascading orgasmic reaction that started at her clit and worked its way to every corner of her body. "Oh God..."

"Pull me in, baby. Like Kegel exercises."

Vaginal walls tightening on their own, she Kegeled and the intensity of her orgasm did the impossible—it increased.

"Oh yes," he moaned. "That's it." Hands gripped on her butt, he repeatedly pressed her into him with a swoop-down motion as he pumped from below.

Toes curling, her climax shook her. She couldn't see how she'd ever get down and didn't care. "So good." She kissed him. "So good." Body calming, she gazed into his eyes.

She'd come, but he hadn't. At least she didn't think he did. Unlike their games, she couldn't see evidence of his climax.

"My turn." He rolled them both over, then lifted her leg and trapped it under his arm and reentered her.

She'd come, but if they kept this up, she'd be coming again. Raising her hips to meet his, she eased her hands around to his butt and gripped. Now this was what a butt was supposed to look like—rounded and firm.

"Ummm…" His hips collided with hers and he threw his head back.

Kegel in full effect, she tried to pull his entire body into her.

"Yes," he said between staggered breaths. "Hell yes! Take every drop." Buried deep within her, he remained still. "Yes…" He drew in and released a deep breath, then brushed his lips over hers. "I love you."

"I love you, too." Wait until she told her mother she was marrying a man she'd met on the Internet. *This should be interesting*, she mused.

Chapter Twenty-One

Alonzo liked Edward, so he decided to save the kid from himself. The boy had called him numerous times asking about the hit. Alonzo finally told him not to call him again until after the job was done. All that phone chatter could lead to issues, plus the less the boy knew of his plans, the better.

Atop a three-story building across the street from the Warren boy's office, Alonzo waited for his targets. Only killing Jonathan would be a mistake that could lead back to Edward. A mass shooting would be a much better cover. One Edward knew nothing about.

"Here we go." Wondering if the Warren boy was banging his assistant, he aimed his high-powered rifle at her head. For the past week, the two always entered the building together at 8:54 sharp. Boy how he loved creatures of habit.

As easy as picking grapes from the vine, he hit each of his pre-selected targets. Two seconds into the shooting spree, panic erupted as people realized what was happening. Everyone was so busy running from the danger, they wouldn't be paying attention to an old business man.

Done shooting, he checked his watch—ten seconds flat. He quickly broke down his riffle and packed the pieces away in a briefcase. Back in his hay day, it would have only taken him seven seconds to pull off the same operation, but he was still happy with his performance.

By the time he reached the exit of the building, people were smashed against the floor-to-ceiling windows trying to see what was going on across the street. Others had poured outside for a better view.

"What happened?" Alonzo knew he shouldn't bring attention to himself, but he'd been out of the game so long, he couldn't resist drawing out his accomplishment high a little longer. He wasn't worried. Unlike when he'd been caught before, he had his bases covered this time.

"Someone shot up the place. Looks like at least six people, maybe even seven, were hit."

Eight, but who's counting, he thought smugly. Shaking his head, Alonzo said, "The world has gone mad."

"Ain't that the truth."

"Stay safe, young man."

"You, too, sir."

Just as police officers arrived, Alonzo walked out and left the onlookers behind. Once clear of the melee, he called Edward from a burner phone. "It's done. Not how you wanted, but in a way that will suit your purpose. Good luck with your girl." He opened his car and set the briefcase on the passenger seat.

"What do you mean?"

"You'll see and be shocked as you should be had you not asked for this favor." He turned on the ignition and checked his mirrors.

"Thank you for everything. I'll take it from here."

Ambulances and additional police cars rushed past the parking lot toward the shooting scene. "She'll be shaken, so don't push too hard."

"I won't. She'll have to book her flight and fly across the country. She probably won't even arrive until tomorrow. I won't call. I want her to see how isolated she is in Los Angeles. Once she arrives, I'll give her family a day to drive her insane, then swoop in to rescue her like I did after her grandmother passed. I've already found a writing coach for her so she can stay close to her family during this hard time and still work on her writing."

"Sounds like you have it all under control."

"This time I won't fail."

* * *

In disbelief, Joy stared out the window of the Maxima Marshall had given her as Sean parked in one of the hospital lots. Their flight had barely touched down in Colorado when a flight attendant said there was an urgent message waiting for her. Not in Joy's wildest imagination could she fathom one of her family members being caught in a mass shooting. Look up world-class prick in the dictionary, and you'd see a picture of Marshall, but she loved and didn't want harm to come to him.

"You okay?" Sean reached over and traced her ear with his fingers.

"No, not really. I just don't understand what kind of monster would do this. Two dead, six wounded. I'm overwhelmed." Her head lulled back onto the headrest. "Mom must be going crazy. We're all her babies. She's protective of all of us. I don't know how to help."

"Being here will be more than enough. Come on. Let's

187

head inside and check on him."

"Okay, but first I need to apologize."

Brows drawn, he said, "For what?"

She held his hand close to her heart. "This is some way to introduce you to my family. Talk about being thrown into the fire. I'd fully understand if you went back to the hotel. I don't want you uncomfortable."

"We're a team now. If you're in the fire, I'm right there with you."

Tears fell from her eyes. "I love you so much."

He pulled her into an embrace. "I love you, too. We'll get through this."

Secure in his arms, she never wanted to leave. "I lost Granny and now this. I have to reconcile with all of my family. They drive me crazy, but I can't lose them."

"I think your being in Los Angeles has been a good break for you, but if you want to move back to Atlanta, I'm game."

"But what about your job?" She gazed into the eyes of the man she loved.

"I'm an investigative reporter who can't remember what the office looks like. Don't worry about me. I'll figure it out. Even if I have to switch to freelance."

"You're amazing."

"Yeah, I know."

A genuine smile tipped her lips. "Thank you for the offer, but moving back to Atlanta is asking my family to interfere in our marriage. If we move, how would you feel about moving to D.C.? At least we'd be in the same time zone as both of our families and there are lots of great stories for you there."

"That's a little too close to my parents." He opened the driver's side door. "We have time to figure it all out. Right now we need to see how Marshall is doing. Are you ready?"

"I should be asking if you're ready. My family is a bit much."

"Let's do this."

Joy barely stepped into the waiting room before she was inundated with hugs from her family. Siblings, parents, cousins, aunts, uncles… you'd think she'd been the one who'd been shot.

"Let me go. Let me go. I can't breathe," she joked. "I love you all, but what was that about?" She reached for Sean's hand, then pulled him near.

"We just miss you is all." Emily held her hand out to Sean. "And you must be Sean."

Head bowed slightly, Sean accepted her outreached hand. "Yes, ma'am. It's a pleasure to finally meet you." He looked up. "It's a pleasure to meet you all. I wish it were under different circumstances."

"You two must be exhausted. Please, take a seat. Marshall's in surgery. So we haven't any new news. I just thank the good Lord his injuries aren't life-threatening."

A round of "thank God" filled the waiting area.

The people in the room were exact replicas of her family physically, but acted nothing like her family. What was up with the love fest when she'd entered? She hadn't been gone an extended period of time or come from a war zone. Why weren't they grilling Sean? Why weren't they grilling her?

Discombobulated, she sat with Sean on one of the most uncomfortable pleather love seats ever made. Thankful Marshall would survive, she asked, "Have you heard anything from the police?"

Her father sat across from them on what she'd bet was the most uncomfortable pleather sofa ever made. "They have a list of all of the victims that they aren't releasing to the public yet. They don't know if the shooter was targeting the location, a business, a person, making a statement…"

"So basically, they know nothing except a lot of people were shot."

"Exactly. How are you doing, baby girl?"

"You look exhausted, Daddy. How are *you* doing?"

"Once my boy is out of surgery and the doctors give the all clear, I'll be fine. We could use a little good news about now. How was the wedding?"

"Incredible." She gave the family a rundown of the ceremony and reception and showed off photos.

"You looked as beautiful as ever." Her father handed her cell phone over to her.

"Thank you." She drew Sean's hand to her heart. "I have some good news I want to share." She gazed into Sean's eyes and her heart swelled with love. "Sean asked me to marry him, and I accepted."

The room burst into applause and congratulations. Now everyone suddenly became interested in Sean, but instead of grilling him, they welcomed him into the family. Grateful her family wasn't acting like her family, she pulled her father into the hallway for a one-on-one.

"Is something wrong, baby?"

"Yes, and no…" How could one ask why their family was behaving properly without sounding ungrateful that their family was acting properly? "I don't know how to say this."

"Just say it and we'll figure it out."

"What happened to everyone? They're all being nice instead of judgmental. Don't get me wrong. I like the change but it doesn't feel genuine. If that makes sense."

Her father let out a deep belly laugh that made her laugh.

"Did you just ask me why the family is on good behavior?"

Still tickled, she nodded. "I guess I did."

"Bertha's death brought a lot of things to light about the family." He took her hands into his. "You moved in with Edward, a man you barely knew, because your family wasn't supporting you."

"It wasn't sexual. I just needed a break."

"I know. We all know. Then you moved from Edward's across the country and don't plan to return. You and Bertha were the light of the family. We took you two for granted. We're tired of the darkness."

"Oh, Daddy…" Eyes filled with tears, she didn't know what to say.

"When I returned from Los Angeles, I set up family counseling."

"Really." Glad they sought help, but hurt she knew nothing about it, she buried her feelings. "You got the entire family to go?"

"Not the entire family, your brothers and sisters. We have a long way to go."

"Why didn't you tell me?"

Walking away from the waiting room, he said, "It's hard to explain. You were born so far after the others that it's like we have two sets of children. We weren't the same parents with your siblings as we were with you. The issues between us and your siblings are rooted in things that don't involve you. Fixing the relationship with them will be different than how we fix it with you." He slowly turned at the elevator bank and walked back toward the waiting room. "Try not to feel left out. Trust me, you'll be included. Just not yet."

"That makes perfect sense," she said, but it still hurt. She'd always been the outcast. Though she knew her family loved her, they never fully treated her as a member of the family. "All that hugging and kissing when I walked in. It didn't make sense. Don't get me wrong. I'll take the love, but it just didn't feel right."

"We also wanted to give you a break from the family. We want you back home, but being with us dimmed your light. That was a hard pill to swallow. Then someone shot Marshall. We knew you'd come home, but we will not have a repeat performance of the reactions after Bertha passed. I gathered everyone and told them things were going to change and if they couldn't handle it, to leave."

"Really?"

"You're a grown, intelligent woman, but we've all been treating you like a baby. You are the baby of the family, but not a baby. While you're in town, I told everyone to get to know you for the woman you've become." He stopped in front of the waiting room.

Beaming with pride, she joked, "So I've earned my grownup card."

"Yes, baby—" he stopped himself. "I guess I shouldn't call you baby."

"I'll always be your baby, Daddy." She wrapped her arms around him. "Thank you for being the best dad ever," she said with sincerity. Even though Bertha raised her, her father always went that extra mile to spend quality time with her and be her dad.

"Ever?"

"Yep. You and Granny were my sanity. Thank you for everything and thank you for getting the family under control."

"I should have never let it get so out of hand." He shook his head. "Like I said, your running away from home was a real eye opener to all of us."

"Running away from home?" She laughed. "Okay, I guess I did."

"We'd better get back inside."

Under no delusion that her family's good behavior would continue, but grateful for the reprieve, she re-entered the waiting room. In the end, you always returned to your nature. Not saying she didn't think the counseling would help. She just knew it wasn't magic or an overnight process.

A doctor was giving an update on Marshall's progress. She must have entered when they were walking off nervous energy. Outside of her parents and Marshall's children, he wouldn't be allowed visitors until tomorrow, so Benjamin told everyone to go home. Joy and Sean lingered around the room while the others left. She wanted to remain with her parents until Marshall was transferred from recovery to his room.

A suit-clad man with a badge she couldn't read stepped into the waiting area. "Judge, the doctors and police department are about to hold a press conference. Victim names will be released. Would you like to make a statement?"

"No thank you. I want to see my son."

The man nodded. "Fully understandable, sir."

"There's nothing you two can do. Go on and get some rest. I'll call when he wakes," her father said.

"I guess we should head on over to the hotel."

"Hotel?" Pain filled her mother's eyes. "Oh, I thought you might stay with us. I just wanted my baby close is all."

"I don't want to put you out."

Pain replaced by hope, her mother said, "You can't put us out. You know the code. We'll see you when we get home." She hugged Joy. "I love you."

"I love you, too."

The drive to her parents' home was silent for the most part. Comfortable silence, as opposed to the uncomfortable comradery in the hospital waiting room.

"That was... awkward." Sean pulled the Maxima into the drive of her parents' six- bedroom estate.

"So you noticed. It was like being surrounded by pod people."

He chuckled. "What do you know about *Invasion of the Body Snatchers*?" He turned off the car's ignition.

"Granny and I loved to watch old movies together. Daddy would come by on Saturdays, and we'd watch movies late into the night."

"Sounds like fun." He nodded toward the house. "I knew your Dad's a retired judge and your mom a retired doctor, but wow. This place is huge!"

Nestled in the middle of a five-acre lot, Warren Manor

could be on the cover of *Home Beautiful*. She'd spent many days swimming in the pool and playing on the tennis court. "I guess we should go on in." The modest three-bedroom home she grew up in looked like a shack compared to her parents' home. Sadness engulfed her.

At the door, her hand hovered over the keypad.

"You okay?" Sean, rolling their bags, approached.

"Don't pay me any never mind. I had a good life with my grandparents." She punched in the code.

He turned her to face him.

Life was good. Her brother would fully recover, her family was seeking help, she was engaged to a great man...

For the longest time, Sean didn't say anything. He just gazed into her eyes. "You loved living with your grandparents."

"Yes. I have no right to complain."

"Is this where your siblings were raised?"

"I think they moved here when Marshall was ten." She re-entered the code and opened the door. "Welcome to Warren Manor. Home to the king and queen of the land." Holding the door open, she stood to the side.

Rolling their bags, he stepped onto the marble flooring of the grand entrance. "This would be the perfect place to film the ball from Cinderella."

"Using a little hyperbole today, huh?" Smiling, she closed the door behind him.

"I'll tell the truth. I know you loved living with your grandparents, but if this were me, I would be resentful that my parents raised my siblings but didn't raise me. There were four of them and only one of you."

How could he know exactly how she felt? "I should be grateful I was raised in a good home. I am grateful. I wanted for nothing." She led him upstairs to one of the guest rooms. Her siblings had all moved out before she was born, so the house had numerous spare rooms. "It just hurts. You know?"

"I understand." He left their bags near the doorway, then crossed over to the bed and sat. "Come, sit with me."

"I can't believe I'm saying this, but I don't want to make love right now."

He laughed. "Okay, I think about sex the overwhelming majority of the time, but this isn't one of them." Hand held out to her, he said, "Come, I want to tell you a story."

She crossed over to him and accepted his hand. "Sorry for accusing you of being a horny toad."

"I am a horny toad, but my heart is hurting and needs a different type of love right now." He released her hand. "How about we call it an early night and just cuddle?"

Touched that he'd called her is heart, she nodded. "That sounds perfect." They'd come such a long way since they first met. No matter how crazy the world, as long as they had each other, everything would be all right.

After they stripped down to their underclothes, he closed the door and they crawled into bed. Dusk quickly approaching, soon the room would be in darkness.

He cupped her into his body. "I love you," he whispered into her ear.

"I love you, too." She turned her body to face him. "We have Granny to thank for our meeting. She was pretending to be me for months."

He chuckled. "You said she was a mess."

"The original hot mess." She shook her head. "I don't know why I'm so upset that I wasn't included in the family counseling. Daddy's right. I wasn't raised with my siblings. I don't know. I guess I just don't understand why they never wanted me."

"They love you."

"Loving and wanting are two different things."

Head rested on a pillow they shared, he said, "I want to tell you a bedtime story, a fairytale."

"You tell the best stories." She did love his stories, but she hoped this one wasn't the usual X-rated type he told. She had sulking to do.

"Once upon a time, in a land faraway, there was a commoner couple who dreamed of ruling the land. We'll call them Benjamin and Emily. People of their status were rarely allowed to do more than work in the castle, so the thought of them ever being rulers was preposterous to most. Ahead of their time, the couple ignored the naysayers and accomplished feats no one thought possible and became rulers of the land."

Her father making it to federal judge and her mother head of the maternity department who both happened to be Black and raised in a south that was torn by segregation and blatant racism was a sign of just how far ahead of the times her parents

194

were. Joy appreciated what her parents had gone through and also knew their struggles were why her mother thought choosing to be a mere grade school teacher was a step backward. In her mother's eyes, they hadn't fought so hard for their child to be average. At least that's how Joy saw it.

"After many hard years of work and fighting against the powers that be, King Benjamin and Queen Emily were ready to sit back and enjoy life, but there was a sadness in both. They'd been so focused on becoming rulers of the land that they'd missed out on much of their children's lives. Now their children were grown and looking to conquer lands of their own."

Joy always resented not being raised by her parents, but though her siblings lived with them, they weren't really raised by them either. The household staff did much of their raising.

"Queen Emily, not one to be beat, went to King Benjamin and said she wanted to have another baby. That this time things would be different. That she wanted to raise her child instead of being an observer. The king, a wise man, knew the queen wanted to raise a child today, but feared she would go back to her workaholic ways. Worried, he summoned Fairy Godmother Bertha for advice."

"Fairy Godmother Bertha agreed with the king, didn't she?"

"Yes ma'am. But the king wanted to make his queen happy, so he agreed to have another child," he held up a finger, "on the condition that the queen not work outside of the castle more than one day a week until the baby was old enough to attend princess school. Then she could work when the princess was in training. The king stressed that he did not want this baby to be raised by others. That he would devote more time to his little one, but he was not ready to give up his seat on the throne. That the queen must uphold her end of their compromise."

"That sounds like a great compromise. So far this story needs more conflict. I think you should go to the writing camp with me."

"Behave, my princess." He kissed her gently. "Or we'll never get to the part about the exceptionally handsome, sexy prince."

"Ooo, I'm intrigued. I'll be good." More than intrigued, she enjoyed the soft timbre of Sean's voice as it caressed her ears. She could listen to him talk all day and night.

"A year later, Queen Emily gave birth to the most beautiful princess ever born. Loose curls framed the baby's adorable face, chubby cheeks begged to be pinched and big expressive eyes captured everyone's heart. It's said that when people saw her, their hearts filled with joy."

"Aww, that's so sweet."

"Everything was going well, but within a few months, the queen realized that raising a child was more difficult than she'd thought. She loved the princess, but being a full- time mommy was just not what she'd thought it would be. Not used to failing, she needed something she knew she could do well to boost her ego. Though she'd promised only to work one day a week, she increased her schedule—with the blessing of the king—to two days a week. Fairy Godmother Bertha was happy to watch the princess an additional day, but warned the king and queen that she saw them both returning to their old ways and to be careful or history would repeat itself."

"History has a way of doing that, doesn't it?"

He nodded. "Indeed it does. With time, Queen Emily wanted to increase her hours outside of the castle to more than two days a week. Ashamed and disappointed that she no longer wanted to follow the extended terms of the compromise, she sought the advice of the sorcerer who lived on the edge of the land. He understood her needs and agreed to watch the princess while she worked the extra hours."

Joy thought back and didn't remember anyone taking care of her before her grandparents.

"All fairytales have a villain, and this one is no different. Unbeknownst to the queen, she'd left Princess Joy with an evil sorcerer who hurt the princess and left her with demons that haunted her."

"I don't remember a sorcerer. This isn't making sense." Darkness encompassed Joy, and not because the sun had gone down. Breathing ragged, her mind became jumbled. She could see a silhouette of a large man holding her hand, but it wasn't her hand. At least not her hand now. This was when she was small.

"Stay with me, my princess." Sean held her close. "Stay with me."

Focused on Sean's voice, she calmed. "I'm here."

"Fairy Godmother Bertha noticed Princess Joy's spirit had

dimmed. The king and queen had no answers to the change in the princess, but had also noticed the change. Determined to get to the bottom of what was going on with the princess, Fairy Godmother Bertha hired scouts to follow and keep an eye on the princess and report everything back to her. You still with me? Do you want to continue the story?"

"Yes. Please continue."

"The scouts were very good at what they do and brought Fairy Godmother evidence of the Sorcerer George harming the princess in unspeakable ways. Enraged, she had the sorcerer banished to the dungeon."

Tears dropped from Joy's eyes. "He molested me…"

He toyed with one of the curls by her ear "And you survived. Your great uncle wasn't the only one who suffered Bertha's wrath. She blamed your parents for what happened to you. They were in a vulnerable place, and she convinced them they were unfit and should sign custody of you over to her. That she had the time and wanted to raise you."

"Wait, wait, wait!" Joy sat up. "They signed custody of me away? How do you know all of this? You're making this up?"

"This story had a co-author." He pulled Joy back into his arms. "Did I ever tell you that Bertha called me?"

"Yeah, but…"

"Besides threatening me, she said that you were an excellent judge of character and should always follow your first mind. That she knew you'd chosen me so she was on Team Sean. She also said she didn't have much time on this earth."

"So you knew all along? Why didn't you tell me sooner?" she said out of curiosity, not anger.

"Bertha wasn't aware that you thought your parents didn't want you until shortly before your trip. She felt horrible that she hadn't realized it sooner. She was dying and didn't want to spend the last of her time with you sorting through what happened to you when you were three. She asked me to ask you to forgive her for being selfish, but she just wanted to enjoy her last days with you."

"There's nothing to forgive," she said honestly. "I'm glad we got to enjoy our final hours together."

"She said she was going to have to trust me to do the right thing. That if you ever mentioned your family not wanting you, I was to tell you what happened. That after your parents signed away custody, they had regrets and eventually tried to get you back, but Bertha had somehow outsmarted one of the top legal minds in the country. The custody agreement was ironclad."

Money. Bertha had a huge bank behind her from her books that her parents knew nothing about. Turned out Granny had a lot of secrets, Joy mused.

"Had they continued to fight for you, it would have gotten worse. She could have even kept them from you completely. She died regretting she hadn't given you back to your parents. That her protection had hurt you. In the end she felt she was no better than the rest of the family."

"Poor, Granny. This was all a big mess."

"Yes."

Refusing to give into the emotions trying to pull her down, she said, "As far as fairy tails go, your story sucked!"

Moonlight sparkled off the blue of his wide eyes. "What? You love my stories."

"I'm already depressed. Why would you tell me a story with a Grimm ending? I want a Disney ending where everyone lives happily ever after." Lips pursed, she said, "I thought we discussed this."

"Who says the story has ended. I never told you what happened with the exceptionally handsome, sexy prince, my impatient princess."

"Pardon, me. Please continue." She snuggled close.

"When the prince came to the land, he wasn't only exceptionally handsome and sexy. He was also extremely angry and bitter. Life had taught him not to trust. That people always let you down and there was no such thing as being in love."

"And I thought the princess had it bad."

"Against his better judgment, the prince had fallen in love with a young maiden. At least what he thought was love. He thought the young maiden returned his feelings. But alas, the young maiden turned out to be an evil witch who ripped out the prince's heart and chopped it up into tiny pieces."

Glad he was opening up to her, she said, "That's just horrible. I'd kick that witch's butt."

"Well, the prince didn't have a kick-butt princess at the time, so he protected himself the only way he knew how. He vowed never to give his heart to another. Sex felt good. His relationships would be based on sex. Over the years, the prince found his relationships weren't fulfilling. He needed more. He wanted someone who connected with him on levels outside of the bedroom. Someone he could debate with. Someone he could explore life with."

"I know someone who fits that bill!"

He chuckled. "Growing up, the princess's powers had grown."

"What powers?"

"Pay attention, princess." He tapped her nose. "As I was saying before I was so rudely interrupted. The princess's powers had increased over the years. When the prince met her, his heart filled with so much joy, that there was no room for the anger. He was now able to forgive and begin to heal from wounds of the past."

Her own heart melting, she hugged him. "I love you so much."

"You want to hear more?"

"Yes please."

"The prince knew the princess was special, and didn't want a relationship with her like he'd had in the past with others. With her he saw he could have more, so he did the impossible, he refused to have sex with her. All of his other relationships had been based on sex. He wanted this one to be based on something different." He covered her body with his. "This was no easy feat. The princess had the most luscious lips that were made for kissing." He nibbled her lips.

Lips tingling, she nibbled back.

"Umm, and she had real breasts." He nudged down her bra and suckled a nipple until it became hard. "What a treat. And don't get me started on her ass."

Joy laughed.

He rolled her over. "This wasn't any ordinary butt, but well-rounded and firm. The perfect consistency for the prince." He ground his hardness between her butt cheeks. "The prince wanted to make love with the princess so bad it hurt."

"I know how he feels." Aching with need, she pressed back into him.

"But he stuck to his guns until he knew he had healed enough from his past wounds to love her and be loved as they both deserved," he whispered into her ear.

"I like this story much better."

"The prince asked the princess to marry him, and…"

He nudged the crotch of her panties to the side, then pressed his hardness into her slowly. No longer caring about the end of the story, she accepted everything he had to give. "Ummm…" How could something so simple feel so good? she wondered. "Why did you stop?" she moaned more than said.

"Savoring…"

"Torture…"

Pulling out as slowly as he'd entered, he whispered, "You want torture. Try having the princess without literally having the princess." Re-entering, he suckled the rim of her earlobe. "You didn't make it easy for me. Now that was torture."

Heat and softness from his mouth, his slow lunges… he was driving her mad. Two could play at this game. Her hand traveled along the inside of his leg. Unable to reach her target, she turned her body slightly.

"What are you doing?"

Fingers at the base of his scrotum, with a slow, gentle pinch, she gathered the flesh between her fingers and released several times.

"Oh God." He pumped faster, harder.

Body humming, she grasped onto the bedding with one hand and stimulated Sean with the other. She'd found this spot when exploring his body. He'd been as shocked as her at his reaction.

"Stop, stop. You're going to make me come. I give. No more torture."

She released him.

"Damn that was too good." He rolled her over, then pushed into her again. "But I want to see your face when you come."

Legs wrapped around his thighs, she matched him stroke for stroke. Too good was right. Making love with Sean felt too good to be true. Body tightening around his, she tightened her stomach muscles to pull him in as deep as she could.

"That's it, princess. Come for me." Pulling out slightly with each stroke, he lifted her leg and trapped it under his arm.

Changing the angle sent her over the edge. Senses spinning in delight, she cried out.

Grunting, he quaked as they climaxed together.

Breathing ragged, heart pounding, her hearing returned

slowly.

He brushed his lips over hers and kissed her gently, then lay and drew her onto his body.

"Incredible..." Sprawled across him, she laid her head on his shoulder. "You are incredible."

"I was just thinking the same thing about you." He slowly ran his hand from her lower back to the base of her neck. "I'm starving."

"That makes two of us. You took a lot out of me." Smiling, she said, "Your story really improved there at the end. For a while I was worried."

"I aim to please."

"Seriously, though. The way you opened up to me meant a lot."

"I thought I was in love before, but was wrong. This is what being in love is all about. I want to share everything with you."

Eyes accustomed to the moonlight, she looked into his face. "I thank God for sending the angry, white prince my way. It's time for our happily ever after."

"To our happily ever after." He pulled her into a kiss.

Chapter Twenty-Two

The next morning...

By Edward's calculations, Joy would arrive late this afternoon. She only took early flights and wouldn't have rushed back across the country for the brother she didn't like. Still upset Alonzo had altered the plan, he barked into the burner phone. "Why couldn't you just do as I asked?"

"Boy, who do you think you're talking to?" Alonzo snapped. "I love you like a son and will beat you like I would my son. You hear me?"

"I'm sorry. It's just..." He gazed out the car window toward Warren Manor. "I needed Jonathan out of the picture. He'll try to stop Joy from being with me."

"I'm saving you from yourself. What is the first thing you think the police ask the family after the shooting? I'll tell you. Do you know of anyone who would want to harm the victim? Who are his enemies? Has he had any major disagreements with anyone lately? Joy is a witness to you and Jonathan butting heads. Had Jonathan been shot, the cops would have her thinking you were involved. As long as you don't start acting like a stalker, she's yours."

"I guess you have a point. I'm sorry." Edward hated being wrong almost as much as he hated not being in control. "Where are you? I went by your place last night."

"If for some reason the cops try to follow my trail, according to this resort, I was checked in and ordering room service at the time of the shooting. I shouldn't need an alibi, but I still wanted one. I'm getting rid of this burner phone. I'll call you when I get back to town in a few weeks."

"Thanks again."

"Take care." The line went dead.

Alonzo was right. Taking out Jonathon would have been a mistake. A mass shooting was the perfect cover. Now all he needed was for Joy to come home to him so he could comfort her as her family couldn't. Last time he'd pushed too hard. He'd have to figure out a way to give her space without giving her freedom.

He drove onto the private drive and up to the home. Benjamin and Emily were early risers, so they would probably be getting ready to head to the hospital. He needed to show his face before Joy arrived to give the illusion that he was there for the family.

Parked in the circular drive, he headed up to the house. At the door, he drew in and released several calming breaths before he rang the bell. This was it. His chance to make a good impression on Benjamin, who didn't like him any better than Jonathan did.

"Hello… Edward." Joy smiled. "What a surprise."

"Joy… What are you doing here?"

Brows drawn in, she looked at him like he'd lost his mind. "Umm, my parents live here." She thumbed behind herself. "Want me to leave?"

"Oh, oh, I'm sorry." He pulled her into an embrace. "I was just shocked to see you." He released her. "I just heard about Marshall and came by to see if there was anything I could do for your parents. I know they must be going crazy." Her smile returned and his heart sang. She'd missed him. He knew it. When she thought he wasn't happy to see her, she'd been hurt.

"They're at the hospital. I was just about to whip up some three-cheese omelets or scrambled eggs depending on how they look when I finish. Are you hungry?" She fully opened the heavy oak door and let him in.

"I was finishing up breakfast when I saw the news, so I'll pass. Thanks though."

"Well, I have onions and peppers to chop."

In the kitchen, he sat at the table. "Do you need help?" He'd missed coming home to a hot meal. After a long day of work, seeing her dance around the kitchen as she finished preparing dinner was just what he'd needed.

"I've got it. Thanks." She washed off a red bell pepper in the sink, then joined him at the table with a cutting board and knife.

"So how is your writing camp coming along?"

"I love it!" She went on to tell him just how much.

The excitement in her voice invigorated him in ways he'd need Angie for after he left. Glad Joy had found a passion she could do from home, he'd be sure to research writing coaches. Once they were married, she could quit her job and write full-time.

"We sent in the manuscript we wanted to work on before

the camp. Now that we're a few weeks into our lessons, they'll be giving us the developmentally edited manuscript. I'm worried. Now that I know more, I know I have a long way to go. My manuscript will probably be more red than anything else."

"But you can turn it around."

Smiling, she nodded. "Thank you." Done cutting the peppers and onions, she set them to the side.

"I thought you were making three-cheese omelets. Where's the cheese?"

"Yeah, we noticed. Sean went to the store for the cheese. I can't wait for you to meet him."

Did she just say her friend Sean was a him? No he couldn't have heard right.

"You okay?"

This was not the time to overreact. So what if this Sean was male. That would end after they were married. "Yes, yes. I'm fine."

Some tall guy walked into the kitchen like he owned the place.

"Sean, this is Edward." Joy wiped her hands on the hand towel, then rushed over and grabbed the bags from the guy. "Edward, this is my fiancé, Sean."

Fiancé, fiancé. No she did not just say fiancé. Holding his anger at bay, Edward stood to shake hands. No, Joy wouldn't do this to him. She loved him. This guy was manipulating her. Innocent and naïve, she didn't stand a chance. He should have stopped her from going to Los Angeles. He'd failed her.

"Pleased to finally meet you." Sean held out his hand.

The jerk had the audacity to say that with a smile. Edward would be sure to wipe that smug look off his face permanently. "The pleasure is all mine." He shook. "I have a long day ahead of me. I hate to rush off, but I should go. Enjoy your breakfast."

Blinded by rage, Edward could barely make it to his car. No way would he let that asshole steal Joy. When you loved someone, you didn't let them go. His family hadn't loved him. They'd just given him away. Well, he'd finally found love and wouldn't let it go. He'd fight for it. Joy needed him.

Seething, he raced his car from Warren Manor. Sean had to go, but first he needed to put Joy somewhere safe. She'd be angry with him at first, but with time, she'd see he was right and forgive him.

A few miles away, his plan came to him. He pulled out his cell phone and looked up the closest branch of his bank, then called Angie.

"Hello, Edward."

"Hey, I'm about to deposit a hundred grand in your personal account. I don't have access to your account, but I need you to do something for me."

"As long as you don't want me to kill anyone, sure."

He liked this whore. She had her head on straight. "It's my girl. She's been..." he trailed off. "I don't even know how to explain it. I need somewhere to keep her safe. She's going to be pissed with me. Probably call me every name in the book and make up new names, but I need you to only listen to me. I love her. I'm saving her."

"Oh my God, what happened? Of course I'll help."

Her sincerity touched him. Even a common whore could recognize true love. "I'll put extra in your account. I need you to start preparing your basement. Joy deserves the best. Do you hear me? I don't want her to feel like she's in a prison."

"Maybe you should just talk to her."

"That's not going to work." He headed toward the bank. "After we get the place set up and I drop her off, I'll have to stay away for a few months. I'm sure I'll be a person of interest. I'll bring a few burner phones to you."

"Are you sure you want to go this route. Once you're in, there's no turning back."

"I love her. I'm willing to risk everything to protect her."

"You're the boss. How will you explain me?"

"While she's in the house, we can't fuck. At least not on premises. I'd never disrespect her like that. I guess I'll tell her you're my cousin."

Angie's laughter filled the line. "Umm, you know I'm Black, right?"

"There are lots of mixed families out there."

"Okay, but maybe you should say I'm an old friend of the family."

"I haven't gotten this all figured out yet. I'll think of something. I'll be there to help prepare the place. If you want out, let me know now. I can give you twenty grand to just walk away, but I'll need the place back."

"Like I said, as long as there's no killing involved, I'm in."

"If you try to double cross me, I'll kill you. You can't run far enough away. That's a promise."

"I understand."

* * *

It's good to be home. So much greatness had happened since they'd left that Charlene was overwhelmed, but in a good way. Thankful for the abrupt turn her life had taken, she was afraid she'd wake at any moment to find it was all a dream. A giggle escaped her.

A gentleman, Tony looped his arm around hers and escorted her along the petunia- lined walkway to the house. "What's so funny?"

"Who knew Prince Charming was the boy next door?"

Smiling, he unlocked the front door to their home. "Do not even think about going inside." He kissed her, then ran back to the car and rolled their bags into the house.

Eyes narrowed on her husband, she folded her arms over her chest. "What are you up to?"

"You'll see." He returned to her and picked her up.

"What are you doing?"

"Be still. You're heavier than you look."

She smacked him on the arm. "I didn't tell you to pick me up."

He carried her over the threshold and set her down. "You're my wife now. I was performing my husbandly duties."

Laughing, she hugged him. "I can't believe we're married." She gazed into his eyes. "I love you so much I don't know what to do. I'm happy. Truly happy for the first time in my life."

Holding her close, he whispered, "That makes two of us."

Frisky, she lifted her skirt and pulled down her panties. "Speaking of husbandly duties. Isn't it your duty to keep me sexually sated? I've been home thirty whole seconds, and you've…" Shoulders hunched, she shook her head. "We'll, I guess I'll have to pleasure myself." She slipped her finger between her legs and circled her clit.

In the ride from the airport, he'd been a distracted driver because he'd been trying to make her come. His fingers had worked her into a frenzy, then they'd arrived home and she'd been taken aback by how far she'd come.

Ready to continue what he'd started, she slipped a finger into herself. "All wet and no dick to ride."

206

"I want to fuck you so bad right now."

"Talk is cheap."

He kicked off his shoes and took off his pants and boxers so quickly, his shadow could barely keep up. He backed her against the entry wall into his hanging coats.

Hands on his shoulders, she squealed in delight as his dick slammed up into her again and again. "Yes, yes…" Legs wrapped around him and back pressed into the coat- cushioned wall, she fucked the man she loved and enjoyed every second of it.

Breathing ragged and climax close, she moaned as her body tightened around his.

Grunting, he plunged harder and harder until they both cried out.

* * *

Fresh out of the shower and dressed in robes, Charlene plopped onto the bed with Tony. "I need two naps." She snuggled under the light blanket with him. They hadn't decided to stay in Atlanta or start somewhere fresh. She was leaning the same way as Tony—move. Hopefully to the West Coast so Edward wouldn't think she was worth the trouble to follow.

"I could use three." He reached over her for the remote control, then flipped on the television. "Hey, that's Joy's dad."

"Who?"

He pointed at the screen. "That's Judge Warren. Joy's father." He turned up the volume.

They watched the snippets of a press conference given earlier and updates from the local police. The more she learned about the mass shooting, the more she knew Edward had to be behind it. Trembling uncontrollably, she burst out in tears.

"What's wrong?" Tony held her close. "Charlene…?"

"It's… It's…" How could she have stayed with such a monster so long? How had she ever thought she loved him? Somewhere between her mind and mouth, her words got lost. "It's… I feel…"

"I feel awful, too. I know there's nothing we can do to help, and they probably have everyone bothering them. I don't know. We'll figure out something to do for support that won't be intrusive. The Warrens are good people."

"No." She shook her head. "No." Pointing at the television, she eked out, "It's Edward. He did this."

"What?" He released her. "What would make you think Edward's behind the shooting?" He turned off the television.

"He's insane."

"Agreed, but that doesn't make him a mass shooter."

"He's obsessed with Joy. There's no way he knew she was going to Los Angeles. He's so controlling, her leaving like that must have pushed him over the edge. The best way to bring her home would be to harm someone in her family."

"But a mass shooting? How could he pull it off?"

"He knows people." Hands to her heart, she said, "Every nerve in my body is screaming tell the police everything, including C'Money's murder."

Eyes wide, Tony shook his head. "No. You can tell them about your suspicions, but they might think you had something to do with C'Money's murder."

"If I go to the police telling them I 'feel' Edward is behind the mass shooting, they'll laugh me out of the precinct. I have to give them something."

Tony ran his fingers through his hair. "Give me time to think."

More than willing to give Tony time to accept what was to happen, Charlene had a lot of thinking of her own to do. Who could Edward have called to pull this off? He was a monster. If the judge's son had been beaten, she'd say Edward had done it himself. He loved boxing and had a hard time finding sparring partners because he often took things too far, but he was not a sharpshooter.

Tony hopped off the bed, snatched his pants off the chair and pulled out his cell phone. "I know who can help."

* * *

Self-conscious, Charlene straightened her blouse and slacks. "Okay, I'm ready."

Tony allowed Joy's parents into the house. "Thank you for agreeing to meet with us on such short notice. I know this is a difficult time for you." He motioned toward Charlene. "This is my wife, Charlene. Charlene, this is Judge Warren and his wife Dr. Warren."

The older couple nodded. "Pleased to meet you."

"The pleasure's all mine. I just wish it had been under better circumstances. May I offer you something to drink?" Charlene backed into the living area. Tony had said the judge was laid back, but that didn't mean he hung out with former prostitutes. Anxious, she drew in a few deep breaths. "We're just returning home from a trip, so we don't have much. Water or coffee is it."

"I'm fine," said the judge, "and please call us Emily and Ben."

Forcing herself to relax, she motioned toward the sofa. "Please take a seat." They would or wouldn't believe her. Once she told them the truth, the ball was in their court to do with what they please. Her conscious would then be clear.

Tony drew her hand to his heart and softly said, "Everything will work out. I promise." They sat together on the loveseat.

"You were saying you think you know who's behind the shooting," Benjamin said.

She liked a man who didn't beat around the bush. Now she needed to do the same, she mused. "I'm afraid so." She looked from Joy's parents to Tony. Words quickly becoming lost again, she drew in an additional deep calming breath that was none too calming.

"It's okay." Tony caressed her face. "You're not alone. Just start from the beginning."

Charlene faced Joy's parents. "I'm sorry. I know this is a trying time for you and I'm just making it harder." *Cut to the chase.* "I'm afraid Edward is behind the mass shooting."

"What?" Emily shook her head. "No. You're wrong. Why would he do such a thing?"

Charlene noticed the judge didn't look the least bit shocked. Seeing the judge was already leery of Edward, she focused on him as she told her story from the time she was a prostitute for C'Money, to Edward murdering him. Grateful the judge seemed to believe her, she relaxed.

"Why didn't you go to the police?" Emily asked.

"Who would believe a whore over a respected doctor? He reminded me of this every day for years. Now I realize it was his way of keeping me in line."

"This is insane. It's too much." Emily shook her head. "You can't be right. He's not that monster anymore. You've changed, he could have changed also."

"Be quiet, Emily," the judge barked. "Stop defending that bastard." He nodded at Charlene. "Please continue."

She explained about Edward becoming obsessed with Joy and admitted she'd taken the job at the school to scope Joy out.

"See, it's you who wanted to harm my baby." Emily pointed at Charlene. "I'll have you arrested."

Eyes narrowed on his wife, the judge warned, "I will not tell you to be quiet again." He faced Charlene. "I apologize. Please continue. There is no need to fear. You will not be the one going to jail any time soon."

"Thank you." No tiptoeing around the facts. She told how she started out with ill intent but became friends with Joy. Her past relationship with Tony and how they fell in love also made it into her retelling of events. Then she went back to Edward. How he'd threatened them and how his controlling obsessive ways could have led to him hiring someone to pull off the mass shooting. "One of his patients... Alonzo something. He used to talk about him all the time. He used to be a hitman. He's an old man now, so I doubt he did the shooting, but if Edward hired someone, he'd go through Alonzo to get him."

Shaking his head, the judge stood and paced about. "I can't believe we put the baby in harm's way again."

"She's wrong!" Emily rushed over to her husband. "She has to be wrong."

Confused, Charlene watched the two argue back and forth. What baby?

"You're the one who left her in the clutches of your fucking perverted uncle. You were supposed to stay home with her and leave her with Bertha when you were at work, but no. You had to do things your way."

"How was I supposed to know?" she shot back.

"Had you done what you'd promised, or hell, perhaps not hide what the hell you were doing like a fucking child, she wouldn't have been molested. Now you've thrown her into the hands of this nut job."

Uncomfortable overhearing their argument, Charlene looked to Tony. "I think we should give them their privacy." They began to stand.

"No. Stay," the judge said without looking their way.

All choked up, Emily cried, "She has to be wrong."

"She's not. And this time it's just as much my fault. I didn't like Edward from day one. I was totally against him having anything to do with Joy, but I sat back like an idiot. What the hell?" He returned to pacing about. "It was my job to protect her. When the hell did I hand my balls over to you?" He faced his wife. "Those days are over. I'm taking my shit back now." Turning toward Charlene, he pulled out his cell phone. "You don't have to worry about anything. I still have connections. I'm about to get you full immunity, and if it turns out Edward has anything to do with the mass shooting, he'll pray to get sent to hell after I get to him."

Chapter Twenty-Three

On a scale that went from sucky to the worse article ever written, Sean's article was closer to the sucky end of the spectrum, but that the article could be on the scale at all bothered him to no end.

Staring at the computer monitor did nothing to improve the article. As a matter of fact, watching the screen made things worse. He could see Edward's reaction to him playing as if a bad sitcom about a stalker. Now he fully understood why Joy was put off by the man. Forgoing the age difference, he was just evil.

It wasn't in what Edward said or even how he acted, but in his eyes. Edward wanted Joy to be his. Sean understood that. The engagement was an unpleasant surprise. Sean got that. Sean even understood why Edward wouldn't like him, but what he saw in that man's eyes went well past dislike, jealousy or anything normal. Hate.

Sean had never been an angel, and there were plenty of people who didn't like him. But hate? He was just getting a full understanding of how strong an emotion hate was.

He scrolled to the beginning of the article. It wasn't due until tomorrow. Maybe he should let it sit a while and come back to it. He shut down Microsoft Word and switched over to the Internet. He hadn't been online in… He couldn't remember the last time he'd entered the chat rooms.

… Angry White Man has entered community room thirteen

Easy Money: Oh hell, here we go. Just when the women started hanging out again, here comes trouble.

Angry White Man: I know you've all missed me.

… Cherry Delight has left community room thirteen

Easy Money: Go away. You're chasing off the women again.

Baby Girl: AWM, what did you do to Sweet Thang? We haven't seen her in weeks.

Smiling, he couldn't wait to tell the crew how much things had changed for him.

Angry White Man: I need to change my username. I'm no longer angry. I'm Happily Ever After White Man. Yeah, that's the ticket.

Baby Girl: And what of Sweet Thang. She disappeared the same time as you. Was it a coincidence or do I need to call the police on you?

Angry White Man: Who do you think I'm engaged to?

Baby Girl: No way!

Easy Money: You lyin' and I don't even care as long as you don't chase away the ladies. XQQQME, you want to hook up? I can come to you.

XQQQME: Go away, Easy Money. Congrats to you and Sweet Thang, AWM. I knew there was something going on between you two.

His cell phone rang.

Angry White Man: She's trying to call. I'm sorry I acted like such a jerk.

He exited the chat room and answered his cell. "Hey, beautiful." He switched the phone to speaker and set it on the desk.

"Hey, handsome, how's the article coming along?"

"It's coming." Thinking he may need to tackle the article from a different angle, he looked at the notepad.

"That doesn't sound good."

"I'll get it together." He tossed his notes to the side. "How's Marshall?"

"You know how a near-death experience changes some people?"

Nodding, he said, "I've heard it does quite often."

"Well, Marshall was a jerk before he got shot and is still one. I needed a breather, so I thought you'd like to have a mid-afternoon snack with me, but—"

"But nothing," he cut in. "A mid-afternoon snack is exactly what I need. Preferably one that leaves us naked and sexually sated." Blood rushed to his dick and set it to throbbing.

"You are such a horny toad."

Light laughter filled the line and his heart. Whether talking, debating, planning their life together, making love or fucking, Joy was his end all and be all. Amazed at how much his life had changed since he allowed her into it, he couldn't express how much he loved her and what they had in words. Words just weren't powerful enough.

213

"It's all your fault that I'm like this. As a matter of fact, I want to taste you right now." Hardening, he stroked the bulge in his jeans. "I have a confession to make. That first night we chatted." Uncomfortable, he unzipped his pants. "When you finally came out of your shell and challenged my mind, I knew I was done."

"I wasn't in a shell. Granny was pretending she was me."

"And I love her for it." He leaned back in the leather office chair. Just as on that first night, he could feel Joy's curious fingers roaming his body. "How far away are you from the house?"

"Are you gratifying yourself?" she said without the least bit of judgment in her voice, reaffirming how perfect for him she was.

"Pull over. I want to make you come."

"Oh no you don't. You're not getting me arrested for public lewd behavior."

"I have bail money."

"Cute, but not today."

He freed his throbbing member. "I really wish you were here."

"I may go back to the hospital. We'll be in bed all afternoon, and you'll miss your deadline."

"So I'm on my own…" Hand wrapped around the base of his dick, he worked his way up. "Your hands are so much better at this than I am. And your mouth. Damn…"

"Umm, I love that little salty treat that forms at the tip of your dick. And the brim. Taking my tongue around, exploring… Do you have pre-cum on your tip?"

"Yes."

"Use your finger to spread it around the bulb."

Eyes closed, he followed her instructions. In his mind, his fingertip was replaced by her tongue. His hand replaced by her hand, slowly stroking.

"Tell me your favorite sexual fantasy that you are afraid of telling me."

"You first."

She giggled. "I guess I should go first. I would love to have sex in a crowded place without others knowing."

"That's a good one. Mine isn't nearly as exciting."

"Tell me."

214

"I dream of working and you come in and fuck me. No foreplay, no hello. You just rip off my pants and fuck me like your life depended on it."

"Now that sounds doable!"

He stroked harder, faster. "Damn, I love you."

"You know what I love? I love watching you come. There's just something about that cum shooting out of your dick and splashing against your chest that excites me. The next time I see you I'm going to pull down your pants and suck your dick. Then when you're just about ready to come, I'm—"

"Oh shit…" His balls constricted and nerve endings sang out.

"Come for me. I want to hear you moan."

Breathing ragged, he stroked with one hand and covered his dick with the other to prevent the hot, sticky cum from splashing onto the furniture. "Ummm…."

"That's it. Music to my ears."

Hands a mess, he took a few seconds to calm. "Next time I see you, I'm going to make you come so hard you cry." He snatched a few tissues out of the Kleenex box to wipe his hands.

"Yeah, yeah, tell me anything. I think I'll stop by the sex shop."

"Not without me! I want to come."

Laughing, she said, "You need to clean yourself up and finish your article. If you're a good boy, I'll drop by and show you the goodies I get at the sex shop."

"You're right. I need to wash up. Call me when you get to the sex shop and tell me about the goodies. Facetime me and I'll help you choose something."

"I think this is something I can do on my own. Love you."

"Love you, too." He disconnected, then jogged upstairs to shower and change into fresh jeans and a T-shirt. *Life couldn't be better*, he mused.

Just as he finished dressing, the doorbell rang. Joy had the code to the door, so she wouldn't ring the bell. Unless… Hoping it was Joy there to do a little role-play, he rushed downstairs and answered.

"Hey…" Upon seeing Edward instead of Joy, his happy mood disappeared. "Hello, Edward. Sorry, but the Warrens are at the hospital."

"Is Joy around?"

"No, did you want to leave a message?"

"Actually, I was hoping we could speak. May I come in?"

"Sure." Speaking with Edward wasn't the last thing Sean wanted to do. Speaking with him was something he didn't want to do at all, but he might as well get it over with. After Edward's performance at breakfast, Sean had a feeling he'd be lurking around. The guy had stalker material written all over him. This was as good a time as any to find out where Edward's mind was and ensure Joy wasn't in danger.

Sean closed the door behind Edward. "Can I take your jacket?"

"Thank you, but I won't be long."

"Would you like something to drink?" Sean didn't like Edward, but no one could accuse him of being a bad host. "I could use a Sprite, but there's Pepsi, various juices, water. Coffee perhaps?" He led Edward into the kitchen.

Once the Warren children left home, there was no longer a need for a live-in maid, so Sean and Joy had cleaned the kitchen back into its spotless glory after they ate breakfast. He sure could use some of Joy's cooking about now. Sex over the phone or in person tended to make him hungry and Joy could throw down in the kitchen. Growing up with her grandmother, she'd spent many hours in the kitchen watching then helping Bertha cook until eventually Joy did all of the cooking. He'd have to start working out more to ensure he didn't gain a million pounds.

"No thanks." Edward stood at the oversized preparation island in the center of the room.

Sean grabbed a Sprite out of the refrigerator, then joined Edward. "So what did you need?" He popped open the can.

"Since Bertha's passing, Joy's had a difficult time adjusting. She's been acting out."

"Isn't she a little old to be acting out?" Sean wasn't born yesterday. This manipulative prick considered anything Joy did without his permission "acting out."

"Bertha was her world and a soft-handed guidance that Joy needs."

"Bertha raised her. Of course she took her opinion into consideration when making decisions, but what does that have to do with why you're here?"

Hate momentarily flashed in Edward's eyes. He nodded and held his hands up slightly. "I'm a patient man," he said calmly. "A patient man who is in love with Joy and understands she's confused right now. I also understand that you took—are taking advantage of her."

"Me?" Hand to his chest, Sean set the can of soda on the island before he began laughing and dropped it. "I'm the one taking advantage of her? Her grandmother died, and you swooped in like a fucking vulture for a carcass. This is ridiculous. Why am I wasting my breath on you?"

"You'll never be good enough for Joy."

"Maybe not, but that's not your decision to make. At the end of the day, Joy chose me, not your old ass. Get over it." Sean walked around the island and headed for the door. "It's time for you to leave."

"You fucking son of a bitch."

"Dude…" Sean turned and was stopped by Edward pointing a gun at him.

"You think because you're younger than me I won't fight for what's mine?"

Having a gun aimed at his head was not Sean's normal, but he'd never let Edward know that. "You're the one hiding behind a gun. Drop the gun and let's do this."

Nodding, Edward backed up. "To show mercy, I was going to put you down like the rabid dog you are, but if you'd rather I beat the life out of you with my bare hands, so be it." He set the gun on the island, then charged Sean.

Running wasn't an option. Bracing himself for the hit, Sean lowered slightly. He hadn't played football since high school, but remembered how to be tackled without being taken out. The force of Edward running into him knocked the wind out of Sean, but not so much that he couldn't hold onto him and take him down to the floor. Turning them as they fell, he made sure Edward would be on the bottom.

"Stop fighting." Having Edward down and subdued were two different things. Sean didn't know his next move. He didn't want to hurt Edward, but Edward was making it hard.

"What the hell's going on?" Joy screamed as she entered the kitchen.

Caught off guard, Sean looked toward her voice. Opening his mouth to warn her, he was stopped by Edward laying a mean uppercut from below, causing him to bite his tongue. Tongue smarting and chin hurting, Sean couldn't talk and could barely keep Edward from landing another blow.

"Edward!" Joy stomped toward the two.

"Get cops," Sean barked. Thankfully, Joy ran out of the room before Edward could work his way from under him. Keeping Edward away from Joy until help arrived was Sean's only focus. No more Mr. Nice Guy. Joy was in danger.

Edward may have fifteen years on Sean, but he was also fast, strong and apparently worked out regularly. Edward rose just a hair faster than Sean, which was enough time for him to grab a chair swing it at Sean before he could prepare for it. A direct hit to the side of the head sent Sean to the floor. This time Edward was on top and showed no mercy.

* * *

Scared and confused, Joy returned to the kitchen with her father's .45 caliber pistol and saw Edward choking Sean. "Get away from him!"

Hands still around Sean's neck, Edward directed his rage at Joy. "You let this fucking punk touch you! I'll kill your worthless ass." Pushing Sean down, he charged toward Joy.

Eyes closed tightly, she pointed the gun forward and squeezed the trigger. The bang of the gun was so loud it made her ears ring. The floor vibrated from the thump of Edward hitting it. Praying she had just stopped his advance, she turned to see how badly she'd hit him. Before she could see, Sean grabbed her into his arms and held her close.

"Don't look, baby. He's dead." He took the gun from her.

Trembling, she uttered, "Oh God. Oh God. I killed him." Crying uncontrollably, her mind spun out of control. "What have I done?" She tried to look around Sean, but he guided her out of the room, then set the gun on the entry table.

Blood, she'd seen lots of blood on the floor and Edward's arm. "Oh my God. What have I done?"

Her face cupped between his hands, Sean gazed into her eyes. "Listen to me. You saved my life. You saved us. That's all that matters." He kissed her gently. "I'm sorry it wasn't the other way around. I should have saved you." He embraced her.

"You stopped him."

"I did my best."

"No, you held him. You stopped him. He would have killed us all. He went mad."

Lost in what had just happened, she somehow ended up

on the front porch swing being held by Sean when ambulances, police and her parents arrived. Everyone spoke too fast and at once. She just couldn't comprehend what she'd seen or what she'd done. One second she's bringing in a bag of goodies from the sex shop for her and Sean to enjoy. The next Edward was trying to kill Sean and then came after her.

"Joy… Joy… Talk to me."

"Daddy?" When had her father arrived and why was he kneeling in front of her. Oh yeah, she remembered, they'd arrived when the police had. Tears fell from her eyes. "I killed him."

He pulled her off the rocking swing into his arms. "I just thank God it wasn't you who was killed."

Epilogue

Eighteen months later…

One of Sean's favorite past times had become watching Joy sleep, especially now that she rarely woke with nightmares of Edward's misdeeds. He still had a hard time believing what had happened.

Had it not been for Alonzo Montoya's arrogance, they may still not have the whole story. Though retired, Judge Warren was still a powerful man—and intelligent. To learn Montoya's level of involvement, he'd had the police release his DMV picture to the press as a "possible witness" of the shooting and asked viewers to contact the authorities if they had any information on the "mystery man."

Infuriated the authorities continued to harass a man who had served his time, Montoya had sent them his proof of an alibi. The alibi would have been airtight had several witnesses to the shooting not sent in videos with Montoya at the scene. One young man had even said they had a conversation.

Joy eased over to Sean's side of the bed and cuddled close to him. They still had a ways to go, but they would make it. Since having his ass handed to him by a "more mature" man, Sean had added martial arts to his workout routine. Joy pointed out, several times, that Edward's background set the odds in his favor in a fight. That it hadn't been a fair fight. Logically, he knew she was correct, but that didn't diminish his feelings of failure. If the time ever came again, he'd be able to protect her.

Waking, she stretched her arms forward. "Good morning…"

"Good morning." This was another highlight of his day. He'd wake early to watch her stretch like a cat. The higher her butt rose, the harder his manhood became. Today, their first wedding anniversary, was no different.

Slowly, he ran his hand along her bare spine to the small of her back as she reached the top of her stretch. Butt cupped, he squeezed ever so lightly. Firm, with just enough give, he had no idea how much of a butt man he was until Joy. Maybe by their next anniversary, she'd be ready to try anal sex. Over the past few months, he'd slipped a knuckle in a few times and she hadn't reacted, which was better than a negative reaction.

Lying flat on her stomach, the sweetest most innocent smile tipped her lips. His sweet thang had sexual mischief on the mind, and he loved it in her.

Unable to resist, he laid a trail of kisses that followed the route his hand had taken. "Time for your anniversary gift," he whispered into her ear. He knew exactly what she wanted, but thought wasn't possible to achieve. She'd been fascinated every time they saw it. If everything worked as planned, she'd see the impossible become possible. If things didn't work out as planned, she'd have the best sex of her life. Sounded like a win-win situation to him.

"What is it?"

"You'll see." From behind, he spread her legs, then pressed the head of his dick into her hot, wet walls. Remaining shallow, he slowly pulled out and pressed back in several times.

Her back arched, a move she did when she wanted him to go deeper, but today he wouldn't oblige. Not yet. Wrapped in her moist heat, he wanted to sink completely, but couldn't.

Leaning on his arms, he suckled along her shoulder, clavicle, neck, up to her ear, all the while continuing his slow, shallow stroke. Glad the additional working out was paying off, he'd keep going until he thought he'd come.

* * *

Joy loved her husband and had told Sean several times not to torture her. Of course she didn't mean it. Body humming, this type of sexual torture drove her wild in all the right ways.

He pulled out completely and straddled her.

"What are you doing?" she asked lazily.

He massaged her neck and shoulders. "Relax. Enjoy."

Hum increasing, he'd get no complaints. She could hardly wait to give him his anniversary gift. She'd been preparing for months. Two things no one could truthfully deny were her gifts as a student and teacher. She'd researched and learned everything she needed to know and was ready to teach him a thing or two.

Best massage ever completed, love, desire and passion burned in his eyes as he lay beside her and drew her close. Ready for him to nibble her bottom lip, he switched things up and licked instead while slipping a finger into her.

Tongue and finger playing the same game, he pressed her against the bed and showed her why she couldn't get enough of his kissing. Flicking and rubbing her clit, his thumb joined the action. Moaning in pleasure, she gyrated.

"That's it." Finger play and kisses still pushing her to the edge, he used his free hand to knead and caress her breast. Nipple aching for relief, he knew the perfect moment to take her breast into his hot mouth.

"Yes..." Fingers weaved through his hair, she fought to let the torture continue. Patience had never been her strong suit, but today, she'd make saints envious.

Fingers working their magic, he tasted little nips of her skin from between her breast down to her panty line. Anxious to see what he'd do next, she propped up on her elbows.

"Relax."

This time she'd continue to do as her husband asked—this time. Sunken deep into the bedding, she'd swear her nerve endings had nerve endings and they were all immersed in an ecstasy bath.

He lowered his mouth to her inner thighs and indulged, working his way up and joined his fingers in play. His tongue looped around her clit and sent her whirling.

Back pressed against the bed to keep from taking off, she cried out.

He flattened her clit with the tip of his tongue and a sensation shot through her.

"Oh no, I need to go pee."

"You're okay."

Urge gone as quickly as it had come, she lay back and enjoyed the pulses surging through her body.

He rose and pressed his palm against her clit and everything in her rang out. She gripped the bedding to hold onto reality.

"Oh, God..." A thick, milky substance gushed out of her, taking her breath with it. Squirting! She was actually squirting. Not like the pornos they'd watched, but she'd take it.

"That's it." Holding his dick, he rubbed the cum around her clit, then he pushed into her. "So hot." Laying over her, he plunged in deep and hard.

Legs wrapped around his thighs, she matched him stroke for stroke. Too good, too good, kept rolling through her mind. This was too good to stop, but she must. "Sean..." she breathed.

Kissing her, he slowed the stroke. "I'm sorry. I'll be more gentle. Just watching you come does something to me."

"You are adorable." She kissed him back, then gently pushed him away.

Confusion lowered his brows.

* * *

Sean didn't know what to think. One second he's having the best sex of his life, the next his wife is making him stop. Dick throbbing, he watched her roll over and grab the strawberry lubricant off the nightstand. She loved to lick it off his dick. "Put on plenty."

What sane man would say no to having his dick sucked by a beautiful woman who could just about swallow him whole? All lubed up, he was ready, but she was still on her stomach.

He loved taking her from behind. He squeezed her butt, then kissed it. This was no normal butt. It couldn't be. Mind made up, he'd have a discussion with her about anal sex later. Right now he needed to reach his climax before his dick went on strike.

Holding onto her hip with one hand, he used the other to guide the head of his penis to her hot, wet pussy. Just as he was about to slip in, she reached back and wrapped her hand around his hardness, moving it up to her ass. She pressed her butt against him.

He wanted to enter, but didn't want to hurt her. From everything he'd read, you couldn't just stick your dick up someone's ass. You needed to start small and work your way up.

She looked over her shoulder and smiled that mischievous grin she'd get whenever she was about to do something to shock the hell out of him. Again she reached back and grabbed his dick, then she backed into him. In sunk the head of his dick. "Ummm," she cooed.

Seeing he hadn't hurt her, he held onto her hips and went deeper and deeper. "Oh…" This was… was… indescribably good. Hot and wet, but tighter. The same as when she was about to come, and she'd tighten around him, trying to pull him in.

In and out. Deep, deep, shallow. Over and over, she was his. All his and he loved every second of it. Climax nearing, he gripped onto her hips and drove in deep and hard.

Holding onto pillows, Joy continued to work her back and

hips into each stroke, seemingly enjoying herself.

"Oh shit!" Orgasm shaking him to the core, he held on tight. "Oh shhh..."

"That's it." Joy tightened her butt cheeks and dipped her back a little more with each stroke, throwing him for another loop.

Panting, he couldn't believe this. He'd been the leader, the teacher in bed, but now she'd flipped the script on him and he couldn't be more pleased with the result.

Body coming down from the high she'd sent him to, he lay beside her and pulled her close. "You are incredible." He brushed his lips over hers.

"I was just thinking the same thing about you."

"We are a nasty mess."

"I know. We need to shower and change the bedding badly, but I'm finding it hard to move."

Surely smiling like a boy who'd just lost his virginity, he said, "I can't believe what we just did. Happy anniversary."

"Happy anniversary."

Deatri's Titles
Romance
Beauty and the Beast
Broken Promises (Interracial)
Christmas Angel (Second Chances)
Diamond in the Rough (Interracial)
Ebony Angel (Interracial)
For Keeps
Hero (Precious Jewels I)
If You Only Knew (Second Chances)
Love's Desire (Free Read)
Journey's End (Interracial)
Santa's Helper (Write Brothers II)
Silk Scarves and Apples (Second Chances)
Someone To Hold
Soulmate (Precious Jewels III)
Sweet Thang (Interracial
Tease (Write Brothers IV)
Tell Her How You Feel (Write Brothers I)
The Drama The Street and the Seduction (Free Read)
The Impossible Possible (Interracial)
The Only Option
The Other Realm
Third Time's A Charm (Write Brothers III)
Trapped In Paradise (Free Read)
Warrior (Precious Jewels II)
Whisper Something Sweet
Women's Fiction
Caught Up
Jodie's Choice
Operation White Rose
Picture Perfect
Suspense (as L. L. Reaper)
Black Widow and the Sandman
Birth of the Black Widow (Free Read)
The Sandman Cometh (Free Read)
Hell Hath No Fury
Nonfiction
Become A Successful Author

www.ingramcontent.com/pod-product-compliance
Lightning Source LLC
Chambersburg PA
CBHW060054150626
46556CB00017BA/426